SWEET MEMORIES

Harley was reminded of a time long ago . . . she was not more than seven or eight and he a stripling of perhaps fourteen. She had caught him trying to steal a kiss from one of the village schoolgirls. When the chit had run away, Coquette, instead of teasing him, had asked for a kiss herself. He had been rather shocked and yet touched. He had asked her why, and she had responded, "Because, Harley, I know you best and I should like my first kiss to be from someone I know."

He had thought her answer sensible and tender and had even promised to oblige her, but not until she was at least eighteen. The years had dimmed the memory in him until this very moment. He smiled, thinking he should like nothing better than to oblige her now, a circumstance which once more reminded him that he would probably have the devil of a time keeping his house clear of undesirable suitors, which, given the size of her fortune, would be excessive.

At that moment, Coquette happened to turn away from the pianoforte, glancing in his direction once more. Again, that powerful sensation gripped his chest. Faith, had he ever seen any lady so beautiful?

Books by Valerie King

A Daring Wager
A Rogue's Masquerade
Reluctant Bride
The Fanciful Heiress
The Willful Widow
Love Match
Cupid's Touch
A Lady's Gambit
Captivated Hearts
My Lady Vixen
The Elusive Bride
Merry Merry Mischief
Vanquished
Bewitching Hearts
A Summer Courtship
Vignette
A Poet's Kiss
A Poet's Touch
A Country Flirtation
My Lady Mischief
A Christmas Masquerade
A London Flirtation
A Brighton Flirtation
My Lord Highwayman
My Lady Valiant
A Rogue's Deception
A Rogue's Embrace
A Rogue's Wager
A Daring Courtship

Published by Kensington Publishing Corp.

MY DARLING COQUETTE

Valerie King

ZEBRA BOOKS
Kensington Publishing Corp.
http://www.kensingtonbooks.com

ZEBRA BOOKS are published by

Kensington Publishing Corp.
850 Third Avenue
New York, NY 10022

All Kensington titles, imprints and distributed lines are available at special quantity discounts for bulk purchases for sales
promotion, premiums, fund-raising, educational or institu-
tional use.

Special book excerpts or customized printings can also be created to fit specific needs. For details, write or phone the office
of the Kensington Special Sales Manager: Kensington Publishing Corp., 850 Third Avenue, New York, NY 10022. Attn.
Special Sales Department. Phone: 1-800-221-2647.

Zebra and the Z logo Reg. U.S. Pat. & TM Off.

First Printing: November 2003
10 9 8 7 6 5 4 3 2 1

Printed in the United States of America

To Troy and Tyler Collins,
my buddies

One

Bedfordshire, 1817

"Are you wearing my boots again?" Lord Harlington called out loudly.

Coquette Millbrook was just barely able to see her nemesis, the seventh Earl of Harlington, through the tangle of her red curls. She was astride her favorite horse, Old George, having just returned from an exhilarating ride about the Chiltern Hills.

Why Harley was waiting for her she could not imagine, although if the past served as an example, he had no doubt come to torment her. Presently, he leaned negligently against the base of the massive stone arch leading to the stables of Barscot Hall, his arms crossed over his chest and a familiar grimace on his otherwise quite handsome face.

Was it possible, she thought facetiously, he was actually disenchanted with her . . . again?

"What if I am wearing your boots?" she shouted back, competing with a sudden roll of thunder to the west. His frown deepened.

She had grown up at Barscot, having been planted in Harley's home when she was but a child of four. Her own parents had died in a fire which had burned their house to the ground, leaving her orphaned and homeless. The sixth Lord Harlington had been a compassionate man and as her guardian not only had he given her a home, but he had been as near to a father as any man could have been.

He had died, however, not a sennight past, having succumbed at last to an inflammation of the lungs. Not even Cook's famous snail soup had been of the smallest use in preventing his death. In truth, his health had been poorly for many years. He had been an invalid for nearly twenty, spending most of his days in a Bath chair. The end had been mercifully swift but had devastated her beyond belief. Now she was left—and Harley, too, of course—to live their lives without him.

She had therefore spent the entire morning and the early part of the afternoon racing about the Chilterns, up and down the undulating hills which traversed much of the county of Bedfordshire, trying to give herself some relief from the monstrous sorrow which had overtaken her. She had been too sad to do anything else before what would soon be the reading of her guardian's will. Not able to find her own boots, she had, of course, *borrowed* Harley's. He detested when she took his things, and arousing his displeasure was just possibly the greatest joy of her existence. Even at four and twenty, she still took great delight in setting up his back. As she drew nearer, she slowed her horse.

"Are you still at your childish pranks," he queried, moving away from the arch to meet her, "that you must take my boots when you know how much I dislike it?"

How wonderful to see him so pricklish. "And did you think there would be no retribution for your having forced me to dance at the assemblies?"

At that, a glimmer of a smile entered his gray eyes. "I must confess, watching you stumbling down the dance, missing half your steps, was the pinnacle of my delight for the evening."

"Then you have just comprehended to perfection my reason for not hesitating in making use of your boots. Besides, what does it matter anyway? You must have a dozen pairs in your wardrobe."

"I have but three, each fashioned by Stultz, and not a one of them suitable for your small feet!"

"Oooh, Stultz!" she cried sarcastically, drawing her horse to a stop in front of him. "Are we now become a Pink of the *Ton,* my dear Harley?"

She watched his cheeks darken. "Just because a man chooses to wear the finest quality, does not mean he is . . . oh, the devil take it, Cokie, you always could make me as mad as fire."

A sudden smile suffused his face and her breath, for reasons quite beyond her comprehension, caught in her throat. Why, she was not certain, but of late, when he would but smile at her she often felt breathless and queasy, yet afterward she never became ill. She could not account for these sensations in the least. She had begun to wonder if she had contracted some manner of odd, lingering illness. However, since the symptoms tended to disappear the moment Harley either quit her presence or began quarreling with her, she could only assume that after so many years of squabbling with the man she had formed some sort of permanent, if not unpleasant, anxiety toward him that commenced the moment he but appeared in a doorway—or, in this case, beneath a stone arch. In fact, so strong was the present sensation that had she been completely witless she would have thought she was actually happy to see him.

There must be some other explanation, she thought, as she continued to watch him through the tangle of her hair. However much she brangled with him, she was still able to appreciate the considerable perfection of his athletic figure. His shoulders were some of the broadest in the county, his waist tapered to narrow hips, and his legs were well turned. Not that these aspects of his person appealed to her in any romantical sense, for she was quite devoid of any such capacity of feeling, but she was able in her more serene moments of appreciating that what nature may have denied Harley in temperament, it had fully redeemed in the absolute beauty of his person. He was as rugged and strong as many of the powerfully built farmers who lived in the vicinity of Barscot.

In addition, his aristocratic birth had given him a compelling countenance that required but the softest of commands in order to evoke obedience. He rode to hounds with a mastery she had never quite equalled, though very nearly so, and he was quite devilish with a sword in his hand. Indeed, more than once she had actually thought of asking him if he would like to join her on her forthcoming adventures, in which she meant to travel to all the most famous ports in the world. In but a few short weeks, on the third of May, she would enjoy her twenty-fifth birthday and officially come into her inheritance. Immediately afterward, she intended to leave Bedfordshire, probably forever, and sail the seven seas. Such an undertaking by its very description would involve some danger, and since she might have need of a man handy with sword, pistol, or even with his fives, as the stableboys liked to say, she knew Harley was that man.

He was a full six years her senior and might have served as an elder brother to her had he not been so determined to send her into the boughs every time he but shared the same room with her. She would have liked to think of him as a brother, she mused, but he was far too remote and challenging for that.

Generally, she enjoyed the company of men, particularly since her interests ranged more nearly with theirs than with those of her female counterparts. However, Harley had never spoken more than a half dozen caustic words to her at any one time. He had never withheld his sharp disapproval from her, and so it had been war for two decades. Since the death of Lord Harlington, however, she had striven to keep her temper, and she knew Harley had been doing the same.

"I refuse to brangle with you," he said. "At least not now. I came only to tell you that Mr. Jennings is arrived."

"I thought he was not due until four o'clock."

"As did I and the rest of my family. But he is here, ready and waiting. Everyone is."

A raindrop struck the top of her head and only then did she realize that somewhere in her jaunts she had lost her hat. Not that she cared overly much. She only wore the deuced thing to keep Lady Potsgrove, Harley's aunt, from flying into a fit of the hysterics. She tugged at the long sweep of curls that had swirled over her forehead and wondered how quickly she could get to her room and make herself presentable. Because of the recent rains, her riding habit was caked with mud to her thighs. She pulled a leaf and a bird feather from her hair and groaned inwardly. Changing her garments would be simple, but her hair was completely snarled and would require an hour's labor in front of her dressing table just to enable her poor abigail to finally work a brush through her curls.

A flash of lightning and another roll of thunder overset the darkening skies. It would be raining hard soon.

"But I am not at all dressed properly," she complained.

"You never are."

The contemptuous nature of his remark set up her hackles instantly. She straightened her shoulders. "In that case, *my lord*, I see no reason why I may not attend the reading of the will just as I am."

"You would not dare," he hissed.

As soon as the words left his mouth, Harley knew he had made a mistake. Of all the flaws he saw in the young, hoydenish woman before him, her stubborness was the worst. A familiar martial light entered her blue eyes. He was not surprised when she merely lifted a brow, visible through a tangled mass of red curls tumbled over and about her face, and, giving Old George a tap with her boots, moved sedately past him like a queen on parade. The brisk wind of the approaching storm flung her hair backward and a twig, suddenly dislodged from the wreckage of her coiffure, struck him on the forehead.

He muttered a long string of invectives as he turned to follow after. Lightning blazed just beyond the great house and a second later another loud rumble shook the land. Before he could even form the thought that he should hasten back to the house, the rain began and quickly became a downpour.

He caught up with her in the stables, intending to try to persuade her that she ought at least to comb her hair, but the strong words readied on his tongue fell aside. Her forehead was pressed against Old George's sleek and now quite wet neck. Her shoulders shook.

He went to her immediately. "Cokie, I am sorry. I should not have said anything to you."

"It's not that," she said, her hands clinging to Old George's black mane. "What shall I ever do without your father? I miss him terribly."

The words wrung his heart, for they reflected precisely how he felt. This was something they both shared now—they were orphans, the pair of them, without mothers or fathers. His own mother had perished some five and twenty years ago in childbed, giving birth to twins who also did not survive. In a moment of painful awareness, he came to realize that this was how Coquette must have felt most of her life, a sensation he could only describe as a rather fierce feeling of loneliness.

Seeing and comprehending the depths of her grief caused his own heart to soften toward her immeasurably. He therefore took her gently by the shoulders, gave her a turn and gathered her up in his arms. For a moment he wondered what manner of insanity had caused him to try to comfort such a thistly female, but when she buried her wet face into his chest and released several hearty sobs, he knew he had acted wisely. "Cokie, 'twill be all right," he said over and over, all the while petting her mass of leaf-laden curls.

Only after several minutes did he become aware quite suddenly and rather acutely that she fit rather perfectly against him. He tried to dismiss such an unwonted thought, but in the next moment he realized that he was also feeling a profound if inexplicable desire to keep her held tightly against him forever.

This passing thought, however, he set aside quickly as having been the result of their mutual grief. "I loved him, too," he said.

"Of course you did," she said, drawing back and sniffing loudly. "No son could have been more attentive. I always admired and appreciated that about you. You were not like so many who take no interest at all in their parents."

He looked into her dewy blue eyes, still partially concealed behind a mat of auburn hair. He wondered suddenly what she would look like if properly taken in hand, her hair shorn, her eyebrows thinned, perhaps a little rouge on her lips. Not that it mattered. Coquette had never cared for such things and had made her intentions clear for years that as soon as she came into her inheritance she meant to live a life more suited to an adventuresome man than a woman.

When she sniffed loudly again, he drew his kerchief from the pocket of his coat and handed it to her.

"Thank you. I did not mean to become a watering pot like Lady Agnes, who always seems to find some excuse to beg for your kerchief."

He immediately took offense. "Lady Agnes," he retorted sharply, drawing her gaze away from the kerchief as she blew her nose, "happens to be one of the finest ladies of my acquaintance." He narrowed his eyes. "I believe you may be jealous of her."

"Jealous?" she responded, clearly surprised. "And in what manner would I possibly be jealous of Lady Agnes?"

Harley did not even know where to begin. The answer was so obvious that he wondered yet again if it were possible Coquette was slightly addled. For one thing, Agnes was very much a lady in every possible respect. She was petite, which Coquette was not, and had the countenance of an angel. She wore her hair in a delicate halo of blond curls which further enhanced her celestial appearance. She was demure and had the peculiar ability to make Harley feel as though he was the strongest man in the world. She also had a wonderfully fetching manner of giving a tug or two on her curls while smiling up into his face. If occasionally he wished she would not play so much with her hair, he certainly set such ungenerous thoughts aside. He was, in truth, very close to offering for the beauty. This, of course, he would never say to Coquette, for undoubtedly she would take to mimicking Agnes in that way of hers that always made him grind his teeth.

Lady Agnes Clifton represented for him the epitome of all that was feminine and beautiful. She was a favorite of his six aunts, which further confirmed his opinion that she might just be the next Countess Harlington. He smiled, thinking with some pleasure on the fact that his nearest relations were a handsome collection. His aunts, all of them, were quite lovely and well bred. Each had a keen eye to fashion and color, except perhaps for Potsy, who was a trifle eccentric and yet who in her day had been quite a diamond of the first stare. Coquette had been the bane of all their lives and no effort on any of their parts had resulted in making a lady of her. It had always seemed to Harley that his father had delighted in setting up the backs of both his sisters as well as his sisters-in-law, and to this end Coquette had proved a most effective and willing accomplice.

These thoughts caused him to frown. "Have you never wished for beaus?" he asked.

Coquette started, then laughed heartily. "Beaus? Whatever would I do with them?" she exclaimed.

"Because one day you will naturally wish to wed, no matter how vehemently you protest against the married state at present."

"I have no use for a husband, as you very well know. I intend to have adventures."

"What of my father's wishes? I know he desired more than anything that you might marry."

"How well I know it," she returned. "It is my only regret

that the future I have chosen for myself was always such a disappointment to him. Although I do think that he should have tempered some of his remarks from time to time, especially where your aunts were concerned." She laughed suddenly. "Do you know he desired at one time that you and I wed? Could you think of anything more ridiculous?"

Harley smiled broadly. "It was the greatest absurdity."

When the laughter subsided, Coquette frowned. "I wish I had been born a man. How I have wished it a score of times."

Though he did not mean to, he glanced at her quite lovely bosom, after which he immediately averted his gaze. She might speak of wishing she were a man, but in this particular respect nature had made it abundantly clear that there was but one opinion on that score. He thought it a great irony that so many much less beautifully endowed London chits made every effort to enhance such a deficiency while Coquette had no such need, but could not have cared less. Her figure was quite wasted on her, therefore, but he still thought it a pity that the outmoded gowns she wore were all made high to the neck.

He cleared his throat, however, and engaged the argument once more. "You ought at least make a push. My aunts are in complete despair. If I might make a suggestion, you would do well to imitate Lady Agnes. Why, even if you followed her example in one or two essentials, you would be improved a hundredfold."

"Hah," she answered sharply. "I'd as lief take her lead as shoot off one of my legs."

He shook his head, unable to comprehend her in the least. "You may borrow any of my hunting rifles, should you feel inspired."

She rolled her eyes and turned away from him, returning to the entrance to the stables.

He caught up with her. "Why must you be so intent on this course, Cokie? Have you never wished to be like other females?"

"No," she answered succinctly. "Not when I have a fortune at my hands. I do not think you realize how restrictive a woman's life is, even in these modern times. Every woman is required to be married and if she is not, she is seen as a perfect oddity. Besides, you must see that were I to marry, I should no longer have the smallest power over my fortune, for it would be given into my husband's hands in every legal sense."

"Not all men are so high-handed."

"Most," she stated emphatically. "You must agree with that."

"I suppose you are right." When he reached the door, the pounding of the rain on the stable roof warned him that a few yards' walk would see them both drenched. He was about to suggest that he procure an umbrella for her, but she suddenly bolted past him and was running toward the house before he could so much as call her name. His boots, he noted in some irritation, flopped about on her feet quite badly.

Forcing his coat up over his head, he once more followed in her wake. True to her word, she did not mount the stairs to her bedchamber but made her way directly to the rose drawing room, leaving a trail of debris behind her.

He caught up with her quickly. "There is one thing I forgot to tell you," he said quietly. "Seames is here."

She stopped in her tracks abruptly, just short of the drawing room and turned toward him. "Whatever for?" she asked, her voice low. "He can have nothing to do with the will, with my inheritance, surely."

Harley shrugged. "Still, Jennings summoned him, so my father must have left something of importance to him. Besides, he is your nearest kinsman."

"I do not like him," she responded, frowning. "I believe he is become a gamester and besides, whenever I see him he is always smiling, far more than is at all necessary or becoming."

At that, Harley laughed. "Well, if he is smiling today, it

won't be because of your hair. With all these red curls, you look just like an exploding firework."

"Oh, do stubble it." Once more she attempted to bring some order to her tangled locks, but to no avail. "Come, let us see what Jennings will tell us before we start brangling again."

"An excellent notion."

Two

Coquette lifted her chin proudly as she entered the well-appointed rose drawing room in the east wing of Barscot Hall. The chamber was rarely used except for grand occasions or, as today, those of the most somber. The decor reflected the room's general function, since it was in the French style which had been quite popular thirty years ago. Scattered down the length of the elegant receiving room were sofas and chairs covered in heavy brocades of rose and taupe and painted tables trimmed lavishly in gilt. Lord Harlington's sisters had tried to persuade him a hundred times to modernize the decor, but he had always refused for the simple reason that his beloved wife had chosen the furniture and fabrics herself. Once having learned of his sentiments, Coquette had treasured the antiquated feel of the furnishings—although at this moment she did not think there could have been a contrast more sharply drawn than the staid function and opulence of the chamber against her muddied riding habit.

Having crossed the portals, Coquette faced an extensive array of Byngs dressed in somber blacks and grays, the very breadth of the Harlington family. Glancing at the shocked expressions she now encountered, she wished she had first returned to her bedchamber and at least tidied her hair. An audible gasp went up from nearly all six females present.

Lady Potsgrove, who had served as mistress at Barscot for many years and who had tried unceasingly to train Co-

quette out of her wild ways, went a step further and exclaimed, "I believe I shall faint!"

Dear Potsy, Coquette thought. How hard Potsy had tried to
make a lady of Coquette, yet she herself was something of an
oddity and since her widowhood of some ten years past had
taken to wearing the most absurd caps. Her present dainty
confection was made of black lace but appeared to have
sprouted a dozen black silk flowers all by itself. When she,
shook her head, as she was now, all the flowers danced as
though moved by a brisk breeze. She looked ridiculous.

"I was out riding," Coquette felt obligated to explain, "and
thought Mr. Jennings would be arriving at four. I did not wish
to keep all of you waiting by retiring first."

An ensuing round of resigned sighs followed. Coquette
knew that not a single lady present had ever known what to
do with her.

There was nothing more to be done or said, so she merely
offered a curtsy and settled herself in a secluded window seat
where she could watch the rain drizzle down the window.
Most of what would be read in the will pertained to Harley,
although, according to Mr. Jennings, there were several specific passages about herself as well which required she be
present.

She glanced at Mr. Jennings, who was an older man with a
perpetually pinched expression, a balding pate, and white
tufts of hair protruding in many directions above his ears. He
wore spectacles but still squinted and spoke in an oddly firm
voice suggesting the time to commence was at hand. When
Harley nodded his acquiescence, Coquette was surprised to
watch the solicitor remove a kerchief from the pocket of his
coat and mop his brow and face. She could only wonder if he
was becoming ill.

His voice, however, was quite steady, and he proceeded
point by point to ennumerate Lord Harlington's wishes. For
herself, within two or three sentences of hearing information

that had nothing whatsoever to do with her, she ceased listening.

Her gaze traveled slowly about the room. She knew everyone quite well and among Harley's relatives she had several favorites. Mrs. Jane Byng and and Lady Marianne both had treated her with kindness over the years. Lady Harriet, on the other hand, was something of a tyrant, while Mrs. Constance Byng and Mrs. Theodora Byng were quite critical, albeit civil enough generally. However, when her gaze settled on Rupert Seames, she felt less content. She could not imagine to what purpose Mr. Jennings had summoned him.

She regarded him for a long moment. He was nothing like her, which of course he would not be, since he was such a distant relation, but it unnerved her that any of her relatives would be such a dandy as Rupert Seames. His hair was a perfect bubble of blond curls and so carefully ordered and put into place, besides being fixed there by incomprehensible means, that he did not look quite real. His eyes were very strange, a pale blue that reminded her of someone. She sought about in her mind for a moment, trying to determine who, precisely, until she recalled Lady Agnes and nearly burst out laughing. Indeed, the pair of them were very similar in their shared sort of angelic beauty.

Only Rupert was no angel. He was constantly in debt to the cent-percenters and was known to frequent gaming hells. No, she had never been able to warm to him and to some degree resented that he was here, since the loss of her beloved guardian was still so hurtful. Rupert had never shown the smallest interest or consideration to the man who had frequently paid his debts for her sake.

Finding that the more she dwelled on Rupert, the more distressed she became, she shifted her gaze to the window, to the rain still running in rivulets down the pane and to the misty vision of the Chilterns rising sharply to the east of Barscot Hall. The rain reminded her of water and the water of the ocean.

Her mind became instantly caught up in the vision of a vast sea, a clear sky, and a brisk wind that pushed every sail of her East Indiaman until the ship was moving swiftly toward . . . which destination this time? China. She closed her eyes. How she longed to see the world, every famous harbor about which she had read and a thousand unnamed ports betwixt.

Maybe she would cut her hair and don a man's clothes: a loose shirt and breeches or maybe the increasingly fashionable trousers. After a few months at sea, when she was sun bronzed, who would ever recognize her? Perhaps she could even change her name.

Her thoughts flew in excited circles until they landed upon one call in particular she intended to pay as soon as possible. Her former governess now lived in Boston. Mrs. Undershaw had been a treasure, indeed, and she had not ceased corresponding with her during the past six years when she first quit her post at Barscot and married Mr. Undershaw. She was quite happily married and had three small children, but Coquette had never quite forgiven *her* Miss Tuttle for not only having deserted her but for having actually tumbled in love, married, and settled in a faraway home to raise a family.

How Miss Tuttle had inspired her. How her words could stoke the fires of her imagination until they were burning hotly. Miss Tuttle had always approved of her plans to see as much of the world as she could in one lifetime. There was even a time Coquette had formed the intention of asking her if she would serve as her companion on the adventures she meant to have. Then Quentin Undershaw, a scientist of some merit, had won her affections and all had changed. Barscot had seemed inutterably dull for at least a year following her departure in 1811, at least until Coquette had learned to fill her life with hiking and riding and frequent trips to the wilder northern counties.

Though Lord Harlington had been an invalid, he had happily joined her during the summer months on long treks, even into Scotland, but more often than not to Lakeland, where he rested beside the clear waters and she hiked the fells until the stitching on all of her half boots gave way. Her evening hours, whether at home or at some distant place, were spent playing whist with her guardian and his friends while occasionally performing sonatas, preludes, and fugues on the pianoforte whenever requested, which was often, for Lord Harlington had loved music very much. She was a bold performer, if not entirely perfect in her execution. She knew she needed to practice more, but unfortunately the stables called to her more often than the music room.

The only time she had ever attended balls or any of the local assemblies was on the all too frequent occasions when one or the other of Lord Harlington's sisters or sisters-in-law would arrive at Barscot for the strict purpose of trying to bring Coquette Millbrook into fashion. Much good it ever did. All of Harley's aunts finally tossed up their hands in exasperation and admitted failure when, a year past, Coquette had been stuffed into a ballgown, her hair gathered into a huge mass on top of her head, and a fan tied to her wrist. The duck pond had not been far from where the coaches awaited the ladies. Coquette had inched slowly toward the pond and, as soon as she was able, fell backward and submerged herself completely, a task which had been no easy feat, since the pond was barely two feet in depth. She came up sputtering and exclaiming in a loud voice how devastated she was that she could not attend the ball after all.

Harley had seen her, dripping with mud and downy feathers, and had laughed himself silly.

Later, the aunts had each sent her quite scornful letters prophesying disaster for her future. However, her antics had at least put an end to the attempts of what dear Potsy had referred to as making a lady out of a 'sow's ear.'

How peaceful her life had been since that night. From that point, so near to the age at which she could claim her inheritance, she had been biding her time knowing that her ship would be coming to her very soon. She read any book she could find on the West Indies, the Americas, the Levant, Cape Horn, India, China, the Japannes and even New South Wales. The only blot, therefore, on the enjoyment of her forthcoming liberation had been the death of her dear Lord Harlington.

Her gaze was drawn away from her reveries for a brief moment when a rather long pause in the reading ensued. Mr. Jennings appeared to be looking for another document. The entire assemblage seemed disinterested, and she wondered how many of Harley's aunts were thinking of anything but the will, just as she was. Most everything had been long since settled. The entire estate belonged to Harley, as was the law, and anything else to be disbursed would of course be of a more trivial, sentimental nature. She could not help but notice that Harley, in particular, seemed quite bored. He sat beside Lady Potsgrove, one knee slung over the other, twirling a monocle he required for reading purposes and which was held by a long silk riband.

A gust of wet wind threw a spattering of rain once more against the windows. She was drawn back to her ship and suddenly on that ship, Harley appeared in a magnificent admiral's uniform, hat and all. He often did that, she thought, positioning himself right in the middle of her daydreams quite without warning and always in a place of prominence and power. For a moment she dwelled on the image possessing her mind. She sighed deeply, not knowing precisely why. He was without doubt the handsomest man of her acquaintance, even exceeding Farmer Flitt in beauty—and Farmer Flitt was the absolute pinnacle of girlish interest among the village maids.

She turned to look at Harley and even forced some of her hair behind her ear that her vision might not be obstructed. His face appeared almost chiseled, his cheekbones well formed, his brows thick and expressive, his jawline absolutely commanding. No wonder he often crept into her daydreams, and, if she were to own the truth completely, into her nighttime dreams as well! That, of course, was a great secret, and perhaps the most incomprehensible part of the whole business where he was concerned. She often actually kissed him in her dreams, though why, she could not imagine. It was not as though she was a ridiculous Lady Agnes Clifton who longed to be mistress of Barscot more than anything in the world.

She wrinkled her nose. Somehow she suspected Lady Agnes had no interest in Harley at all beyond his title and fortune. What a novel thought! Yet she felt in her bones she was right, that Agnes's interest in Harley was purely to get a handle to her name. Why else would she constantly be pulling on her curls in his presence except for the guilt she carried in her heart? Ah, well, it was hardly her concern, and he was certainly well able to tend to his own interests. Although if he did decide to wed Lady Agnes, Coquette would be able to take the constant delight of knowing that Lady Agnes was plaguing him to death every morn, noon, and night of their life together.

When he suddenly looked at her, Coquette felt very conscious of the fact that she had been staring at him and meant to look away. But when he made that particular face of his indicating he disapproved of her, she felt relieved, pulled a face of her own, and reverted to staring out the window. This time, though, he was still aboard her ship, she had the crew pounce on him, bind him, and throw him overboard. Though just before he splashed into the water, she wondered if Harley ever dreamed of her.

Harley was utterly disgusted. His gaze had drifted to Coquette's skirts, and there he found what would undoubtedly amount to a pound of mud attached to the bottom of her gown. Her—rather, *his*—boots were caked, of course, and now that she was indoors and the mud was drying, chunks had started falling off and collecting on the floor around her. She was a complete scapegrace, and he no more understood her than he did half the legal words of the document Jennings was reading in his monotonous voice. Earlier, he had re-

viewed most of the essentials with Jennings and understood
fully his inheritance, and had for several years, since his father had included him in the process of estate managment for
a very long time.

As it was, he was hardly listening and therefore had time
to ponder many things. For one, he was not happy that Coquette intended to launch herself upon the world the moment
she succeeded to her inheritance. He thought it foolish beyond permission and wished there might be something he
could do about it. Of course, she was a difficult, ridiculous
sort of woman, but he had essentially grown up with her and
he supposed he wished good things for her. He considered the
possibility of trying to persuade her to take short journeys for
a year or two, to Spain and France, for instance, before attempting a voyage across the sea with her own crew aboard
the ship she intended to purchase.

He glanced at her. Would she listen? To him? Good God,
no. Not in a thousand years.

Another pause in the reading occurred, and Lady Potsgrove
leaned close to him, whispering, "What is to become of her?"
she asked. "I have seen you watching her closely, even grimacing, my dear Harley. Only what is to become of our dear
Coquette?"

Harley answered quietly, "She will travel the oceans, I suppose, as she has always wanted to."

"You do not mean to let her?"

He shrugged. "On the third of May she will be five and
twenty, in full possession of her quite substantial fortune, and
far beyond the desire of advice from a guardian."

"It is strange to think that you are her guardian now," she
offered, still speaking quietly. Since Mr. Jennings was again
searching for another document, several small groups were
chatting.

"For a scant few weeks. Hardly significant. Besides, I
would not interfere in her affairs anyway. She is a woman

grown, she knows her own mind, and though I do not approve at all of her professed plans, I will not stop her."

"She will be killed in a hurricane off the coast of Bombay. I am convinced of it. Oh, I feel faint suddenly."

He could not help but chuckle. "Do you know, Aunt, your imagination is your worst enemy."

"How is that?" she asked.

"You tease your vapors, spasms, and nerves by your fanciful predictions and reveries."

She giggled. "I suppose you are right. Well, I guess there is nothing to be done now about Coquette. I blame your father, of course. He spoiled her, in every possible sense of the word. I believe he kept her head full of all these outrageous ideas and he certainly did nothing to check her."

"I am convinced you have the right of it, save that I do know he pressed her to find a husband, to marry."

"He did?" she asked, obviously surprised. "I had no notion."

"Indeed, he had even suggested I might make an excellent spouse for her."

At that, Lady Potsgrove nearly lost her composure entirely and barely suppressed a peal of laughter, which she hid behind a black lace kerchief held tightly over her mouth. What resulted were several strangled choking sounds. When she had recovered herself, she whispered, "That was very cruel, Harley, making me laugh like that, and at so solemn an occasion."

He smiled suddenly, but his heart felt a deep twinge of sadness. "Just the sort of thing Papa would have approved of."

"Oh, you are so very right. He always was one to insist on liveliness and joy, even when the worst happened. I do not know how many times he said to me, 'Now, none of your vapors, Potsy. I shall not have you oversetting the servants.' Oh, dear, now I shall cry."

He patted her arm and, indeed, tears did trickle down her cheeks.

"Alfred was always my favorite," she murmured. "But did he truly think you should wed Coquette?"

"I have no doubt it was the merest grasping at straws and that he regretted not seeing her settled properly, but by then the hour was too late. But she was always quite headstrong."

"That she was. However, I am still trying to picture you, a Corinthian, with Weston fashioning every coat, and with even the thumbs of your gloves sewn to such precise specifications, married to that?"

As one, they both looked at Coquette. Another clump of mud dropped to the floor.

"What is that hanging from her hair?"

Harley squinted. "Good God. I believe it is a bird's nest."

"Oh, no, do not say that, for I am like to go off again!" She was silent for a moment, then added, "Harley, are those your boots she is wearing?"

"Yes, I fear they are."

Mr. Jennings began reading again.

Harley shook his head as he once more glanced at Coquette. What a complete curiosity she was. He wondered suddenly just why it was she was so intent on leaving England and why she had so little interest in the things which so wholly possessed the minds of most females. At the same time, the disgust he felt at her appearance had never dimmed. From his earliest memories, the most certain sign of a well-bred woman was the general femininity of her attire and her demeanor. His mother had been just this sort of woman, as were his aunts. Not that he wished Coquette to lose any of her daring and evident joie de vivre, but nor would he have her continue in this hoydenish, quite ridiculous vein.

The thundershower ended quite suddenly and, without warning, the sun broke through, setting Coquette's profile in strong relief. With her matted hair still stuck behind her ear, he was a little shocked to see an almost perfect flow of forehead, nose, lips, and chin. *Good God,* he thought, *she is almost beautiful!*

The realization that she was possibly a diamond of the first water beneath her layer of independent zeal truly made him wish that there was something he might be able to do for her. But as another clump of mud struck the Aubusson carpet at her feet, his enthusiasm faded.

It was not to be. The moment she came into her fortune, Coquette would purchase her longed-for East Indiaman and he would choose a wife. The time had come for both of them to embrace the future—she, her dreams, and he, his obligations as the seventh Earl of Harlington.

A great sadness swelled over him like a strong tidal bore. He wished this day had never come.

After a time, the delightful sunlight became too strong on Coquette's face and she turned into the room. Though she had not been paying attention in the least, she realized at once something extraordinary had just happened. For one thing, all of Harley's aunts wore expressions of extreme astonishment and at least two of them were clapping, laughing, and glancing at her in wild fits and starts. But it was Harley who caught her attention completely. His complexion was nearly the color of a beet, but not in embarrassment. He was utterly and completely enraged.

"What?" he thundered, rising to his feet, his question directed toward Mr. Jennings.

All eyes now became fixed on the poor fellow, whose color was also quite high and who began mopping his brow in earnest as he had earlier. Coquette wished that she had been paying attention, for something untoward and clearly unexpected had just happened. Had Harley somehow been disinherited? But that was impossible. He was Lord Harlington's legal heir. Nothing could alter that. What, then?

Another glance about the chamber and her gaze became fixed on Rupert. His smile was so broad, so pleased, that he appeared just like the cat who had caught the mouse. Only why?

"Explain this to me at once!" Harley thundered again.

"Yes, m'lord. Of course, m'lord. I tried to persuade your father to speak to you about this, but he would have none of it. He said it would be best for you to know on the day the will would be read and not a moment sooner. I know it must not seem in the least fair to you—"

"Fair!" Harley cried. "Absurd! Ridiculous! Completely unheard of! How the deuce do you expect me to find that creature"—and here he leveled a most coarse finger in Coquette's direction—"a husband."

All eyes now turned upon Coquette, even Harley's. The room fell silent except for Lady Potsgrove, who murmured, "I feel as though I might faint. Jane, dear, may I have the use of your smelling salts for a moment?"

"I fear not," Jane Byng responded, her eyes wide. "I believe any moment I shall have need of them myself."

With so many eyes upon her, Coquette rose to her feet. "What is the matter, Harley? Why are you pointing at me and speaking of husbands? You know I haven't the smallest intention of marrying."

"Were you not listening, Cokie?"

"No, not especially. I knew the will pertained to your inheritance, not mine."

"Well, it does now."

"In what way—and why are your aunts beginning to smile, and why are they looking at me in that peculiar manner, from head to toe, as though I were a horse at Tattersalls?"

Harley pressed a hand to his brow. "I still cannot credit this is true. Jennings, are you certain?"

The solicitor held up a sheet of paper. "It is all here," he responded in a resigned fashion. "And if I may say so, my lord, I advised your father against this. I am not even certain it is entirely legal."

"But what does all this have to do with me?" Coquette asked, stamping her foot.

Harley's Aunt Harriet was suddenly beside her and pushing the hair back from her forehead. "I have always believed it could be done!" she cried.

"Lady Harriet, I beg you will desist. Will someone please tell me what is going forward?"

Harley's brow was thunderous. "Only the worst farce imaginable. Somehow my father has made both our inheritances conditional, yours wholly, mine until the first of May."

"Upon what condition?" she asked.

"That you are to marry before either of us inherits and that it must be before May first!"

"What?" she shouted. She felt her own color rise hotly not just on each delicate cheek but beginning at the base of her neck and traveling in a wave over her entire face. "I am to marry? But this is horrible, ridiculous! Rupert, is that why you have been smiling?"

"I refuse to answer that," he said, tidying one of his tight blond curls. He appeared quite smug.

She then narrowed her eyes, a terrible suspicion overtaking her. "Pray, what does Rupert have to do with any of this?"

Here, the entire chamber grew very quiet and she sensed no one wanted to impart this next portion of Lord Harlington's conditions to her. Even Lady Harriet, so intent on looking at each of her features, carefully stepped away.

Lady Potsgrove, apparently feeling she needed support in this moment, approached her and gently took her hand, but Coquette would have none of it. "Tell me. Now," she commanded, jerking her hand free.

Once more, Harley informed her, "If you are not wed by the first of May of this year, your entire fortune is forfeit to Mr. Seames."

Coquette weaved on her feet. She reached toward Lady Potsgrove and clutched at her arm.

"Steady, my dear," Potsy said. "What are you doing? You

are pulling on my arm? Do be careful, or I shall . . . oh, dear! Goodness gracious!"

Coquette had released Lady Potsgrove but weaved on her feet. "I . . . I feel quite ill," she said. "Unaccountably so." She sank where she was, in the middle of the carpet, near to casting up her accounts. Before she could beg them not to, Harley's aunts had surrounded her and had thrust at least two vinaigrettes and one vial of smelling salts beneath her nose. Lady Marianne wafted her feathered fan over Coquette's face.

"Married?" Coquette murmured, her gaze barely recognizing the faces peering down at her in a perfect circle over her head. "I had rather be eaten by wolves."

She then fell into oblivion.

Three

Several hours later, when the Byng ladies were having their fashionable lie-downs before dinner, Coquette found herself sufficiently recovered from the shock of Lord Harlington's will that she went in search of Harley. She was generally not given to the shedding of tears, but she had shed a few this afternoon, especially while her abigail brushed out her tangled curls. Her entire life had just come to a sudden and abrupt end. She did not know how to think of the future without her wonderful dreams, and the very thought of taking a husband made her shudder.

Still, there remained within her a small whisper of hope that something might be done to release both Harley and herself from this most wretched of predicaments. She had been pondering several ideas and meant now to present them to Harley, if only she could find him.

She walked the long halls of the Elizabethan mansion. The storm had passed, leaving the landscape drenched in not just rain but light as well. However, in the early springtime, the evening came quick on the heels of afternoon and the lovely light was fading fast. She thought perhaps Harley was dressing for dinner, but after inquiring of Stiles, Harley's butler, she was informed that he had last been seen in the billiard room and that he had not as yet sent for his valet.

The billiard room was empty, as was the library. All of the receiving rooms were completely silent. She would not be deterred, however, and finally found him on the terrace, a muffler wrapped about his neck, supporting a book of Shakespeare's sonnets in the crook of his crossed leg and sipping a glass of sherry.

"You will not have sufficient light in but a moment or two," she said, pulling her shawl close about her shoulders.

He glanced up at her, his monocle dropping to dangle on its riband, and smiled, if falteringly. "Very true. I have been straining for the past several minutes." He paused for a moment. "How do you fare, Cokie? Your—our—plight has been weighing on my mind, yours more nearly."

She drew a chair close to his. "I cannot remember being so sad in my entire existence. I have shed more tears this afternoon, I vow it is so, than dear Potsy did all of last year."

He laughed. "So many, then?"

"I cannot credit that your father, who I know loved me, would decide to consign me to such an unwanted, undesired fate."

He closed the volume of verse and rubbed his forehead. "It is a mystery."

"But I have sought you out to discuss the matter. Do you think we might have legal redress?"

He shook his head. "I discussed the matter at length with Jennings. I might have recourse, but you most certainly do not. Papa was your sole guardian and your father's will left him with enormous discretion on every count. You must marry. There can be no two opinions on that score."

"Very well. Will you marry me, Harley?"

He laughed outright. "What the deuce?"

She leaned forward and overlaid his arm with her hand. "You could wed me and then in a few weeks or months divorce me. Then I would have my fortune—and I do trust you sufficiently not to gamble it away beforetimes—and I could buy my ship and hire my crew and sail away. You would never hear from me again!"

"Oh, my dear. You forget. There would be a terrible

scandal, for which I don't give a fig, but what of my aunts, uncles, and cousins? Would you use them so badly?"

"Yes," she answered, her throat feeling tight again. "For it is not by my fault that this thing has come down upon me. I loved your father. I was as devoted to him as any daughter might be, and he used me so ill."

He lowered his voice, and in turn covered her hand with his own. "You would wound others so easily?"

She did not mean for it to happen, but another tear escaped her eye and trickled down her cheek. "Yes," she responded, but her voice sounded very small.

"I do not believe it. Whatever you may be, you are not by nature cruel."

She was surprised and met his gaze fully. He had given her a compliment, something he had never before done. "That was very sweetly said."

For a brief moment there occurred a faint tingling sensation all about her, the way she often felt just before a sudden shower. However, there was not a cloud to be seen in the sky, just a few twinkling stars. In the dim light, Harley's eyes were nearly coal black, and for some odd reason she found herself completely incapable of looking away from him. She felt as though she wanted to say something, but no words either framed themselves in her mind or made their way to her lips.

"You deserve sweetness and kindness in this moment," he said. "You were an angel to my father." He suddenly lifted her hand and placed a kiss on her fingers.

The tingling sensation Coquette had been feeling became a river of lightning that traveled up her arm, suffused her face, and sped down her back, leaving a trail of gooseflesh the entire distance. She was stunned—and something more, something so pleasurable her breath caught in her throat. "Why did you do that?" she asked.

She watched as he looked at her fingers, as though he was unaware of what he had done. A frown split his brow, after which he gently released her hand. "I have not the faintest notion," he responded quietly. "I suppose it was merely in response to my compassion for your situation. I hope I did not offend you."

"No, but it was very odd. Very odd, indeed."

He seemed suddenly offended. "I beg your pardon, Cokie," he responded facetiously. "I did not mean to wound your sensibilities."

"Oh, what nonsense, Harley. You know I have no sensibilities."

"Then why so pricklish? I kissed your fingers. Gentlemen do such things all the time."

Here she laughed. "Not to me."

At that, he regarded her appraisingly. "Well, they would if you did something with that red lion's mane of yours besides holding it back, and that not so very well, with a ribbon. And also if you were not such a badger about everything."

"Is that how you see me?"

"Yes," he responded succinctly.

"How am I to get a husband, then? Oh, Harley, please marry me. Nothing could be simpler, and I think your family would understand and not fly into a pelter."

"You do not know my aunts, then."

"We could keep the entire affair very private, even secret," she said earnestly. "Indeed, we could."

He released an exasperated sigh. "You are forgetting. A divorce, for me, would require an Act of Parliament. And, believe me, there is nothing subtle or private about an Act of Parliament."

"Oh, God, I had not thought of that," she said, flopping back in her chair. "Then it is hopeless. I am lost forever."

He was thoughtful for a moment. "Not necessarily. Cokie, you have never permitted yourself to even ponder the possibilities of love and marriage. I am persuaded that were you to choose the right sort of husband, you would not find the married state so completely abhorrent."

"But I would not have the freedom to do as I pleased."

"The right gentleman would be able to grant you all the freedom you desired."

"Even to enjoy a Turkish bath in the Levant?"

"Is that what you wish to do?" he asked, the expression of his gray eyes inscrutable.

"Of course. That and a hundred other things that would cause palpitations in even the strongest of men."

At that, he laughed.

"Tell me I am wrong, then. Would you permit your wife to travel to Turkey and bathe as the natives do?"

He tried to picture Lady Agnes in such a setting but could not. At present, she shuddered at the mere mention of ocean travel. Even taking the small packets from Dover to Calais caused her to wince. "I can't say that I have given it much thought, to be quite honest."

"Then let me ask you the same question but in a different manner. Were I your wife, would you permit me such liberty?"

He frowned, then smiled. "I suppose I would, but then I have known you for ages and I know it would please you."

"Harley, you mystify me, really you do. Why are you being so kind?"

He did not answer for a long moment, but regarded her steadily. It was a rare day indeed when they were not brangling. Rarer still when kindness was the order of the moment.

Finally, he said, "Perhaps I am merely being selfish. After all, until you are wed, I cannot take over the full reins of Barscot and must discuss with Mr. Jennings every matter of import. You cannot imagine how sorely this grates with me."

"I see. It must be aggravating in the extreme being treated as though you were still green behind the ears instead of, well, a man of thirty years. Regardless your motive, I do appreciate that you are not tormenting me just now. I do not think I could bear it."

"The truth is, Cokie, I have never seen you so sad in my entire existence. Generally, your spirits are so powerfully air-borne that I have no small degree of difficulty in bringing you to earth on occasion. I must confess, I dislike enormously seeing you this way and . . . I am sorry."

She sighed. "There is nothing for you to be sorry about. Only, I cannot credit that your father could be so cruel—especially when I loved him so very much." With that, she found herself overcome and rather than disgrace herself by once more either fainting or becoming a watering pot, she excused herself and returned indoors. He called to her, the tone of his voice quite tender, which only served to make her pick up her skirts and run.

During the next three days, Coquette spent her days and nights separated from Harley and his anxious aunts. She knew that for some perverse reason, the ladies of the family were itching to cut her hair, pluck her eyebrows, give her lessons in deportment and fashion, and construct an entirely new wardrobe for her. Why they had not descended on her like a gaggle of geese after a morsel of bread she did not know, but it appeared they were restraining themselves purposefully, and for that she was grateful.

She walked the halls of the enormous mansion late into the night and during the day spent most of her time in the saddle. She shed more tears than any lady ought to shed in a lifetime and certainly more than she ever would have believed were within her. She felt as though her life had ended, certainly all her long-cherished dreams. But there was nothing to be done but accept this incredibly horrible thing that had happened to her and to reconcile herself to the equally wretched fact that she must very soon place herself in the hands of the Byng ladies in order to become, at long last, a lady of quality.

On the morning of the fourth day, she presented herself for the first time since the reading of the will in the breakfast room, where the entire family was lounging over an assortment of breakfast foods and a collection of periodicals. All eyes turned to her, after which several gentle greetings were sent in her direction. She thought it a bit curious, especially when this was followed by the aunts each settling their gaze upon Harley, as though waiting for him to speak some pronouncement.

She watched him, not quite understanding what was going forward until he finally scowled and then addressed them all. "I absolutely insist you wait until she has partaken of her breakfast!"

Comprehension dawned on her and she cast Harley a faltering smile of intense gratitude. He, clearly, had been the reason that the Byng ladies had left her to her own devices for so many days together. She had now only the enjoyment of a single breakfast, sort of a last breakfast of freedom and independence, before all would change. She therefore lingered over each dish set on a side table, demanded of the butler that fresh scrambled eggs and a tart or two be procured for her from the kitchens, and piled her present plate so high that when she took up a seat, a general groan sounded from all the ladies.

There was so much that was ridiculous in this circumstance that she began to smile and eventually to laugh. Oh, how absurd life could be at times, no less so now than that while she was enduring the lowest point of her entire existence, six ladies were nearly bursting with a kind of euphoric excitement about which she happened to be the very center. She therefore chuckled through her large meal, enjoyed the scrambled eggs and apricot tartlets Cook sent with her blessing, and lingered for an extra fifteen minutes over a cup of coffee which she insisted upon refilling twice.

When she had taken her last sip, she caught Harley's eye and formed a thank-you on silent lips. His answering smile was both sympathetic and hopeful. She grimaced in response, but to the Byng ladies she said, "Well, why do we dawdle even a moment more when I've a husband to get?"

It was as though the heavens burst open and released a

thousand doves, so spectacular was the ensuing chorus of expressed excitement that reverberated through the walls of the breakfast room. Indeed, because of the female nature of the sound, the gentlemen, almost as one, raced from the chamber, leaving even half-finished articles unread in the need to escape so much feminine commotion.

Coquette spent the next entire week in one form of agony after another. The gentlemen, having been effectually banished from Barscot, were led by Harley to his hunting box in Lincolnshire with nearly the full complement of his stables in tow to enjoy some riding and what hunting the cold spring days might allow before the entire party dispersed. For herself, she was grateful they were gone, since more than once her screams of either pain or frustration could be heard echoing down the long halls. She could not imagine a greater form of torture for anyone, man or woman, than the plucking of eyebrows, one after the other, dozens of them, until she was certain Jane Byng had plucked her brow bald.

Her long curly red locks were brushed, combed, and scissored free of mats and tangles. Lady Harriet wanted her hair cropped short in the mode of Emily Cowper, which suited Coquette's notion of a hairstyle to perfection, but none of the other Byng ladies would have a jot of it.

"With the elegance of her nose and chin, only the Greek will do!" Constance Byng exclaimed.

Lady Harriet was quite overborne, and so it was that only half the extreme length of her hair was removed. Even so, her curls were smoothed with hot irons and then curled again with tongs until a dozen different styles were achieved and subsequently taught to Coquette's abigail.

If this were not bad enough, however, when the dressmaker arrived with a wagon loaded with bolts of silks, satins, calicos, cambrics, muslins, and tulles, Coquette soon found herself standing for hours at a time. She was measured, sized, pinched, fitted, and trussed with a corset, for heaven's sake, until she felt like a Christmas goose. Standing in but her shift in front of so many ladies, especially when a great deal of the comment was on the beauty of her figure and the perfection of her bosom, her cheeks became the color of a strong summer sunset. She had never paid much attention to her shape, but with the corset pulled so tightly, she glanced down only to find that she could not see her feet, not even her toes, for the uplifted nature of her breasts.

At that moment, panic struck. "No, no, no!" she cried, startling the dressmaker and her seamstresses. She turned around and ran from the room. Her bare feet slapped against the wood floors as she made her way to her bedchamber, where she threw herself on her bed, face first, and screamed into her pillows until the fight had finally left her. When she sat up, yet another mirror shouted at her, at the changes being made in her, of her red hair caught up in copper bands and her brows but two thin lines. She touched her face and wondered where she had gone. She touched the mirror and once more the sadness of this new life crashed down upon her.

An hour later, Lady Potsgrove came to her, finding her sitting in the dark, the bands pulled from her hair.

"Are you feeling better?" she asked. "It is no wonder you had a fit of the hysterics, what with everyone staring at you and plucking at you and making all manner of comment about you as though you were nothing but a bit of statuary. I am sorry, my dear. We do mean well."

"I know, Potsy," Coquette said quietly.

"Shall I have your dinner sent here?"

"I should appreciate it very much."

"Harriet, of course, thought you ought not to be coddled, but then she would feed her own children to the dogs did she think it would benefit them. However, I was very firm and suggested that you ought to be spared any more measuring until tomorrow. Will that suit you?"

"Yes, very much. I am sorry to have kicked up such a dust, indeed I am. I will do better tomorrow. Everyone has been so kind in helping me."

"Stuff and nonsense. We have not had so much fun in years."

Coquette chuckled. "That much is evident to me, but I cannot for the life of me comprehend why."

"Well, in part because fashion and taste are the meat of many of our discussions, but for another, we really do want to see you happily settled."

Coquette drew in a deep breath. She did not in the least understand so much compassion. After all, she was not a Byng and never would be. She thought it very generous of Harley's relatives to be so concerned for her.

On the following morning, Coquette found her spirits greatly restored and for that reason was able to bear with at least a modicum of equanimity the renewed efforts of the Byng ladies to make her quite the lady of quality. She practised crossing the long ballroom in front of them, trying to adopt all the suggestions cast in her direction for the purpose of developing a poised countenance. Unfortunately, each crossing, as she drew back her shoulders, tucked her buttocks, pulled in her stomach, bent her knees slightly, and kept her head high, all the while pretending to greet a dozen friends, sent a round of groans echoing off the high ceiling of the elegant, domed chamber.

"Whatever is to be done?" Lady Marianne cried.

"She walks like an elephant," Jane complained.

Theodora, the youngest of the matrons at three and forty, shook her head. "I have no more suggestions left in me. I begin to appreciate now how my own mother used to pinch at me about walking and sitting. I believe I even may have resented her, but no more."

"This will not do, not in the least, but whatever are we to do?" Lady Harriet queried.

Coquette turned to the bank of ladies who had given voice to so many hapless criticisms. "Is it so very bad?" she asked, unable to credit why.

Once more the groans reached the ceiling and returned

again. It would seem that thinned eyebrows and a corset were not going to satisfy these exacting ladies. She approached Lady Potsgrove, whose expression was so anxious that she looked as though she meant to cry. "And what do you say, Potsy?"

Lady Potsgrove pinched her lips together and sighed heavily. "Oh, my dear, though I risk offending you, I do fear that you look just like a big bear I once saw at the village when a fair was come to Bedfordshire. You have this wretched manner of weaving from side to side. It must be from having spent so much time on horseback. You do not seem to have a sense of the earth."

When all the ladies exclaimed their agreement with this assessment, Coquette could only stare at them. Walking was walking. She did not know in the least what they meant and certainly had no way of offering a remedy.

Lady Harriet, however, suddenly jumped from her seat and walked briskly to the bellpull. "I have it!" she cried. "I know precisely what may be done."

The ladies each demanded to know what notion was rattling about in her head, but she merely smiled in response and waited. When Stiles appeared, she demanded a tea service. "No, make that two."

"Two, my lady?"

"Yes," she returned with some degree of asperity. "I have said so."

"Two," he returned, bowing low and disappearing down the hall.

"Why, how kind of you," Lady Potsgrove gushed. "To be thinking of us in our sufferings. Tea would suit me to perfection."

"The tea is not for you. It is for Coquette."

"But we distinctly heard your order two complete services," Theodora stated. "You cannot expect Coquette to be drinking it all."

"We shall see."

Jane frowned. "Harriet, I do believe you may have gone mad."

"And again, we shall see."

Coquette, for her part, took up a seat as well. She had begun to feel like a bear, at least the ones she had seen at fairs who were kept too long at the mercy of barking dogs and shrill children and finally roared with displeasure. She felt like roaring now, but the response from the ladies would be so swift and cutting that she dared not. As she glanced out the windows that appeared in regular succession along the north wall, she watched the beech trees on the far hill dancing in the wind. The day appeared to be perfection, with a blue sky shining above the beeches and calling to her. She suddenly longed to be astride Old George, no lady's saddle on this day, and pounding across the turf and up the tall hill until she was riding the crest.

She was brought back to earth abruptly by Lady Harriet calling to her. "Come, Coquette. I wish for you to try this. I recalled once seeing a progression of servants, each bearing a tea service held aloft like this with one arm." She tried to demonstrate, but with the teapot so full she was unable to raise it at all. "I suppose you will get your tea after all," she said, addressing Lady Potsgrove. "The pots will need to be emptied before my plan will work."

The ladies, clearly ready for a restorative, rushed to the tea services and began pouring, preparing, and drinking their tea. Even Coquette was needed to help empty the first of the ornate silver pots. Lady Harriet encouraged her sisters and sisters-in-law to empty the second while she worked with their student. Coquette inwardly grimaced at this latest tactic of trying to establish some means of grace in her movements, but accepted the challenge of balancing first one, then two trays laden with several objects as she moved across the floor. After so many years dedicated to every manner of sport, she was not too surprised that she was sufficiently strong to bear the trays. Nor, apparently, was Lady Potsgrove.

"Just as I suspected," she whispered. "You could lift a small horse out of a peat bog."

Coquette merely laughed and strove to find the exact position required to hold the trays. The first thing she noticed was that in order to keep them aloft and not allow any of the articles to move, she had to stand very tall and straight and at the same time bend her knees for balance.

"Good. Very good," Lady Harriet called to her. "Yes, keep walking. Thank goodness you are a strong female. Do you feel the rigidity of your spine?"

"Yes."

"That is how you should feel while walking into a room."

"And you are certain I do not look like a broom?"

Lady Harriet laughed. "No, you look the best I've ever seen you. How does it feel?"

"Very strange, like I have a pole through my back." She glanced at Lady Harriet, who had begun to smile.

"Now you have it."

Coquette continued to walk across the floor and heard the chattering of the aunts suddenly stop. "I cannot believe it," she heard Jane cry. "You have done it, Harriet."

"Indeed, you have," Lady Marianne's youthful voice intoned.

"May I stop now?" Coquette inquired, her arms beginning to feel weary.

"No!" the ladies cried as one.

"Not until your back understands what is required," Lady Harriet explained. "If your arms grow weary, you may rest them, but only for a brief spell."

Coquette began to march to and fro. Every once in a while a command would issue from one lady or the other to the effect that she must lift her chin or take longer strides, or shorter steps, or pull her shoulders back a trifle, or whatever element seemed to be lacking. Eventually, however, she seemed to have satisfied them, for they had begun to ignore her entirely, sharing the latest on dits. She could not hear everything they said, and some of it, particularly if it referred to the confinements of one of their numerous daughters, she found both incomprehensible as well as uninteresting.

However, when Rupert Seames's name was brought forward and she happened to be near enough to hear all that was said, she was a little shocked, especially by Theodora Byng's revelation. "William was telling me only a sennight past that it is believed he is in debt to the cent-percenters to nearly eight thousand pounds."

"Indeed?" Constance murmured, clucking her tongue. "And he has but a paltry allowance upon which to live."

"How do such men manage?" Jane asked pragmatically.

"I haven't the faintest notion," Lady Potsgove responded, her graying brown curls, which peeped from beneath one of her absurd caps, shaking with her disbelief.

Lady Harriet, now sipping a cup of tea herself, declared, "I only wish he would not smile the way he does. As you know, I am not a fragile sort of female, but I vow when he casts me one of his smiles, it is as though he has thrown a handful of dirt on me."

All the ladies agreed, but what more was said of him was lost to Coquette's ears as she continued her progress to the end of the chamber. When she passed by the Byng ladies again, the subject had changed completely, which she felt was much more to her liking. She did not care for her kinsman in the least, but having them speak so harshly, if truthfully, about her only relative caused her some degree of mortification.

The new food for fodder was far more intriguing and caused her to slow her steps, for the ladies were actually wagering on which of Harley's latest favorites he meant to offer for.

"A guinea on Agnes Clifton," Constance called out.

"Oh, no," Lady Harriet cried. "She will not do at all for Barscot."

Jane said, "She may not do for Barscot, but I believe she will do for Harley. He is in love with the chit."

"No, he is not!" Theodora exclaimed hotly, as though the matter at hand was as serious as proclaiming war. "You only think he is because you are a particular friend of her mother's. Anyone can see that he favors Katherine Godwin, and who would not? She is by far the prettiest of all the ladies who has caught his eye. I shall wager five pounds that he chooses Miss Godwin."

"You will lose five pounds," Lady Marianne stated in irrevocable accents. "He is destined for Olivia Dazeley."

"Olivia!" Jane and Theodora protested in unison.

"That Long Meg," Lady Harriet added in some disgust.

"I am persuaded that whatever you might think of Miss Godwin and Lady Agnes, Miss Dazeley will win the day because she has something more than straw in her head."

This comment, so provoking for the champions of the other ladies, caused something akin to a brawl among the women. Not that they were engaging in an exchange of fisticuffs, but at the very least, the interchange of words became quite heated. For her part, Coquette was happy to be ignored so that she might set both trays down, pour herself a cup of tea, prop her feet up on an adjacent chair in a most unladylike fashion, and listen in some enjoyment to a variety of descriptions of Harley's dainty women.

Of the three, she had met only Lady Agnes, who was quite pretty and demure but who she had to agree with Lady Marianne was rather bacon-brained, even if she could walk like a queen. So it was with some interest she heard of the tall Olivia Dazeley with green-gold eyes and a habit of bending her knees slightly in order to appear shorter among the gentlemen of her acquaintance. Katherine Godwin, it was agreed, had a little more wit than poor Lady Agnes, and she did possess the most extraordinary large cornflower blue eyes, but had anyone noticed her proclivity to always have the correct opinion on *any* subject?

Coquette slouched in her chair and slurped her tea happily, all the lessons of the last several days set aside completely.

Her enjoyment of her tea and of the nature of the gabble-mongering ended, however, when Lady Potsgrove exclaimed, "Coquette! What in heaven's name are you doing?"

This unfortunate comment brought her brief respite to an end. The ladies turned at once to her, and the cackling which had been directed previously toward one another in the brangling over Harley's favorites was once more cast in her direction. How could she be sitting so? No lady elevated her legs in that fashion and certainly did not show so much ankle! And why was she drinking her tea like a hog at his trough? Had she learned nothing?

Coquette settled her teacup back on the table, rose from her chair, and once more took the trays in hand. After an hour had passed, a new exchange drew her attention away from her efforts to keep the pole in her spine in place.

"But Saturday is far too soon!" Jane exclaimed.

"She does not have much time," Lady Harriet reminded all the aunts. "She must be wed by the first of May, which means she ought to be in London as quickly as possible. Besides, I am persuaded she will be ready. We have three days yet."

Coquette returned to the ladies and relinquished the trays to Lady Potsgrove. "Of what are you speaking?"

"Harriet wishes to give a soiree on Saturday so that you might practice what you have learned. It is one thing to walk up and down a ballroom devoid of guests. It is quite another to maneuver through a crowded room and still maintain one's dignity, posture, and deportment."

An argument ensued. At least three of the ladies felt another sennight was necessary to the achievement of their ends, but Coquette considered the very short time she had in which to find a suitable husband and made her pronouncement. Keeping her shoulders well back, and feeling as though a pole had indeed been formed in her spine, she said, "I should be happy to attend a soiree on Saturday evening. I believe Lady Harriet's idea is precisely what is needed."

The Byng ladies regarded her with mouths agape. Constance blinked several times and whispered, "By all that is wonderful, I vow she is learning!"

With that, Coquette began to smile. Perhaps she was learning, perhaps they could even make a lady of her, but would she be able to find a husband by the first of May who would neither revolt her nor rob her of her inheritance?

Four

"The gentlemen are returned," Lady Harriet announced, a smile softening her usually harsh features.

Coquette felt her stomach twist into a knot. A rainstorm had drenched the land from the early morning hours and there had been some doubt as to whether Harley, his uncles, and Mr. Seames would return in sufficient time to enjoy the soiree. With Lady Harriet's pronouncement came the end of any such anxieties but a whole beginning of new ones.

Every time Coquette but looked in the mirror she had to pinch herself to determine if the reflection was truly hers. She had not thought she could look so very different with only her hair cut and curled, her brows shaped, a dusting of powder to diminish her freckles, and a light rouge on her lips. Of course, she was also wearing an extremely fashionable gown in the Empire style, cut low across the bosom, and made up in a lovely shade of sapphire blue.

I ought to be wearing black, or at least gray, she thought. Indeed, whenever she reflected on her most recent loss, she had no desires beyond this. She had even attempted to persuade the Byng ladies that she ought to be strict in her observance of this custom. They, in turn, were adamant that she not do so. They understood to perfection her desire to honor Lord Harlington in this fashion and honored her for it. However, not one of them saw how it would be possible for her to get a husband if she wore a color that would make her look as pale as death itself.

"And it will be allowed in you," Lady Marianne assured her. "For though we knew you stood as a daughter to our dear brother, society will see you only as a disinterested ward. But if you wish, out of respect, you could wear black gloves on occasion."

"At the very least, I do wish it so."

"Then consider the matter settled."

Reminded as she was of her present predicament, she said nothing further in an argument over proper mourning attire.

The Byng ladies had tried to keep to the whites and pale colors more suited to young maidens, but given Coquette's auburn curls and light complexion, her appearance suffered dreadfully. An hour had been spent, therefore, in the early days of selecting complementary fabrics, settling just which colors would be best suited for her reddish beauty. None of the ladies wished to offend the more exacting of the London hostesses by presenting Miss Millbook with gowns more suitable for matrons. On the other hand, white simply would not do, unless of course it was well embroidered.

However, the greater difficulty in seeing their protégée wed before the first of May eventually took precedence so that Coquette's entire wardrobe would be full not of white muslins and faded shades of blue and pink, but of more vibrant colors that would enhance her natural beauty.

All along the way, she had had her doubts about the choices the Byng ladies had made on her behalf, but now, seated as she was in front of her looking glass and wearing an exquisite shade of sapphire blue, she had to confess that she would never have believed she could look so well, so different, so pretty! Only, what would Harley think of her? She truly hoped he would not make jokes at her expense. Of course, she had no reason to believe he would, for he was a well-mannered gentleman who was for the most part beyond behaving in a rude fashion, at least in company. At the same time, she had provoked him so sorely for so many years that she would not have blamed him even a trifle were he to avenge himself now.

She turned to regard Lady Harriet. "Has Lady Potsgrove returned from the village yet?" She had gone there earlier to deliver several baskets of food to families in need, and Coquette in particular had wanted her near when the evening's festivities began.

"No, I fear she has not. But you know what she is, a very great gabblemonger. I am certain she could not resist drawing out every morsel of gossip possible, which I have always believed was her foremost purpose in giving the baskets in the first place."

The remaining Byng ladies laughed, for it was quite true. Lady Potsgrove loved gossip above all things.

Jane Byng fussed a trifle over the curls on Coquette's forehead. "You need not worry, Miss Millbrook. Even if she arrives late, we shall be beside you the entire way. Although, if I may say so myself, you hardly need anyone to remind you of what you ought and ought not do. You have been a very apt pupil. Even now! Do look at your carriage! You are sitting ramrod straight!"

Coquette opened her eyes wide and once more caught her reflection in the looking glass. So she was, not even the smallest stoop, slouch, or slump to be seen. A miracle indeed.

"Shall we adjourn to the drawing room?" Lady Marianne suggested. "I daresay the gentlemen will join us as soon as they are able, and I for one would enjoy a glass of sherry before they do." This last hint set all the ladies in motion.

Coquette rose from her chair, smoothed out her blue silk gown, and gave a final tug on her black gloves. How peculiar she felt, as though for the first time in her existence she belonged to the society in which she had been born. There was a feeling of comfort in the sensation, which was as pleasing as it was surprising.

A quarter of an hour later, Coquette sat with the Byng ladies in one of the smaller chambers, the green drawing room as it was known, which happened to be a favorite of hers. Bookshelves lined two of the walls, giving the chamber an intimate feel, while the various wood tables were an elegant mahogany. The sofa and chairs were covered in a gold and cream striped silk, while the walls and draperies were both of a medium shade of green. A small pianoforte sat in the corner, adorned with a stack of music. She had known hundreds of happy hours with Lord Harlington, always before dinner, in just this room.

She was sipping a glass of sherry and remembering the earl fondly when Lady Potsgrove entered the chamber. "Where is our dear Coquette?" she exclaimed, glancing from visage to visage. She wore a black pelisse, as was proper given her state of mourning, and a black bonnet. "I know I should have dressed for dinner first, but I had to discover how she fared. Well, where is she?"

Coquette smiled and was about to speak, but when she realized that Lady Potsgrove did not know her, she could not help but remain silent a little longer.

"Well?" she asked again, seeming slightly agitated. "Do not tell me the chit did not have the courage to join you. She may be lacking many things, but not pluck! Oh, I see we have a guest."

She squinted slightly, then moved toward Coquette. "And a very pretty one. Are we known to one another?" She seemed very confused.

Coquette heard the Byng ladies choking on their laughter.

"Lizzie, you have been in need of spectacles for these two years past!" Lady Marriane cried. "And this is what has come of it. Do you not remember the lady before you?"

"Indeed, I . . . I cannot say. Are we very well acquainted?"

Coquette did not think it fair to keep her in such suspense. "Yes, I believe we are, Potsy, quite well, indeed!"

Lady Potsgrove's hazel eyes opened as wide as they were able. "Coquette!" she cried. "I confess that I am in some need of spectacles, but truly I did not know you, even after all this week of watching you transform. Oh, my dear! How charming! How elegant! How *beautiful!*" She clasped her hands to her bosom. "Oh, my dear, you will cast them all in the shade. I must say, I am feeling rather odd. Why is the room spinning in just . . . that . . . "

Coquette watched her drop into a lump of black bombazine.

"Good heavens!" Lady Harriet cried. "I do believe that in all these years, after so many threats that she might faint, our dear sister has actually accomplished the deed."

The knowledge that the alteration in her appearance could be so profound sent a shudder through Coquette. As the Byng ladies clustered about Lady Potsgrove, all her former anxiety returned to her. This was not the life of her choosing. This was not the path for her feet. She did not belong here, and she was certain to overset everyone in the process. Surely if she had had even the smallest amount of resolution she would have simply turned away from her inheritance and cast herself upon the world, intent on surviving by her own wits and nerve.

However, such resolve did not exist within her. The world was a harsh place for penniless women, as Lord Harlington well knew when he assigned such dreadful stipulations to her inheritance.

Lady Potsgrove recovered quickly, and after sitting for a few minutes in a chair near Coquette and partaking of a small glass of sherry herself, her complexion resumed its normal rosy hue. "I vow you are the prettiest lady of my acquaintance," she said. "We shall have such fun in London, perhaps an adventure or two that will satisfy even you."

Coquette knew that Lady Potsgrove's notion of adventure meant a visit to a subscription library or a museum. She resisted the sigh that threatened to erupt from her throat and instead murmured politely, "I believe we shall." She forced a smile to her lips, which caused Constance Byng to nod approvingly.

"You will do, Miss Millbrook," she said quietly. "Indeed, you will." She then smiled in a knowing manner and raised her glass to her.

Coquette acknowledged the compliment with a nod of her own and lifted her glass in response. After that, there was nothing left to do but to wait for the gentlemen to begin arriving. A feeling of dread soon overtook her, upon which even the sherry had not the smallest effect.

A quarter of an hour later, she was standing near Lady Potsgrove when Harley, the first of the gentlemen, arrived in the doorway of the drawing room. His expression was pleasant enough, quite amicable in fact, but when his gaze landed upon her, his color first faded, then grew quite heightened. "Good God," he murmured, immediately making his way toward her. "Is this possible? Is this, indeed, you, Cokie?"

She lowered herself into a smooth curtsy, then rose. "Miss Millbrook if you please, my lord."

He stared at her for the longest time. "I had always thought, I had always known or at least believed . . ." He shook his head. "You are lovely, a diamond of the first water. I congratulate you."

"Not me," she responded. "I did nothing. You must offer your compliments to your aunts, all of them. They have slaved for days hoping to make me presentable."

"And you are," he responded, a slight frown between his brows. "Even . . . even how you carry yourself."

She leaned forward and whispered, "They made me carry heavy trays in order to learn to balance myself properly."

He smiled and at that moment, when his handsome features were softened, she felt her breath yet again catch in her throat. She had seen him a thousand times in the course of her existence. Why now did she feel overcome?

His gaze caught hers and held. She had all those strange sensations again—a queasiness in her stomach and her knees trembled slightly. What did it mean, she wondered. Was this the way Harley was with all the ladies of his acquaintance, or perhaps just with those he meant to conquer? His underlook, so famous in fashionable circles, so deadly to the feminine heart, was in prime twig, as evidenced by the rapid beating of her pulse, which she could feel even in her throat.

Of course, the idea that she might be even in the smallest sense susceptible to his advances struck her as so absurd that she began to laugh so heartily, her head tossed back, that it was but a few seconds before she realized all the Byng ladies were frowning her down. She quickly schooled her features and resorted to merely grinning at Harley. He, in turn, had begun to scowl at her.

"Oh, now, do not you come the crab," she cried. "I could not help but laugh. Was that your 'underlook'?" she added with some innocence.

"My *what?*" he fairly thundered.

"Harley!" Lady Potsgrove called to him. "We are attempting to show our dear Coquette how to conduct herself. This cannot be accomplished by your deciding it is appropriate to set up a caterwaul."

"I beg your pardon, Aunt," he responded properly. To Coquette, however, he immediately reverted his attention and queried again, only in softer accents, "My *what?*"

"Pretending ignorance does not at all become you," Coquette said. "You know very well to what I am referring. The entire *beau monde* is perfectly well acquainted with your underlook, so I beg you will refrain from feigning otherwise."

"Well, well," he responded, a familiar grimace set to his lips. "I see my aunts did prepare you for the Season after all. To hear you speak of 'the entire *beau monde*' as though you had done so since you were in the cradle is something I never expected to hear. I not only congratulate you, I applaud you."

She clasped her hands to her bosom as she had seen Lady Agnes do any number of times. "Do I give offense, m'lord?" She then batted her lashes in what she hoped was a wholly provoking manner.

Harley did not answer her but instead offered a disgusted

grunt and moved away. His thoughts, however, remained
fixed with her. Coquette had always been able to raise his
hackles, but in this instance, she had not offended him in the
least, except perhaps in her ridiculous reference to his underlook. Good God, his *underlook!* Of all the absurd starts. She
made him sound as though he was a poetic creature, like
Byron, who used all manner of arts to seduce the ladies of his
acquaintance. He might take some measure of enjoyment
from engaging in a flirtation now and then, but he hoped he
was not so bacon-brained as to be obvious in his tricks.

He threw himself into a chair near the door, from which
vantage he could hear Mr. Seames and one of his uncles conversing in the antechamber. He watched Coquette move in her
newly acquired elegance to stand by the pianoforte and flip
through the music laid out on the closed lid. He still could not
credit her utter and complete transformation. His stupefaction
was eclipsed only by his admiration.

She was beautiful, a diamond of the first stare, as he had
already told her. But even now, observing her, he felt an enormous pressure on his chest, as though the mere sight of her
was holding him in a tight grip. A terrible thought powered
through his head: *This is how she will affect all the gentlemen
she meets from this moment on.* Perhaps he should have been
pleased with such a truth, but instead he found himself disliking the notion immensely, though why was less clear.

Perhaps it was because until now, Coquette Millbrook had
been thoroughly unspoilt. He may not have approved of her
unladylike conduct all these years, but at least she was, well,
real. A Season in London beneath the admiring attentions of
the *ton*'s finest bachelors and fortune hunters would turn her
head completely. She would undoubtedly grow proud, perhaps even haughty, as so many beauties did. He did not wish
to see her in such a state and grew determined to set himself
against her did she show even the smallest predilection of
doing so. She was his ward now. Therefore he had a certain
responsibility toward her not just to see her wed, but to see

her present transformation grow deeper than just the beautiful flow of her auburn hair cascading in banded waves down her back, or the graceful manner in which her dark blue gown curved to reveal the beauty of her figure, or the way her black gloves fitted her long fingers quite to perfection.

He pondered the color of her gloves for a moment and was reminded suddenly of the occasion which had forced so many changes in her. A quick, hurtful wave of sorrow passed through him. He did not want to go to London, nor should he, given the recent death of his father. But the will had changed everything and had dictated in this instance that some of the niceties must be set aside.

Glancing again at Coquette, he realized that his aunts had made several excellent decisions on her behalf. She most certainly could not have appeared in London in complete mourning attire. Had she been dressed in black, she would have looked like a crow wearing a red bonnet. No, such a dark shade of blue suited her quite well.

He regretted suddenly that their ways would part by the beginning of May. She would marry and undoubtedly move to a different county to begin her life as a wife and a mother. He could not help but smile, thinking that never before had he envisioned her in either of these roles, yet somehow he knew she would excel at both. There was a tenderness in her which he had witnessed on many occasions over the years, and something more.

He was reminded of the silliest memory of her. She could not have been more than seven or eight and he a stripling of perhaps fourteen. She had caught him trying to steal a kiss from one of the village schoolgirls. When the chit had run away, Coquette, instead of teasing him, had asked for a kiss herself. He had been rather shocked and yet touched. He had asked her why, and she had responded, "Because, Harley, I know you best and I should like my first kiss to be from someone I know."

He had thought her answer sensible and tender and had

even promised to oblige her, but not until she was at least eighteen. The years had dimmed the memory in him until this very moment. He smiled, thinking he should like nothing better than to oblige her now, a circumstance which once more reminded him that he would probably have the devil of a time keeping his house clear of undesirable suitors, which, given the size of her fortune, would be excessive.

At that moment, she happened to turn away from the pianoforte, glancing in his direction once more. Again, that powerful sensation gripped his chest. Faith, had he ever seen any lady so beautiful? She smiled and shook her head, then moved to sit beside Lady Potsgrove. Her expression was cloaked, causing him to wonder which of his aunts had taught her that particular skill of concealing her feelings. Only what were her thoughts and sentiments now that her entire world had been turned upside down?

Coquette let her gaze flow along the lines of the patterned Aubusson carpet at her feet, a finely woven rug in muted shades of peach, green, beige, and blue. She was schooling her features, just as Lady Harriet had taught her to do. In this particular case, she was glad of it, for Harley had looked at her again in just that way—as though he meant to take command of her mind as soon as he was given the smallest opportunity. The odd thing was that he did have an effect on her, inexplicably so, something she did not want him to know. Her heart was racing, her breathing had grown strangely shallow, and her knees were still trembling.

But this is ridiculous, she thought, turning to glance at Lady Potsgrove, who was telling an anecdote in a most animated fashion to Jane Byng. She feigned listening, but her thoughts ran round and round, dwelling upon the extraordinary circumstance that with but a few plucked brows and a pretty coiffure, Harley had given every evidence of being much struck with her. And that after all these years! It was most peculiar and, of course, wholly unwelcome.

Still, she was oddly flattered, but she did not want him to

know any of it, and so she continued to still the smiles, frowns, chuckles, grimaces, and sighs which had heretofore escaped her person in a happily haphazard manner. She supposed, as she withheld another sigh, she was becoming a lady after all.

A rather strangled gasp from the direction of the doorway caused her, as well as the ladies near her, to turn toward the queer sound. She was surprised to find Rupert Seames, nearly as white as frost, staring at her, his pale blue eyes bulging in his thin face. "Good God! Is that you, cousin?" he queried.

Coquette could not help but smile, although she had to admit he appeared very near to fainting. "Indeed, yes," she responded.

He forced a smile. "But how comely you are," he stated, clearly attempting to regain his composure.

Coquette believed she understood him to perfection. His smiles a week ago during the reading of Lord Harlington's will had indicated a great measure of triumph, his certain belief that no one would desire to wed such a hoydenish creature as she had been. He had been right, of course, but he had certainly misjudged both her own determination to retain her fortune as well as the abilities of the Byng ladies. She could also see a measure of bitterness in the cold lines of his face, as though he felt cheated of an inheritance which had never belonged to him.

Since she made no response, he added, "What miracles your benefactresses have wrought in but a sennight."

This of course was no real compliment, so she merely nodded politely, with a slight inclination of her head. Lady Harriet, seated near her right, murmured, "Well done, Coquette. Well done, indeed. One would think you had been in London every Season for the past six."

This was no small accolade, and she turned to cast her an appreciative smile.

What Mr. Seames might have said next was lost to the announcement that dinner was served.

Later, with the soiree fully under way, Coquette found herself surrounded by the same young gentlemen with whom she used to hunt and fish and ride hard to hounds. A daring lot, but in this moment they hardly gave any evidence of it, gawking at her like a bunch of striplings still green behind the ears. She fanned herself and smiled as she had been taught by Constance Byng, but she did not know whether to be flattered or disgusted, though the latter seemed to be the more dominant sensation. How could a group of such virile, fearless, headstrong men be reduced to puddles of incoherent compliments merely by a smile, a batting of the lashes, and a flutter or two of a lace fan? Really, it was both marvelous and ridiculous.

Finally, she had had enough. She missed her childhood friends and abruptly rapped each of them in turn on the forehead with her fan, not gently like a flirtatious miss, but with a stinging *thwap* that caused each of them to cry out.

"The deuce take it!" Thomas Adcock cried.

"Of all the blasted starts!" Richard Chalgrave exclaimed.

"What a baggage you are, Cokie, and I'd thought you'd changed!" Nicholas Wilstead cried heatedly. "Damme if I won't have a welt the size of a walnut."

"And less than you deserve, Nicky!"

"You ought to at least warn a fellow!" he retorted. "Not go dressed up like, like some goddess, then smite him with thunderbolts when he ain't looking."

At that, Coquette could no longer keep her countenance. She began to laugh, so loudly that all the Byng ladies were frowning her down again and at least two of them had begun to move in her direction. She could not help it, however, and between gasps, cried, " '*Smite him with thunderbolts*' . . . I hit you with my fan! *My fan!* " She laughed so hard that she began to weep, more so when the imprint of her weapon became clearly visible on each forehead.

She probably would have continued laughing at their expense had not Lady Harriet intervened abruptly, sending each of the gentlemen to attend to other ladies present while she propelled Coquette by the elbow to a quiet corner.

"Miss Millbrook!" she cried on a harsh whisper. "Do cease this instant."

"Oh, but I can't," she whispered in return, still swiping at mirthful tears that streamed down her cheeks. Her repressed giggles became chuckles until she was laughing almost violently once more.

"Enough of this nonsense," Lady Harriet hissed. "Or I shall make it impossible for you to attend the London Season, and don't think I can't or won't do it. I have not exerted myself so rigorously on your behalf this past sennight to have the whole of it undone because you do not have the smallest command of yourself."

These words had a strong, sobering effect on Coquette. She did not comprehend in the least why Lady Harriet should be so adamant. After all, this was just a soiree in Harley's home, not a ball among prestigious London strangers. She said as much.

At that, Lady Harriet straightened her back. "Do you want your reputation to precede you, Miss Millbrook? For I promise you that if it does, if even one of the persons present regales our London hostesses of your antics tonight, you will be torn to pieces before you have even begun. London is a fierce, competitive place where many matrons with less beautiful and less well-dowered young ladies for daughters will be happy to see your career quickly overturned. Believe me when I say that they will be waiting to pounce, happy to overlook you for the next event and the next and the next until you are no longer welcome anywhere in the first circles. Well, I can see by your expression that I have your attention at last."

"Indeed, you do, my lady. I . . . I beg your pardon. I was not thinking."

"Very well." She turned and waved to Harley, who immediately crossed the room to join them. "See to Miss Millbrook," she commanded. "Prevail upon her, if you are able, to conduct herself properly the remainder of the evening. I have little doubt that Mrs. Dazeley will be happy to report her conduct to Princess Esterhazy, with whom she is intimately connected, and then Coquette will be in the basket."

When she moved away, Coquette queried, "Princess Esterhazy?"

"Yes. She is one of our most famous hostesses and a patroness of Almack's as well. My aunt is quite correct in giving you a hint. Whatever possessed you to abuse your friends so sorely?"

Coquette felt all the excitement and joy of the evening dwindle to a sensation quite near to boredom. "Oh, it was ridiculous. They were staring at me with mooncalf eyes, and I couldn't bear it a moment longer. I was with Nicky when he broke his arm cramming a hedge and with Thomas playing at army in the hills beyond his house. I would never have believed that they could be such simpletons. So I struck them."

"Do but look at Mr. Adcock now," he suggested, giving his head a jerk in Thomas's direction.

Coquette shifted her gaze slightly and watched as Olivia Dazeley, Mrs. Dazeley's eldest and quite pretty daughter, was dipping the corner of a kerchief into an iced cup of champagne and dabbing at Thomas's 'wound.' Olivia was one of Harley's favorites, with whom he was conducting one of his protracted, if misleading, flirtations. She was tall, quite a Long Meg, in possession of green-gold eyes, and wore her light brown curls caught up in a pretty knot atop her head.

As she watched the tender scene, however, all she felt was disgust, particularly if that was the way she was now expected to conduct herself. For that reason, she turned back to a nearby window and stared into the dark night. Very little was visible beyond the ring of light reflected from the mansion's windows. Clouds obliterated the starlight and apparently not even the moon was able to penetrate the veil.

When Harley followed after her, she said in a low voice, "I should not be doing this. Indeed, I should not. I shall make a thousand blunders before the first week is out."

He was silent a moment, then said jovially, "I should like to see that, Cokie! Indeed, I should. I believe it will atone for at least a score or more of your wretched scrapes over the past twenty years."

At that, she turned to him and smiled faintly. "I have absolutely nothing to atone for," she retorted. "Since you delivered ample justice of your own every time."

"I did no such thing," he stated.

"What about the time you plucked me off my horse and tossed me in the stream?"

"Oh, that," he mused. "But then you had taken my newly purchased bay out for a three-hour ride when I had not even put him through his paces."

"But that is my point, Harley. You never let anything rest. You always made me pay for my misdeeds, so at this point I believe our scores are well settled."

"Hardly seems like very much fun, does it?"

At that, she laughed, something of her despair leaving her. She realized suddenly just how unhappy she was at the prospect of going to London and doing the pretty. Oh, if only Lord Harlington, her dearest friend, had not done this thing to her, she would even now be heading to Bristol to see if she might find the right ship to purchase.

"Now, now, Cokie," he whispered. "You were doing much better earlier, keeping your sentiments to yourself, schooling every expression. Right now you appear as though you wish to sink into the earth and never be seen again."

"I do, Harley. I do, if it means I could escape going to London."

"Well," he mused, "you could always relinquish your fortune to Mr. Seames."

She turned to look in the direction of her distant cousin and saw that he sat in the corner of the room, a knee crossed elegantly over the other. While eyeing himself in the reflection of a nearby silver candlestick, he was plucking tenderly at one blond curl after another. She shuddered. "Is he as much in debt as I have heard?"

"More, probably. Living on the expectation."

"The expectation of what?" she countered. "That I might take charge of his debts?"

"Perhaps, but then he does not know you, does he?"

"No, he does not," she stated firmly.

"Then make certain he sees not a tuppence of your fortune, for he would not rest until he had command of the whole of it. And especially try not to give the tabbies food for gossip."

"I'll try to do better the rest of the evening. You needn't attend to me further, I promise."

He eyed her for a moment, his gaze slipping once to Miss Dazeley, who was still laughing and chatting with Thomas Adcock, though she had at least ceased her ministrations.

"Go to her, Harley. Indeed, you may trust me now. In fact, I mean to oblige my aunts and play for all of you."

At that, he brightened. "Excellent. I've always enjoyed your performance."

She laughed, thinking he could not be serious.

"No, Cokie, I am in earnest. You do not play with complete perfection, but there is something bold, even commanding in your performances, rather like the woman herself." With that, he bowed and moved in Miss Dazeley's direction.

Coquette stared after him. Was it possible he had truly complimented her . . . again? Good God, it was a night of miracles. She watched him go, thinking that everything was changing right before her, like leaves turning and twisting in a brisk, unpredictable wind. Even Miss Dazeley's smile as Harley approached her seemed cautious, almost peevish. She had met the young woman for the first time and was not overly impressed. She seemed in the mold of Lady Agnes, at least where her ambition was concerned. She felt a lump of ice would have had more real affection for Harley.

She did not like Miss Dazeley at this moment, extending her hand to Harley as she did, like a long claw ready to grab hold and never let go.

She turned and walked somewhat blindly toward the piano-forte. Was she really leaving for London so soon, in just two days' time? A feeling very near to homesickness descended upon her. And yet she did not belong to Barscot, not really. Harley was not her real family, nor the Byng ladies, not even Lady Potsgrove, who had resided at Barscot for the past decade. She had no real ties to Bedfordshire, so what did it matter that she was leaving and going to London?

As she took up her place before the ivory keys, she glanced again at Harley, who had taken up a seat beside Miss Dazeley. He was smiling brilliantly down upon her and suddenly all her pique at being forced down a road she did not want to travel rushed over her. She was as mad as fire all over again that her plans were to be set aside because of the wretched conditions attached to her inheritance.

She therefore set into the keys with a vehemence that brought all conversation to a complete stop. She had nevered played Mozart so quickly before, but never had Mozart been the brunt of her fury before. When the sonata ended, her performance was greeted with a stunning round of applause, but her anger had not abated, not even a trifle. She bowed politely several times, and when Thomas and Richard rushed forward to express their admiration for her execution of the piece, she realized she could bear no more of so ridiculous a farce.

She made her escape as quickly as possible, expressing her need to withdraw for a time, which the gentlemen permitted her to do, and before she quite knew how it had come about, she was running in the direction of the stables. There was only one possible remedy for the fires that raged in her, a ride with Old George.

A stableboy had just placed the bit in poor Old George's mouth, entirely at her prickly insistence that he be quick about it, when Harley appeared across the gravel drive, completely out of breath.

"I know you too well, Cokie!" he cried. "You might have fooled Adcock and Chalgrave, but not me. What the devil do you think you're doing?"

Coquette realized she did not have time to wait for the now exceedingly anxious stableboy to saddle Old George. Harley could easily keep her from the ride she needed. She grabbed the reins, and with all the ability of a woman who had lived with horses her entire life, she hoisted her skirts up above her knees and swung herself up onto the bare back of the horse with the agility of a monkey swinging from branch to branch. A cold night wind was against her cheeks before even two seconds had passed. She heard Harley calling to her, his voice echoing against the distant Chilterns. Wetness whipped at her face and only when the lights of Barscot had faded from the lanes did she realize she was weeping.

Harley felt a sadness so deep as he watched her disappear into the black hole of the distant lane that his throat ached almost unbearably. He realized he felt as she did, as she must, that life was belching fire beneath both pairs of feet and neither could be content.

"What is it, Harley?" Lady Potsgrove called to him as she crossed the lane to join him. "Where has she gone?"

He sighed. "She never could bear the bit between her teeth."

Lady Potsgrove, whose cap was askew, shook her head. "Why on earth did she put a bit in her mouth in the first place? How very unclean."

Harley chuckled as he turned toward her. "I beg you will never change. You delight me enormously."

"Harley, you are making no sense. Are you to be as addled as I believe our dear Coquette is become?" She then glanced at the stableboy, who was still standing nearby with a saddle in hand. After a moment she gasped. "Was Coquette actually riding without a saddle and in a, oh, dear, a completely improper position?"

"Though I daresay I shall cause you to swoon by saying it, my dear aunt, our Coquette could easily ride for Astley's Amphitheatre."

Out popped Lady Potsgrove's fan. "Oh, dear. Oh, my. And I am to be her chaperone . . . for two months! However shall I bear it? She will cause a great scandal, and I shall never be welcome in London again! I wish to heaven your mother were here. She would have known how to manage Coquette all these years, but one thing is for certain, she never would have approved of this."

"Of course not," Harley responded numbly. His mother had been the ideal of all that was ladylike, while Coquette was in every sense the opposite. He found himself therefore torn completely in his sentiments toward her. He could not help that he admired excessively the passionate independence which framed Coquette's character. At the same time, no lady would have just mounted a horse bareback. She hardly deserved the term, even if her brows had been recently plucked.

"Come, Aunt, let us return to the soiree."

"But what shall we tell everyone? We can hardly say that she rode off into the night with her garters on display."

He laughed loudly at that, for indeed he had seen her garters—and much more. "No, we cannot. I suppose we shall simply have to say she was overcome by the headache and is now prostrate on her bed."

"Yes, yes, that will do very well, indeed. A lady may always lay claim to the headache and still remain above scandal."

"How very true—but might I suggest that once we reach London we let it be widely known that our darling Coquette is prone to such headaches?"

"Why ever would we do that?" she asked in her quite witless manner

Five

Two days later, Coquette descended the stairs slowly as if in a dream. She could not credit that she was actually leaving Barscot Hall, undoubtedly never to return—the place of her childhood, the only home she had ever truly known. How very different this was from how she had originally planned to depart. Presently she wore sedate traveling dress, from half boots of a soft, well-worked tan kid to a pelisse in a lovely shade of green, to a bonnet slung over her wrist and dangling from long cherry-red ribbons. She was all the crack, as Harley used to say in his salad days.

In her original scheme, she had always thought to steal away at midnight, having left a brief note behind saying she had gone to Bristol to buy her ship. Even the thought of it made her smile. A second more and a familiar sadness swept through her of vanished dreams and the real grief that she had so recently buried her dear Lord Harlington.

A cool wind, laden with the smell of an approaching rain shower, blew in from the entrance hall doors, which had been thrown wide open. Beyond, in the gravel drive, servants moved to and fro among at least three coaches and two wagons. The removal to London had always been a significant undertaking. It was odd to think that she had never truly wished to go to the metropolis before, except that had she gone, she would not have been permitted to see the city as most gentlemen saw it, the city pierced by a long winding river that had connected London to the world for centuries.

She would have gone as she was going now, pinched, plucked, and trussed, ready for sale.

As she reached the bottom step, her thoughts turned to Mr. Seames, who had left Barscot on the day before with the rest of the party. In that, she felt she was quite fortunate, since she had very little affection for her relation and no respect for him at all. He had gone as he had come, with hardly a polite word to her. How wretched that her closest relative, and that so distant as to be neglible, was such a worthless fellow.

Lady Potsgrove called down to her from the second floor. "Coquette, my dear, did you remember your kerchief and your smelling salts?"

"Yes, Potsy."

"And pray, stop calling me that terrible name. It will not do at all in London, you know."

Coquette turned fully and stared up at her. Lady Potsgrove was retying the strings of a cap that sported so many layers of lace that Coquette thought she looked like a pastry of some sort. "But, *Potsy,* I had always thought you liked your pet name."

"You are a wretched girl, you always were," was the strong retort, softened by the smile she wore as she turned away to instruct one of the footmen on how to properly carry a trunk.

Coquette might have stepped outside, but Lady Potsgrove had something further to say to her. "And do stand up straight. You are slumping again. You look just like a pump handle."

By the habit formed after having been lectured by six ladies for a full sennight, Coquette pulled her shoulders back, tucked in her bottom and tightened her stomach. At the same time, she pulled a face, but it was far too late to have an effect. Lady Potsgrove had already set ferociously upon one of the upper maids who had dared to drop a bandbox right in front of her. For a brief moment, she wished that the Byng ladies had not all departed on the day before, since she had been left wholly into the care of a woman who had taken to having the charge of her with all the relish of a dog gnawing at and guarding a favorite bone.

For one thing, she had endured a complete hour's dressing down about how she was never, *never*, to ride bareback in London. Coquette had tried to assure her at the outset that of course she would never do anything so scandalous, but Lady Potsgrove was not in the least convinced and had scolded her severely.

"Why do you look so peevish, Cokie?" Harley called to her, drawing her instantly out of her reveries.

He was just emerging from a heavily draped antechamber to her left. She turned in his direction and for a very long moment, she forgot everything but how handsome he looked, especially since a several-caped greatcoat was slung over his broad shoulders. Given a pair of rugged Hessians that gleamed with all the expertise of a truly gifted valet and the absolute perfection of his athletic figure, she found herself swallowing quite hard. A slight dizziness seemed to accompany her present appreciation of his manly beauty and only by the strongest effort was she able to answer his question at all. "It is your aunt. The moment the remainder of your family quit Barscot, she felt compelled to begin her own instruction, which I vow has not ceased one minute in two from the moment of their departure."

"It cannot be all that bad," he offered, a half smile on his lips.

She could see he was being completely unsympathetic, so she said, "Indeed? What if I were to tell you"—and here she linked his arm and drew him away from so many potentially listening ears and into the well-draped connecting room—"that your aunt informed me just after I had partaken of my breakfast that I was to be wary of the attentions of all gentlemen, since each was likely to attempt to steal a kiss from me, if given the smallest encouragement?"

"What?" he cried, laughing.

"Yes, well you may stare, but so she did." She drew him

well into the recesses of the chamber. "I feel compelled, therefore, to ask you if it is true."

He feigned a heavy sigh. "Alas, quite true, I fear. Perhaps I should offer you a little advice of my own."

"No, I beg you, do not!" she cried. "I have been the brunt of so much advice of late that my brain feels stuffed full of feathers."

"I imagine it would. My aunts were tireless, I fear. Only tell me, do you feel prepared for the Season, truly?"

She shrugged, swinging the bonnet a little. "I suppose. I do not cherish going in the least, as well you know, but there is one thing that has been plaguing me since breakfast. Harley, you must know that I am wholly without experience. Would you, I mean, I recall once when I was much younger, perhaps by fifteen years, I asked you to kiss me, and you promised you would."

"Wait," he said, laughing once more. "You cannot be asking me to kiss you now."

"Well, of course I am. You have no particular feelings for me, nor I for you, so it would be perfectly simple and—and unencumbered. I simply do not want to meet a score of young men and not have known what it was to be kissed. Oh, I suppose that must seem ridiculous, but I have not attended to matters as I should have and now I am suddenly faced with taking a husband before barely another month will have passed. Most girls . . . oh, never mind. I suppose it was a ridiculous notion."

"Poor Cokie," he said, smiling kindly down upon her. "You meant to be going out to sea by now. Instead, you are going to London. Of course I shall oblige you. A promise, after all, is a promise."

"Then you do remember?"

He nodded. "Very much so."

"Excellent," she cried, tossing her bonnet aside as though it had been an old toy.

Coquette braced herself, thinking he would simply lean

down and place a peck on her lips. She was not prepared, however, for how gently he stepped very close to her and took her up in his arms. Clearly, he was a man of some experience.

"Oh," she murmured.

"I just want you to know," he murmured softly, "how strange I think this is, since you are so different now, yet not different at all." Then his lips found hers.

At the first sensation of pressure, her mind was quite scientific in approach, for she could ennumerate the various qualities of what she was experiencing. His lips were soft, even a trifle damp, but not in an unpleasant way. His arms held her firmly, she could feel his chest pressed to hers. He smelled of shaving soap and something that might have been gun oil.

Then something quite odd happened. Her brain stopped functioning entirely. Instead, she fell into the most marvelous place of sweetness and light, the way she often felt when she read Byron's poetry, as though magic was crackling all about her and daring her to be everything she was not. The crackles became explosions and suddenly she felt as though her whole body was on fire, the flames coursing through her, teasing her and bringing something new and unexpected into existence.

How long the kiss actually lasted, she did not know, but somehow it seemed an eternity.

When he drew back, if but slightly, there was a frown between his brows.

She blinked, more than once, trying to see him as she had always known him to be, as merely her nemesis, Harley, who would as likely throw her in the duck pond as bid her good morning. However, she could not. Something seemed changed, forever perhaps, but what? "Is it always like this?" she asked, her voice little more than a hoarse whisper.

His head moved slowly from side to side. He appeared to be in as much of a fog as she was.

"No?" she inquired again.

"No, not all the time."

"But sometimes."

"Yes, I think so."

"Well," she said, releasing a sigh. "I should like to do more of that."

The expression of sudden concern, possibly even horror, that skidded across his face made her smile. "What is it?"

"I cannot credit you would even say such a thing."

She scowled. "Harley, in that moment just now when you spoke, your face darkened like a cloud covering the sun. Whatever is the matter with you? How could you possibly object to my saying I should like to do a little more kissing? Surely you would not have me priggish, particularly if I am to be married, and that so soon!"

How could he tell her when even he did not know? But the mere thought of other gentlemen, other *men,* holding Coquette in their arms, kissing her as he had just kissed her and making her feel the way she apparently felt, so disturbed him that for the most ridiculous moment he felt like taking her back to her bedchamber and locking her within until she had grown up a little more, say in thirty or forty more years!

The truth was, when she had asked him if kissing was always like that, he had told a whisker. He had never in his entire existence had so much delight, even pleasure, in kissing before. He remembered suddenly how, over a sennight past, he had taken her in his arms in the stables just to comfort her and how he had thought she fit him so perfectly. That was what kissing her had been like, perfection! But how was that possible when it was merely Cokie he had kissed and not one of his favorites?

He had no comprehension at all as to what had just happened. He could not explain why kissing her had felt like racing into the wind on the back of his fastest gelding, flying across on open field neck or nothing. His heart had become yet again gripped tightly by the same force that had captured him so recently while seeing her first transformed under the guidance of his aunts.

Was that the solution to this riddle? Had kissing her felt so extraordinary because she was changed?

In the midst of his reflections, he became aware that he was still holding her in his arms. He began to release her slowly and observed as he did so that she seemed wary, even suspicious suddenly.

"What is it?" he asked.

"Nothing," she responded. "That is, you appeared very peculiar just now, almost dazed."

"Well, I am not. Merely a trifle confused."

Coquette straightened her shoulders. "Well, I am not confused in the least. I mean to collect a dozen beaus and kiss them all. Perhaps I shall even choose my husband based on how well he can kiss. Oh, Harley, I did enjoy it very much."

"Coquette Millbrook!" he thundered. "Promise me right now you shall do no such thing! You cannot possibly go around encouraging men to kiss you. Your reputation in no time would be utterly shattered and then no gentleman, no real gentleman, will want to marry you."

She regarded him consideringly. "Is that what I am pursuing, then? A real gentleman?"

"Of course!" he fairly shouted. "Faith, but you would try the patience of a saint! What sort of nonsense are you speaking?"

She reached down to pick up her bonnet and settle it over her curls. She was glad what she had said had set up his back, for now she could be easy again. She did not know why it was, but just after the kiss, when he was looking at her so strangely, she had felt swamped with a terrible panic. Why, precisely, she could not say. Except that, while he had held her in his arms, she had suddenly desired more than anything else on earth to remain there forever, something which could never happen. After all, Harley despised her, and she disliked him equally as much. She realized now that she never should have asked him to kiss her and even wondered what precisely had been her impulse to do so. Had she secretly been desiring to kiss him all these years? No, that was quite impossible. Then why? To pretend, perhaps, that she belonged to him and to Barscot so she might remain connected to what was for her the only home she had known?

Oh, she did not understand such things, except that everything about today's departure seemed painfully familiar. She wondered if this was how she had felt as a little girl of four, leaving her home that had burned to the ground so many years ago.

"Promise me," he said again, some of his temper apparently dissipating as he took hold of her arm and held it tightly, "that you will not behave so foolishly. It won't do, Cokie, not by half. You must see that."

"Very well. I shall promise to be both exceedingly careful and discreet and shall kiss only those gentlemen whom I believe would suit me as a prospective husband."

Harley looked into her eyes, into hard, stubborn blue eyes, and grimaced. "Very well. I suppose I must be content with that."

"Yes, I believe you must."

"Do not think for a moment, my dear, that I shall not be watching you closely!"

"Oh, Harley," she said, jerking her arm out of his grasp. "Now you are beginning to sound like Potsy and I tell you, I will have none of it!" With that, she moved into the entrance hall.

He followed slowly behind. He found himself disgusted all over again. Coquette had not changed, not even one whit. She was stubborn, willful, and a hoyden by every standard, which made it all the odder that he had enjoyed kissing her so very much in the first place. He supposed he was as much a fool as any other man, his head easily turned by a beauty with now lovely brows and elegantly coifed locks and who was dressed like a queen in a velvet pelisse trimmed with fur. What a simpleton he was after all.

Coquette would always fall short of his view of what a lady

was. She was nothing to Lady Agnes or Olivia Dazeley, and certainly not near the equal of the elegant and gracious Katherine Godwin. These were his favorites, one of whom he believed would become the next Countess of Harlington. These young women each epitomized, though in varying ways and degrees, the true notion of good breeding, refinement, and feminity. Coquette was nothing to them, nothing at all.

He glanced up the stairs. A maid carrying two bandboxes was descending with great care. In his mind's eye, he could see his mother descending as well, moving in a graceful descent, her head erect, an amiable expression on her face. A feeling of pride swelled in him. She had loved Barscot and had been a very fine mistress of the ancient house. He would always think of her as the paragon by which all other women should be measured.

When Coquette suddenly picked up her skirts and ran up the stairs two at a time, with her ankles and even her knees fully exposed, he sighed heavily and shook his head. A hoyden, indeed! How his dear mama would have recoiled at such a sight just as he did, except that he could not help but notice, again, how beautifully turned her ankles were and that her legs were lean but quite shapely in appearance.

The sudden quiet at the front door drew his attention away from the stairs. Two footmen, carrying what appeared to be a very heavy trunk, had stopped in their movements and were also staring up the stairwell. Each appeared to be in complete shock. Neither blinked.

He chuckled to himself. "Move along," he called out, a sufficiently forceful command that brought them both back to their senses. They each begged pardon and continued their labors.

He suddenly wondered just what the Season was going to be like if this was Coquette's notion of proper conduct.

He walked outside, where his valet joined him, handing

him his hat and gloves. "Thank you, Humphrey. Are we very nearly ready, then?"

"Yes, m'lord." The valet bowed, then moved away to where he had clearly been supervising the storage of his own trunks and portmanteaux in one of two wagons being loaded for the journey.

For her part, Coquette knew it had been entirely and utterly improper to race up the stairs as she had, but she did not care. Time enough in London to behave like a well-bred young miss. For now, she needed to say good-bye one last time to her bedchamber and to pretend for a moment that all had not changed. She looked around the beautiful room, which had been decorated in a blue chintz floral, and shed a few more tears. How much she wished she could continue living in just this space, where so many memories rose up even now to enchant her.

"Good-bye," she said aloud. In this simple farewell, she knew for certain that all had indeed changed. There was nothing for it now but to go, not to look back, and to embrace the future as best she could.

Six

Once in London, Coquette soon learned that her general impression of dear Potsy as that of a dog guarding a bone was entirely accurate. The moment she set foot in Lord Harlington's extraordinary town house in Grosvenor Square, her lessons in manners were renewed with the fervor of a religious zealot. In particular, Coquette became well acquainted with one of the *beau monde*'s most gifted dancing instructors, Monsieur Dubois, whom Lady Potsgrove hired not only to guide Coquette through the intricacies of the rather complicated quadrille, but to further her education in the art of deportment as well.

On the fourth day of their arrival in London, Lady Potsgrove entered the ballroom in which Coquette had been practising alone and announced her intention of making a most important call this afternoon, again without Coquette's company. When Coquette inquired about the nature of the call, Lady Potsgrove merely smiled in a most infuriating manner but refused to tell her anything.

"You will know all soon enough," she added, as she drew on her gloves. "Your posture is improving, I must say, but why does your left hand flop about when you make your turns?"

"It does not!" Coquette retorted heatedly. Even if it probably did, she was sick to death of so much criticism.

"Now, now, there is no need to fly into a pelter. I shall return in time to dine with you and Harley. Oh, my dear, if you could just learn not to slurp at your soup!" With that, she was gone.

Coquette, exceedingly frustrated, stamped her feet several times. Then, for good measure, she hiked up her skirts and performed a cartwheel.

"I hope you do not mean to do that at the next ball," Harley called out to her.

Coquette's hands flew to her face, which grew quite hot beneath her fingers, but she began to laugh. "I never would have done so had your aunt not made me as mad as fire."

"You have been rather cross of late. I noticed as much last night."

"Why would I not be cross?" she responded irritably. "I have been in London nearly a sennight, fully prepared to get a husband, and what must I do but remain imprisoned in your home, however lovely it may be, kicking my heels and learning one country dance after another!"

"I thought as much. I have come, therefore, to offer you a little diversion. How would you like to take a drive, to Kensington Gardens perhaps?"

"Oh, Harley, I would so much appreciate it. Only this morning, when I saw what a fine day it was, I—"

"Just as I thought!" Lady Potsgrove cried from the doorway. "Harley, what are you thinking? Have you gone mad! If you take her now and she offends even one of our hostesses through some chance encounter—which always occurs when one is least expecting it—then she will be sunk. Our presence in London is already suspect given the recent demise of my brother, and if Coquette's manners are not impeccable I have every fear we shall receive the cut direct. And then where will we be?"

Coquette laid a hand on Harley's arm. "Do not listen to her!" she cried. "She is become deranged with so much power as she exerts over me. I beg you, take me to the gardens. Please!"

Harley turned to her and smiled in that maddening way of

his. "I fear in this instance I must bow to my aunt's superior knowledge of how your 'coming out' must be managed."

"No," she whined.

"Now, none of that," he reprimanded sharply. "Even I can tell you that a lady always responds with grace and dignity."

"Oh, do stubble it, you, you wretched nodcock!" she retorted.

Harley merely lifted a single brow, then turned on his heel and quit the ballroom. Lady Potsgrove, however, was horrified that Coquette would lose her temper so easily and spent the next several minutes asserting the absolute necessity of being in command of herself at every turn.

"But it was only Harley," Coquette stated in her defense, her arms crossed over her chest.

"Yes, my dear. But what sets my nerves on fire is the fear that at some unforeseen moment when you get on your high ropes again, only this time in the midst of a ball or soiree, you will forget yourself entirely and speak as though you were bred in the stables instead of my brother's house. Do you understand?"

"I would not be so foolish," she returned, lifting her chin.

"Will you but trust me a little?" Potsy queried.

"Potsy, I just need a husband, not all these lessons. Why do you not find a perfectly amiable gentleman for me? Bring him home and I will happily wed him. Think of all the time we could save."

This suggestion, however much it was made lightly, caused Lady Potsgrove to shake her head. "On no account. We must allow for Cupid to have a chance in your circumstances. You do wish for love, do you not?"

"Love?" she queried, then began to laugh. "I have no confidence in love whatsoever. Give me a sailing ship and a fine crew. That is what I truly want. That is what will satisfy the longings of my heart."

At that, Lady Potsgrove rolled her eyes and took Harley's

lead by merely turning on her heel and leaving Coquette alone in the ballroom.

That evening, Coquette sipped her turtle soup as quietly as possible, all the while staring at Lady Potsgrove from beneath her lashes. She was discussing several of the upcoming balls, soirées, and fêtes with Harley, but there was something in her manner that was not at all in her usual style. She had never seen Potsy's hazel eyes glitter in just that fashion, as though she had an enormous secret she was trying to keep. That she also kept fluffing the pink ruffles of her enormous cap also added to her general appearance of excitement.

Finally, Coquette interrupted the conversation. "So, tell me, my lady, am I sipping my soup properly?"

"Yes, dear, I suppose you are. Now, Harley, as I was saying, I think it would be best if we stayed the first ball until at least a fortnight—"

"Potsy, am I sitting properly?"

Lady Potsgrove turned with a slight frown and cast it over Coquette's head, neck, and shoulders. "Yes, dear. Very nice. You are making excellent improvement. More each day." Her smile was perfunctory, even patronizing. "Now do let me settle things with Harley."

Coquette made no answer but began to sip her soup, gradually introducing a series of ever-louder slurps until both Harley and Lady Potsgrove turned to stare at her.

"Coquette, whatever is the matter?" she asked. "Are you slurping merely to infuriate me? For I must say you are succeeding."

"Not by half," Coquette answered truthfully. "I simply wish to know what it is that has set you all a-flutter. You are keeping a great secret, and I will not cease my slurping until I know what it is." She stared very hard at Lady Potsgrove, a smile on her lips.

"Cokie, really," Harley chided. "I think your conduct the

outside of enough. I believe you owe Potsy an apology at the very least."

"Do I?" she responded provokingly. She then rose from her seat and made her way to Lady Potsgrove's chair. She began fluffing the pink ruffles in a teasing manner. "I really don't give a fig, for if you must know I noticed from the beginning that you, my dear Potsy, were fairly brimming with some sort of secret or news that you can scarcely contain, and I would wager half my fortune it's about me."

She then leaned about Lady Potsgrove's shoulders and forced her to meet her gaze.

At having been discovered, Lady Potsgrove began to beam. "Very well, you have found me out! Oh, my dears! It is more than I had hoped to achieve! You will not credit it when I tell you what has happened."

Coquette returned swiftly to her seat. Lady Potsgrove's countenance had never appeared more lively than in this moment.

"As you both know, I have been making the rounds of all our most famous hostesses, and today I called upon Mrs. Marston." She appeared fairly near to swooning, her ectasy was so acute. "Coquette, it is such a triumph, you cannot imagine. But she has agreed to receive you tomorrow, and if she approves of you, she will persuade one of the Almack's patronesses to give you vouchers. What do you say to that?"

Coquette knew perfectly well that there was no requirement more necessary to any young lady's success in London than vouchers to Almack's. However, some little measure of devilment prompted her to tap her chin, look away and squint, and say, "I had rather have a new set of sailing charts."

When she glanced back at Lady Potsgrove, the crestfallen expression on her face was so pronounced, that Coquette shot out of her chair and returned to kneel beside her. "No, no, no, Potsy! I was only teasing you! I promise I was! Do not look so downcast. Indeed, I should not have made such a joke. So this is what you have been doing for me every afternoon? Campaigning, as it were?"

"Yes, precisely so," she responded, her sensibilities clearly wounded.

"Forgive me, dearest," she said, placing her cheek on Lady Potsgrove's hand. "It was a beastly thing to do and I do apologize, a thousand times!"

"Well, since you put it that way."

Coquette lifted her head and met Potsy's gaze.

A slow smile dawned on Lady Potsgrove's lips. "It really was a triumph."

"Then I wish to hear every word," Coquette said. "Every single word of how you achieved it!"

Harley watched in some bemusement as Coquette took up a seat very near Lady Potsgrove, quite at a distance from her own turtle soup, and gave her complete attention to his aunt. She leaned her elbow on the table, her gaze never wavering from Potsy's face, as she listened to what soon proved to be a lengthy recital of her comings and goings and how difficult that hostess had been or how easy the next had surprisingly proved. The subject would have tried the patience of his own ears and he believed was hardly of the smallest interest to Coquette. On the other hand, she attended to his aunt with a great deal of fortitude, her expression never anything but of the most profound interest, at least until the second remove had arrived and Coquette was forced to return to her place.

Even then, she continued to encourage his aunt with a well-chosen word here and another one there, a circumstance which forced him to admit that there was indeed much that he approved of and admired in Coquette, especially when it was only after some few minutes that Lady Potsgrove finally exhausted the subject.

"A triumph, indeed, Aunt," he said, smiling at her.

"It was. Oh, it was, it was. I am still so happy I can hardly speak, for it is not that Mrs. Marston can know anything of Coquette, she merely chose to honor my word, which is why—" She broke off and nervous fingers touched her lips for her gaze had slid to Coquette, who now had both elbows on the table and was swirling her wine about in her glass. "Oh, dear."

Coquette laughed heartily. "Potsy, I adore you! Do you know how readily you rise to the fly?"

Lady Potsgrove tried to smile but the result was a wavering, worried expression that extended up the full height of her face.

On the following day, Coquette followed Lady Potsgrove into Harley's fashionable, crested barouche and took up a seat beside her. She felt oddly excited, as though she were beginning a race on the back of Old George and meant to do her very best to win. Was she prepared, she wondered, to move well, if not easily, among the tonnish Londoners? She believed she would know in very short order.

As was proper, Lady Potsgrove was gowned in black, from the frilly lace cap she wore beneath a black bonnet to her black leather shoes, a very striking contrast to Coquette's fiery-red curls peeping from beneath a dark blue bonnet trimmed with white ruching and a matching pelisse which bore fashionable gold-fringed epaulettes. When Lady Potsgrove smoothed out the skirts of her pelisse, Coquette did the same, which prompted the older woman to take her hand and give it a squeeze.

"You will do brilliantly," she said with a firm, confident nod of her head.

Coquette drew in a deep breath, "For your sake, I certainly hope I shall."

"For both our sakes, then. Just remember not to put on any false airs. Mrs. Marston is a stickler for many things, but she is known to despise artifice of any kind."

Fifteen minutes later, Coquette found herself being ushered into Mrs. Marston's drawing room, a very fine, high-ceilinged chamber decorated *en suite* in a soft peach silk damask on both the furniture and the walls. A patterned Aubusson carpet in beige, brown, peach, and cream supported the elegant sofas, occasional tables, and a very fine rosewood pianoforte. Coquette did not know when she had seen such a charming chamber.

Upon being introduced to Mrs. Marston, she said as much as she took up her seat beside Lady Potsgrove.

Mrs. Marston thanked her for the compliment, nodding approvingly, then began what Coquette could only feel was a lengthy interrogation for the next several minutes about her family, her connection with Lord Harlington, and the reasons for not having been properly introduced in London when she was eighteen.

Coquette, who felt Mrs. Marston's manner to be ridiculously imperious, answered each of her somewhat impertinent questions slowly and with the elegance of manner as had been drilled into her by the Byng ladies in recent weeks.

After at least a quarter of an hour, Mrs. Marston leaned more fully back in her chair and nodded. "You have the look of your mother," she stated at last.

Coquette was surprised. "You were acquainted with her?"

"A little. She was a considerable beauty, just as you are, and was in possession of an extraordinary fortune, as you are. She could have had Harlington, you know—or did you not know as much?"

"No, ma'am, I did not." She was shocked and yet somehow, given the sixth earl's devotion to her, his preference for keeping her at Barscot now made even more sense to her. "He became as a father to me."

"As was proper, I think. No gentleman was more besotted than Harlington, but many of the gentlemen were at the time. I enjoyed playing partners at whist with her. She was quite intelligent. Your father no less so, of course, but he hadn't a feather to fly with." Mrs. Marston shook her head, her gaze flitting about while her mind rested in the past. "She could have been the Countess of Harlington and instead she became a mere Mrs. Millbrook. We were all shocked."

"That she chose love?" Coquette asked.

Mrs. Marston sat up straighter, her gaze flying instantly to Coquette's. "Do I disappoint you? Are you so provincial that you do not understand the value of a proper alliance?"

She felt Lady Potsgrove stiffen beside her and for that reason, besides the hard expression on Mrs. Marston's face, she knew she must take great care in how she gave her answer. She sought about for a polite, indifferent response, but somehow she knew she should speak her mind, if nothing more than for her own dignity.

"I shall always be happy for my father that he found both love and a proper alliance."

Mrs. Marston narrowed her kestrel eyes and nodded slowly. "A clever response. At least you have your wits about you, or appear to. However, I would strongly suggest that you take great care, Miss Millbrook, to temper your opinions when amongst the *haut ton* in general, or you will find your success exceedingly limited in the first circles. Have you understood me?"

For some reason, Coquette could not help but smile. "Perfectly."

She thought she saw Mrs. Marston's lips twitch, but she could not be certain. Lady Potsgrove's fan made a sudden appearance. "How very odd, to be sure, for I suddenly feel quite warm. Is that a new clock upon your mantel?"

Mrs. Marston did not even glance in the suggested direction. "Of course it is not," she responded abruptly, at the same time rising to her feet. "But I must bid you good day. I have several calls of my own which I promised to make."

Lady Potsgrove shot up out of her seat as though propelled by a cannon. Coquette joined her and after taking her leave as politely as possible to a woman to whom she would truly have enjoyed delivering a well-constructed setdown, she was soon seated beside Lady Potsgrove in Harley's barouche.

"A complete dragon," Coquette stated crisply. "Do you truly account her as a friend?"

Lady Potsgrove turned to stare at Coquette as though she had gone mad. "She is far more to me than a friend," she returned icily. "She is a prominent hostess who, until this moment, made certain I was invited everywhere." On these last words, spoken as a lament, she suddenly burst into tears.

Coquette was not certain at all why her benefactress had suddenly become a watering pot, but she believed the agitations of the moment had descended on her like an avalanche. "Do not cry, Potsy!" she said, slipping an arm about her shoulders.

Potsy, however, would have none of her comfort and shrugged her off with a quick jerk. "It is all your fault, Coquette! How could you! And for a moment we were getting on so famously! Did I not tell you to hold your tongue?"

Lady Potsgrove continued in this vein for some time. Coquette soon saw that there was little she could do to reassure her on any count, so she merely turned her attention to the passing scenery, which soon caught her attention. She was sorry that Potsy was so overset by Mrs. Marston's display of hackles, but for herself she was enjoying seeing the various streets of Mayfair that had been denied her for the past week. If only Harley had been able to take her to Kensington Gardens.

Lady Potsgrove was still weeping when they arrived in Grosvenor Square, and Coquette had half a mind to slip away from her and take a very long walk around the neighboring streets. As soon as she began inching her way backward toward the door, however, Lady Potsgrove's attention became fixed on her. "Oh, no, you do not! You have done quite enough mischief for one day! Back to the ballroom!"

Coquette would have made a fuss, but the sight of Lady Potsgrove's completely woebegone face turned her feet in the proper direction and nothing more was said.

She did not see Lady Potsgrove again until she entered

the drawing room before dinner, where she found both Harley and Potsy waiting for her. Harley shrugged his shoulders, but Lady Potsgrove, still as mad as a peahen, merely turned her shoulder and sipped a glass of ratafia. She remained in this state even into the second remove when the butler, Jenkins, who served exclusively in London, presented a missive to her.

"I beg your pardon, ma'am, but this is just arrived and the footman is waiting for a response."

Lady Potsgrove opened it at once, read the contents, and pressed a hand to her bosom. Her hazel eyes open very wide, she lifted the missive, whereupon a second smaller sheet of paper drifted to her lap. "Good God," she murmured. "If I were not sitting down I should faint."

"What is it?" Coquette asked.

Lady Potsgrove glanced at Harley, then back to Coquette. She blinked several times in rapid succession, quickly grabbed the paper on her lap and read it over very carefully, then handed it to Coquette. "A voucher for Almack's!"

Coquette was stunned, nearly as much as Lady Potsgrove appeared to be. She was under no illusion as to just how valuable these vouchers were, for they fairly guaranteed a young lady a certain amount of social success no matter how platter-faced or ill-bred she might be. She glanced at Harley, who gave her an approving nod and a smile.

Turning back to Lady Potsgrove, she cried, "Almack's? You mean Mrs. Marston actually approved of me?"

"I know! It is completely incredible!"

Coquette might have been offended by the comment, which expressed her benefactress's complete lack of faith in her, but at the moment she was too amazed by this extraordinary turn of events. Indeed, she could not comprehend how she had actually won Mrs. Marston's approval, especially since she had nearly brangled with her. "Well, I must say," Coquette said, "that I think these vouchers are due primarily to your influence, Potsy, and for that I do thank you."

"It was not me at all," Lady Potsgrove responded frankly.

"She says in her note that she had always had a great fondness
for your mother, and because of her warm memories of her
and the fact that you were sufficiently well-behaved not to
cause her any degree of concern, she sought out Emily Cowper and the deed was done. But there is more, and this causes
me the greatest anxiety."

"What, pray tell?"

"She has extended you an invitation to her ball tomorrow
night." Her hazel eyes grew very wide, indeed. "And we must
accept, because not to do so would cause her the greatest offense. Yet you are not in the least prepared."

"Oh, but Potsy—" she began, intending to reassure her that
she could manage herself at a ball, that she knew her steps
sufficiently, but Lady Potsgrove threw up an imperative hand.

"You are not ready. You must trust me in this! Oh, dear,
what shall we do! What shall we do?"

"Calm yourself, Aunt. I believe you do not give Coquette
enough credit."

Lady Potsgrove cast him a glance which said that he knew
nothing of the matter, being only a man, and continued on.
"Well, there is only one thing to be done. We must summon
M. Dubois at once, and we will have you dancing all night, if
need be. Harley!"

She snapped his name so ferociously and with such purpose that Coquette jumped in her seat. She would have
laughed at Potsy's clear panic, except that she had already
begun to comprehend that the next four and twenty hours
would be some of the least pleasant of her existence.

"Yes," Harley responded, eyeing his aunt suspiciously and
not at all with an appearance of goodwill.

"You must go out at once and gather up enough young
ladies and gentlemen so that at the very least Coquette can
practice the quadrille. I shall fetch one of the Misses Long
from next door, for any one of them can play the pianoforte
sufficiently for our needs. Well, why do you sit there? Do go
at once!"

When Harley merely sipped his wine and stared maddeningly at his aunt, she rose from her chair and said, "Anthony Byng, if you dare to disappoint me in this moment, I . . . I shan't speak to you again as long as I live!"

Coquette saw him open his mouth and knew he meant to say something provoking, so she quickly rose as well. "Yes, please, Harley. Will you do as much for me? I would be very grateful."

He seemed a little surprised at her plea, but it had the effect she desired. He set his linen on the table and rose from his dinner. "Oh, very well. I can see that you are both determined on it, but I shan't make any promises as to how soon I shall return. I dare say everyone I know is already engaged for the evening."

When Lady Potsgrove appeared ready to take him to task for this parting shot, Coquette once more intervened, this time by addressing Lady Potsgrove. "Perhaps you should send a servant next door at once. After all, we must have someone to play for us."

"Yes, yes, you are quite right." With that, she quit the table to compose the necessary note, dragging Jenkins with her.

Coquette, therefore, found herself alone in the dining room save for a footman, whom she begged to refill her wineglass. The evening, she now understood, would undoubtedly prove both long and painful.

Seven

Later that evening, Coquette stood beside the pianoforte in the ballroom, flipping through several pages of music. The youngest of the Misses Long, just seventeen and seated before the instrument, was still not formally out and so had been available to assist Lady Potsgrove in a final, hurried practice for Coquette in the art of performing any number of social dances. Miss Long, though not permitted to join her three elder sisters in their nightly round of social engagements, was allowed a limited enjoyment of the sights of London. She had come back just that afternoon from an excursion to the Royal Academy in which she had seen so many paintings of such a fine and accomplished quality that she told Coquette she had all but decided to give up her use of the watercolors entirely. Coquette, who liked her very much, told her not to be a silly goose. "If you enjoy painting, what difference does it matter whether you excel as the masters do?"

"I had never thought of it in that fashion before," she said, looking up at her with shining eyes. "And I do enjoy it ever so much."

"Then it is settled." She had meant to continue the conversation, except at that moment voices could be heard in the hall just beyond. A moment more and an entire party flowed into the ballroom. Harley had been as good as his word and had returned with not only the dancing master in tow but a large group of his friends as well, both male and female.

"Oh, dear," Miss Long murmured. "I fear Mama never would have let me come had she known how large the party was to be."

Coquette patted her shoulder. "Then I for one shall never tell her."

Miss Long giggled.

The dancing master joined them, and since his concern of the moment was with Miss Long's skill on the pianoforte and in which order he wished to execute the various dances, Coquette moved away.

She watched as Harley strode briskly into the chamber, his arm slung about the neck of one of his friends, laughing loudly and talking to him in an undertone all the while. His friend, after a moment, tossed his head back and roared. Since the contingent following behind all demanded to be told what had afforded them so much amusement, the progression drew to a halt.

Coquette smiled, thinking how well Harley appeared in this moment as he related an anecdote. His manner was quite free, his gray eyes sparkled, and his entire demeanor was relaxed. She found herself sighing quite warmly as a surprising swell of pride washed over her.

"Good God!" the gentleman closest to Harley cried out suddenly, only his gaze was fixed upon her.

Coquette wondered suddenly if she had dirt on her face or if her coiffure had become tangled and unpresentable. She felt the most ridiculous urge to turn about and run.

Harley immediately drew him forward. "Miss Millbrook, I believe you have met most of my friends at one time or another at Barscot, but I should like to introduce each to you a little more formally just now. May I present Lord Henry Binyon. Henry, Miss Millbrook."

"How do you do?" she said politely, offering a bow.

He bowed in response, his expression doltish. "Very well, indeed! Harley, you did not tell me she was *beautiful!* Where have you been keeping her?"

"He has not been keeping me anywhere," Coquette felt obliged to explain.

"And your voice is as lovely as your face," Lord Henry said. "Only tell me why you have not come to London sooner."

She wanted to tell him he was being absurd and was about to say as much, but Harley hooked her arm and drew her around her new admirer. She was thereby introduced in quick succession to Mr. Evan Templar, Lord Waltham, Sir Francis Olney, Alice Waltham, who looked to be of an age with her, and Mary Needham. "And of course you are already known to Lady Agnes Clifton."

Lady Agnes could not completely hide her shock, though she made a valiant attempt through a trembling smile. "How do you go on, Miss Millbrook," she said, her voice barely more than a whisper. "How . . . how different you look, so very fashionable and . . . and—"

Sir Francis finished her sentence as he held up his quizzing glass. "Exquisite."

"Just so," Lord Waltham intoned.

"Indeed!" Mr. Templar agreed.

For one of the first times she could ever remember, Coquette found herself blushing. To be introduced to such a lively set of gentlemen and at the same time to have them exclaim over her was more attention than she had ever experienced in her entire life. She thanked them all for their kindness in coming to help her, which thrust the gentlemen into a new cascade of compliments and well wishes for a happy first Season in London.

In the midst of their exuberance, Coquette watched Harley take Lady Agnes's arm and draw her apart. The petite young woman stood very close to him as they conversed, her body seeming to curve and arch with each word she spoke, like a snake preparing to encircle its victim. Harley appeared to be completely unaware of her predatory stance, and Coquette could not help but wonder if he needed to be warned that what appeared to him to be a well-bred female was really a reptile in disguise.

She shuddered faintly. She had never thought very highly of Lady Agnes and seeing her now so obvious in her purposes made Coquette feel rather ill. She was grateful, therefore, when Lady Potsgrove entered the chamber, clapping her hands and marching straight across the ballroom toward M. Dubois.

Her quick movements, however, caused air to billow beneath the layers of her lavender cap so that she appeared as though she had a rather strange bird on her head which only quieted its feathers once she drew to a stop beside Miss Long. Coquette glanced at Harley, who met her gaze, and she saw at once that he had seen his aunt's cap dancing as well, for his lips twitched and he winked at her.

This was something she thought she would miss quite dreadfully once she was finally married and had begun her new life—all those odd little moments with Harley when they would share in a mutual comprehension of some absurdity or other. A sinking sensation attacked her stomach, a familiar feeling by now. Yes, there would be much she would miss in the new life laid out before her.

She realized she would soon succumb to a fit of the dismals if she continued pondering such sad, hopeless thoughts, so when M. Dubois called the party to order and began his instructions, she found herself grateful for the diversion. When a country dance was ordered, she performed quite well with Lord Waltham partnering her, but even so Lady Potsgrove had many suggestions to give her and, indeed, each was of some merit. Whatever her ladyship might be, she certainly excelled in the social arts.

Quite soon, what might have been a rather mortifying experience for Coquette became a rather joyful occasion because of the informal nature of Harley's relationship with his friends. There was a general liveliness among the group and, far from being critical of her missed steps, each of her partners tended to apologize profusely as though the fault was their own. The ladies, too, with the exception perhaps of Lady Agnes, were kind in their suggestions and hints, so before long she was beginning to be even more confident in her knowledge of each dance. Harley as well was on his best behavior, restraining his usually biting comments. At one point he actually told her quite sincerely that she danced with a considerable amount of grace.

"You are not serious!" she cried, astonished.

"Never more so," he responded, a half smile on his lips. "Only I find it rather distressing that you would be so shocked that I might offer a compliment."

"That is because you never do. You never have!"

Harley opened his mouth to speak, then thought the better of the words that had flown to the tip of his tongue. He had almost said, 'You have never deserved a compliment until this past sennight,' but such a comment he felt to be far too unkind, particularly when she was making such a valiant effort to learn her steps.

As he moved through the paces of the dance, he could not keep from glancing at her more often than not. She was dancing quite well, he thought, certainly better than he ever would have expected. She was even able to offer snippets of conversation to her various partners as she continued going down each dance. His friends were certainly taken with her. And why wouldn't they be, since she was quite one of the fairest damsels in London this Season? Although he strongly suspected that part of their eagerness to win her notice was due more to her openness, even artlessness, than to her elegant profile or the swan slope of her neck.

She is so changed, he thought. And yet she wasn't, not in essentials, not in temperament. She was the same yet different, if that was even possible. In some respects, as her progress through the present dance continued without error, she put him in mind of his mother. At that, he chuckled. Never were two women so different than his mother and Coquette. However, tonight he saw a gracefulness emerging in the latter that had not even characterized his parent.

She missed her step suddenly, and Waltham nearly tripped over himself in making his own apologies. Harley realized that his good friend was completely besotted, and he found himself frowning. Waltham would never do for Coquette—or, rather, Coquette would never do for Waltham. He was a fine chap, plenty of bottom on the hunting field, and the very best of friends, but he would never find marital happiness with such a contentious creature as Coquette for a wife.

The dance drew to a close and Templar rushed up to her. "Allow me to partner you in the next dance, Miss Millbrook. I promise I shan't tread on your feet so often as Waltham has."

"I say!" Waltham cried.

Harley watched as Coquette immediately intervened, saying, "I fear it is Waltham whose feet have been severely bruised this evening, not mine."

Waltham regarded her warmly, even more so when she thanked him for the dance, then took up Templar's arm. There could be no doubt of Waltham's interest.

M. Dubois organized the next country dance and Harley found himself opposite Lady Agnes again. She immediately engaged him in conversation, and he was almost diverted by her, except that after a few minutes he could not help but notice how lively Coquette's conversation had become with Templar. What the deuce were they discussing and what had she said to make him laugh so loudly?

"Are you out of patience with me?" he heard Lady Agnes say.

Reverting his attention to her with some difficulty, he responded, "No, how could I be?"

She pouted as she moved in a circle about him according to the dictates of the dance. "Because you are scowling quite fiercely."

"I am?" he asked, surprised.

"Indeed, you are."

He realized with a jolt that he had been thinking only of giving Templar a hint that Coquette was something of a fishwife, and hence must have borne a harsh expression on his face. He had been committing a grave sin himself in so badly ignoring his partner. And how kind and tactful Lady Agnes had been in drawing him back to her.

Ah, Lady Agnes. Now, she was quite the epitome of excellent good breeding and everything that he admired in a proper lady of quality. As his attention became fixed on her, he considered again the possibility that he should ask her to marry him. He had been pondering the notion for several weeks now, more so of late with the passing of his dear father. Perhaps by June he would be ready to offer for her.

When Coquette's laughter, however, rose above the gentler conversation of the party as a whole, he once more glanced in her direction.

"Harley," Lady Agnes called to him. "You are scowling again. I wish you might not be so ferocious in your dealings with Miss Millbrook. She must think you a complete tyrant."

"Cokie? Not by half." He cleared his throat. "But if I seem distracted, you must understand that my aunt is greatly concerned that she perform well tomorrow night at Mrs. Marston's ball."

Lady Agnes, making her next turn smoothly, returned to him and glanced at Coquette. "I have every confidence she will. I suppose you will be obliged to dance attendance upon her the entire evening."

He knew a hint when he heard one. He smiled and said, "Not the entire evening. Certainly I shall be free to dance the cotillion, if you would oblige me."

Lady Agnes dimpled her smile. "I should like nothing better, m'lord."

He felt a swell of pleasure, as he often did in her flirtatious presence. She had certainly made her interest in him perfectly well-known and for that he supposed he was quite indebted to her, really. He was entirely cognizant of where he stood with her and for that reason knew that an offer of marriage, sometime in June or perhaps July, even August, would be the easiest thing in the world to manage.

When the dance came to an end, M. Dubois suggested it was now time for the waltz. For reasons perhaps he would never comprehend, Harley felt obliged, even compelled, to make certain Coquette was his partner. At first, he told himself that he was merely concerned for her, that only a strong partner would be of use in this situation. However, the moment he took her into the circle of the dance, holding her back firmly as well as her hand, he realized with a start that he had simply not wanted any of his presently overzealous and somewhat ardent friends to have the schooling of her. That, he felt, was his duty and in this moment, his privilege.

The moment the music started, he became aware of how she moved. He had never before danced the waltz with her and found her to be quite capable, even something of a joy. M. Dubois had previously stated that he felt she excelled at this new dance, but until this moment, he had not known how much.

The dancing master's voice called out many instructions, not just to Coquette and himself, but to the others as well. He often stamped his foot to keep the rhythm marked, and on occasion even clapped his hands to keep Miss Long and the dancers moving as they were supposed to. Harley found himself smiling. He enjoyed the waltz—or an excuse for hugging, as it was generally known. Who could argue with the delight of that?

"Why do you smile?" Coquette asked.

"I like waltzing," he whispered.

"Well, I must say you excel at it. I was never so at ease, not even with M. Dubois."

"You are an excellent partner," he returned.

"Now you are shamming it," she said.

He looked down into her sparkling blue eyes. She had used a bit of stable slang just for his amusement, and he found himself grinning in response. "Will you dance the waltz with me tomorrow night?"

"Indeed, yes! That would make me quite comfortable, for if you must know, I feared good Mr. Templar would ask, and he is not nearly so graceful a partner as you."

He was not certain that he was content at being described as 'graceful,' but he accepted her compliment nonetheless. He chuckled. "Poor Templar. With all the good intentions in the world, he does tend to go down his dances as though he is chasing hares across a lumpy field."

"Precisely," she murmured, also giggling.

"You know, you really do dance quite well, and you are even able to converse, which is a true sign of the proficient."

"Thank you, m'lord," she responded. She then batted her eyes in a mocking, teasing manner and cocked her head.

In that moment she had assumed Lady Agnes's usual demeanor, and he narrowed his eyes at her. "Enough of that," he murmured.

"Yes, m'lord," she added, in much the same manner.

He looked away from her because he knew if he did not he would begin to laugh and was uncertain where the end of it would be. He cleared his throat several times until he felt he had mastered himself, then glanced at her again.

For some reason, a peculiar expression had overtaken her features. "What is it?"

"Nothing," she responded softly.

"You are thinking something," he said. "I can see it even now in your eyes."

"Only that I find myself so very grateful in this moment to you. I shall be at ease tomorrow night as I know I would not have been had you not brought your friends here. But why are you smiling and now laughing?"

He shook his head. "Do you know, in the score of years

that I have known you, we have never gotten along so well as now. Are you aware that you just *thanked* me?"

"Good God," she said. "How very right you are. Perhaps I am becoming ill."

He found himself smiling again. Coquette had always had the ability to send him into the boughs, but she had also been able to make him laugh as she was doing now.

Indeed, there was just such a warm camaraderie between them, unexpected yet pleasing, that he began to swing her wider with each movement until they were well out of the pattern of the dance. She followed him easily and was soon partaking fully of his antics. A few moments more and all the couples were behaving as badly, but M. Dubois did not stop them. If Harley heard several *Mon dieus* coming from his direction, he noted as well that Miss Long continued the marked three-quarter-time music until the entire party was out of breath and everyone fell to laughing and bumping into one another.

"That was famous!" Coquette cried as he finally twirled her to a stop at what proved to be the far end of the ballroom away from the pianoforte and the rest of the party. For some reason, however, he did not release her but looked down at her, at the color rising on her cheeks, at the brilliance of her eyes. She was so beautiful! What was it that caused such beauty as she possessed to so capture his heart? For in this moment he vowed, had he not actually known better, that he was smitten with her. He had that sensation again that he did not want to let her go, now or ever.

Coquette felt the smile drift away from her face only to be replaced with a strange sense of wonder. Who was this man still holding her in the loose circle of his arms, his hand still clasped to hers, an arm still supporting her waist? Was this Harley, indeed? "I feel as though I have never really known you," she said, her voice little more than a whisper.

He began to release her slowly. "Nor I you, I suppose."

"You have been so kind to me, Harley."

"And you have not bit my head off but once or twice since we arrived in London. Really, it is astonishing."

She was not in the least offended. "Quite." She then laughed.

A strange silence developed between them in that moment, like mist swirling up from a river path at night. She did not know what next to say to him, a circumstance quite unusual in itself since she always had something she was most happy to say to Harley. He seemed to be in a similar quandry and only after he suggested they return to the group and they began walking in the direction of Miss Long and the pianoforte did he finally ask, "Has Mr. Seames been to call since you arrived in London?"

Coquette glanced up at him. "No, he has not, although I must say I really do not give a fig if I ever see him again. Pray, do not scowl down upon me as Potsy does. To you I hope I may always be frank. I cannot like him. I do not trust him."

At that, Harley's expression softened. "Nor I," he whispered in return as they reached M. Dubois and the remainder of the guests, all of whom were still recovering from what Lady Potsgrove was castigating as a completely unacceptable romp.

Coquette moved away from Harley but somehow her gaze returned to him again and again. He was more handsome than any gentleman ought to be, she thought, and one glance at Mary Needham and Alice Waltham told her they, too, found him equally attractive. She felt awkward suddenly, as though caught by emotions and sensations quite unwelcome to her, only what was it precisely that she was feeling? Attachment? That was what came to her. She was in some inexplicable manner attached to Harley, perhaps because she had grown up with him. But such an attachment, even one based on familiarity, was not something that she desired or even felt should be encouraged. She stepped away from the party and observed how they spoke to one another, laughing and carry-

ing on in a happy, contented manner. These were not her peo-
ple. They were Harley's, his friends and one of them perhaps
even his future bride.

She had felt this way so often at Barscot, in particular when
any of his aunts, uncles, and numerous cousins would arrive. Of course they were kindness itself to her, even if she did
scandalize them by her riotous conduct and propensity to be
climbing trees rather than embroidering samplers. This is the
way she had always felt, as though she belonged nowhere,
which was probably her most powerful reason for wanting to
take to the high seas. Perhaps there, in some distant port, she
might find the home she had never truly had, a place where
her strong, independent soul might find a resting place.

She felt the need to steel herself against the warm sensations which had characterized the waltz with Harley, and
when M. Dubois announced the quadrille, she put herself in
Mr. Templar's path, who in turn quickly solicited her hand.
She could now be content, for she would need to concentrate
very hard on the patterned dance and give her attention prin-
cipally to Mr. Templar.

Fortunately, M. Dubois insisted that the quadrille be prac-
ticed again and again, which further allowed Coquette to
be distanced from Harley. After the quadrille, she went
down the next country dance with Sir Francis, whom she
found to be an excellent partner and who gave her many
hints along the way that made the mastering of the dance
more gratifying.

Hearing Lady Agnes trill her laughter, however, just as
the dance concluded, caused her to glance in her direction.
She saw Harley take her up suddenly in the position of the
waltz and twirl her brightly the length of the ballroom, which
set the young lady to gasping, squealing, and giggling the entire way. A very dark sentiment took strong hold of Coquette's
bosom, a place from which she was certain, if nourished,
vipers could spring given the smallest opportunity. Who was

Lady Agnes to be granted such a waltz with Harley and that without the smallest hint of music?

Mary Needham drew close. "I know precisely how you feel," was all the young lady said, as she let out a very deep sigh.

At last, after several more country dances had been practised, M. Dubois pronounced that he was certain Coquette was sufficiently ready to enjoy her first London ball. A rousing cheer rose up from the assembled group.

Coquette was so grateful to them all that she said, "Thank you so much for your help, but somehow I strongly suspect that tomorrow's ball will not hold a candle to how enjoyable this evening has been for me. I will forever be in your debt."

"Very nicely said," Lady Potsgrove commented. She then won the appreciation of the entire assemblage by announcing that a light supper was awaiting them in the gold drawing room.

Coquette thanked Miss Long for the hours spent playing for them all and insisted she stay for supper, an offer which brought a rosy blush of pleasure to her cheeks. She then turned to M. Dubois and extended a similar invitation. The happiness which crossed the face of the aging Frenchman, who had escaped Paris just before the Reign of Terror, made her smile.

"Come, M. Dubois," she said, hooking his arm. "I know very well that you would prefer to be doing anything other than teaching hopeless young women to dance, and do not deny it, for I have seen it in your eyes."

He placed a hand on his chest. "If I have for one moment," he murmured, his accent laying gently upon his words, "done anything to truly give you such a wretched notion, then you must forgive me, even now."

"Forget that I said anything," she assured him.

He remained silent until they reached the hall. "I have seen such a look in your eyes as well," he murmured.

She looked up at him and laughed. "I had meant to have

adventures, not come to London. My first port of call was to be Marseille, not Mayfair."

"There have been moments," he said, looking down at her, his dark eyes concerned, "that I saw something in you, of sadness, *peut-être?*"

"Oui," she murmured.

"But there is a saying, 'joy is not around you, it is in you.'"

"That is a philosophy I must learn to embrace, I suppose. Are you much content then?"

He shook his head. "Not by half, as you say in this country."

She laughed heartily, thinking she liked M. Dubois very much.

Harley watched her enter the parlor with the dancing master on her arm and Miss Long trailing behind. He was at first startled, but quickly overcame his initial disapproval. Of course these two, who had so kindly sacrificed their evening's entertainments, ought to be rewarded a little, Miss Long in particular knowing quite well that she would be able to crow loudly over her elder sisters on the morrow once it was learned how many of London's most cligible bachelors had danced to the tunes she'd played. As for M. Dubois, had it not been for the French Revolution, he would have even now been roaming through the aristocratic homes of Paris. No, Coquette had done well and properly. He only wished M. Dubois would not have taken her arm in that manner, as though he possessed her, for even now he was patting her hand and smiling down into her face.

Good God, was it possible Coquette was considering wedding him? But this was an entirely ridiculous notion. M. Dubois was easily thirty years her senior.

After a few minutes, as he watched Coquette fill her plate with a variety of fruits and cold meats, he drew near and sat down beside her.

"Peckish?" he queried.

"A trifle," she responded, smiling warmly up at him. She

then lowered her voice. "I know I ought to pretend to have the appetite of a hummingbird, but not tonight. I must say that your aunt is a woman of some skill," she added, biting into a strawberry. "Nothing could have been more delightful than this."

"Talking with your mouth full?" he chided. "And now you have strawberry juice on your chin."

"So I have," she responded happily, wiping away the trickle she now felt heading toward her gown. "Do come off your high ropes! I provoked you purposely by talking with a berry in my mouth. What have I done now to so displease you?"

He glared at her and his scowl deepened. "You always were able to know what I was thinking."

Coquette raised a brow and rolled her eyes. "With a little study, the stupidest hound could do as much. You are not all that careful in concealing your sentiments."

He was surprised.

She continued. "But I have never found it a bad thing for I always knew your opinion before ever you opened your mouth. Of course, I suppose I have given you cause for many years to practice your scowling. Only, if you do not cease at once, all your friends will begin to wonder why you are so out of reason cross."

"I am not out of reason cross," he countered, unwilling to let her believe she was right. "And I am not scowling."

She laughed. "What is on your mind, then? For I can see that you are anxious to tell me."

He was exasperated but decided to broach the more critical matter at once. "If you are thinking of wedding M. Dubois, it would be a dreadful mistake. He has no family, no connections."

"M. Dubois?" she cried, then quickly lowered her voice. "When did you begin to think anything so absurd, so . . . oh, because I marched in here upon his arm? What a dolt you are! For heaven's sake, I had been thinking no such thing . . . at least not until now. You may have given me the answer for which I have been searching. We are two of a kind, M. Dubois and I, no family, no place to call home."

"That is ridiculous. Barscot is your home. It always will be."

Coquette was stunned and turned to regard him steadily. "But, Harley, it is not. It never was."

He seemed quite taken aback, almost dumbfounded. "Don't be ridiculous. Of course it is . . . was. You lived there most of your life—or did you think I meant to bar the gates once you were gone and make certain you never returned? Cokie, never, never. I swear it!"

She chuckled. "And I have never seen you so overset, but you do not understand. Because there is no blood tie, we will eventually become but memories to one another, in a year, perhaps two. You will have no reason to include me in your family's events and celebrations and I will have no reason to return."

A quiet expression took hold of his face. She could not know what he was thinking. "You are mistaken," he said. "Greatly so." He did not, however, choose to illuminate the point, but rose from his seat to refresh his glass of champagne.

"What is the matter with Harley?" Lady Potsgrove said, taking her nephew's place beside Coquette. "He seemed quite distressed."

"He was most anxious to warn me against eloping with M. Dubois," Coquette said.

At that, Lady Potsgrove laughed so suddenly, so heartily that even Coquette could not keep from smiling. "How could he even think such a thing," Potsy cried at last. "Why, he could be your—your grandfather!"

"I fear Harley is one step from Bedlam on that score."

"I should say so!"

Later that night, Coquette climbed between the sheets feeling quite low. Somehow, the brief conversation with Harley had served to remind her of her circumstances, something she struggled to avoid remembering. The thought which made her blue deviled the most, however, was that she would probably visit Barscot but rarely, certainly once she wed—unless, of course, she made one of Harley's friends her object.

With these thoughts, in particular just who she was to wed, she fell into a suprisingly deep slumber.

Eight

On the following afternoon, Coquette walked Mr. Templar to the door. "Good-bye," she said, extending her hand to him. "I look forward to our dance this evening very much. And thank you for the roses. They are lovely."

Mr. Templar bowed over her hand. "The least I could do. Quite pretty. You, not the roses." He turned pink to his forehead.

"How sweet you are," she said, opening the door. "Good-bye."

Once the door was shut, she leaned her head against the wood feeling quite dazed. Templar had been her seventh visitor that morning—seven gentlemen in all, and a total of eight offerings of flowers. She turned to look at them, arrayed upon a table in the center of the entrance hall, a sense of utter astonishment still causing her to feel quite dizzy. She had never received such attentions before and could hardly comprehend why she was so suddenly beset with suitors.

The door opened behind her. "What the devil was Templar doing here?" Harley called to her.

She could not keep from smiling in what she hoped was a very provoking manner. "Calling on me," she returned, batting her lashes.

"Why?" he fairly thundered.

"I beg you will lower your voice! Your aunt is having a lie-down until it is time to dress for the ball."

He pinched his lips together tightly. "Only tell me what the deuce Templar was doing here," he demanded, though more quietly this time.

Coquette knew he had returned from his own engagements a very short time ago, so of course he would not have known what the past three hours had been like for her.

She watched him stop suddenly in the center of the foyer and stare with a rather horrified expression at the collection of bouquets covering the round, inlaid table next to her. "And what are these?"

"All from my admirers," she said.

"But you have not even been to one soiree yet, let alone a ball. Who are all these from?"

"If you must know, three of them are from my Tom, Richard, and Nick. It would appear they have each come to town to support me."

Harley stared at her. "Your friends from Bedfordshire?"

"Precisely so." She knew that because he was several years older than her childhood playmates, he had never become well-acquainted with any of them.

"I hope they intend to behave whilst here and not overset your chances of making a proper alliance."

"Harley, do you have a thistle in your breeches?" she asked. "For I cannot comprehend even the smallest mite why you are in the boughs merely because your table is covered with flowers. And why must you choose in this moment to sound as though you are at least a hundred years older than I by speaking to me like an irrascible parent?"

"I am doing no such thing," he retorted irritably. "But I think this is ridiculous. And do not tell me the remainder of these offerings are from my friends, for I will not believe it."

"Have it as you will. They are not from your friends."

"Good God, it's true! Have they all gone mad?"

"That is certainly no compliment to me. Perhaps your friends are behaving as gentlemen ought, instead of like cretins, like one of my acquaintance who I shall not mention."

His expression softened a trifle. "Forgive me, Cokie. I do

not know why I am coming the crab. It is just all so sudden, all this interest and intent. Do you mean to marry any of them?"

She threw up her hands, exasperated. "How the deuce should I know?"

"That was not very ladylike!" he countered, scowling at her.

"You mean to reprove me? Harley, you are behaving like an imbecile, and as for wedding one of your friends or mine, I do not know. I had never considered the possiblity of marrying anyone until but a few days ago. Nor, I might add, have I been the object of so much attention. I do not know what any of it means, let alone whether I ought to marry a gentleman who sent camellias or chrysanthemums. Your friends, for example, are well enough in their way, but—"

"But what?" he countered. "How could you possibly find fault with any of them? They are each as fine a man as you will ever encounter."

Coquette was thoroughly bemused. "Are you then recommending all of them as potential husbands?"

"No! Why are you twisting everything I say?"

"You are making no sense at all."

"Nor are you, but one thing I know for certain, you should not even consider allowing Templar to court you. He is far too sensitive in nature to be your husband. With your fishwife's tongue, you would have him sliced to ribbons before the wedding cake had been eaten."

"How you do flatter me, my lord. I am all a-quiver."

"Well it is true. I shan't mince words with you, Cokie. Remember, I have grown up with you and I know what you are!"

"And you would throw that at my head? Of all the sapskulls I have ever known, you are the very worst, when you must know that I am dreading this evening!"

She turned on her heel and moved into the adjoining library. She was as mad as fire, a state Harley could arouse in her with but a few hastily tossed words in her direction. She moved to stand by the window and watched a parade of horses and carriages go by. The hour of morning calls was nearly past and many were heading to Hyde Park, as was customary.

"Maybe they all want your fortune," he said.

She turned toward him, her eyes stinging a trifle with tears. "As do I," she stated, lifting her chin defiantly. "Which is the only reason I have come to London in the first place, and why you must pinch at me in this horrid manner is wholly beyond my comprehension!"

She tried to move past him, but he caught her arm. "Are you still going to waltz with me this evening?"

"Of course. I have said as much." With that, she jerked her arm free and moved into the hallway beyond.

Harley didn't understand himself either, in particular why the knowledge that Templar had called on her or that she had received seven bouquets from both his friends and hers had distressed him so. After all, the moment he had first seen her transformed, he knew what would happen once she arrived in London. He just had not expected his friends, in particular, to pursue her, especially not one and all!

He heard her call to one of the servants, "Beth, do come here. I am in great need of your assistance."

Now what the deuce was she doing? He then listened in some surprise as she began to assign each of the bouquets to one room or the other, including the maids' quarters and the kitchen.

"This must be the latest, but how lovely!" he heard her cry. He stepped into the doorway and saw that she was lifting a small bouquet of violets to her nose. "I vow it is my favorite, but who is it from?"

"I cannot say, ma'am."

Her interest in the violets, however, served to lay his spines. He could even smile.

A card was tucked into the silver holder and she withdrew it. He watched her read the inscription, then turn to regard him, her brow pinched tightly together. "Oh, Harley, you can be such a beast! Just when I was prepared to despise you anew!" With that, and with the violets he had sent her in hand, she mounted the stairs.

Harley watched her go, the airy demi-train of her morning gown, a pretty confection of yellow patterned silk, dancing up the steps in a lively rippling of ruffles. In truth, he did not know at all why he had pinched at her, but he thought it the outside of enough that just because she was now sporting a lovely cut to her auburn curls and had gained enough polish under the instruction of his aunts that half of London must now be in love with her! It was ridiculous and aggravating, wholly incomprehensible. Nearly as incomprehensible as his own mounting determination that she marry only someone of whom he approved.

When Coquette reached her bedchamber, she lifted the bouquet to her cheek, the small petals soft against her skin. She read the card again, "To a wonderful Season. You will do famously. Harlington."

Later, when Coquette entered the drawing room before dinner, Harley approached her at once. "You must forgive me. I was an absolute bear this afternoon."

"Yes, you were," she retorted, but not without a smile. "Whatever did you mean by any of it?"

"I haven't the faintest notion." He shrugged and handed her a sherry, which he had had readied for her.

She took it gratefully. "Thank you. I shall probably require another. My nerves are tormenting me. Do I look all right? Passable? Or will I appear like a thorn among roses, as I was wont to do in Bedfordshire?"

He took her fingers in his and placed a firm kiss on her gloved hand. "Surely you have a looking glass in your bedchamber?"

"Your aunt insisted on three that I might see myself from

every angle. But if I knew you were satisfied that I would not
cause even the smallest mortification to your family, I could
be content."

Harley told her to take a slow turn about the room. If she
truly wished for his opinion, then he would give it to her, although from the moment she entered the drawing room, he
had the impression that he was viewing a heavenly apparition
rather than the vixen who had tortured him for the past twenty
years.

She moved slowly and elegantly, as she had been taught in
recent weeks. Her hair was caught up in a cascade of curls
separated in the Greek style with gold bands. Her freckles
had been hidden behind a delicate layer of powder, her brows
were beautifully arched, and the lovely oval of her face enhanced by a sprinkling of curls over her forehead. Her lashes
were darkened a trifle, her lips touched with rouge, and a
pearl necklace enhanced with a gold and pearl pendant complimented her beauty to perfection. She wore a pale
aquamarine and cream striped silk balldress with a demi-train
trimmed in lace. The sleeves were puffed and the skirt made
high to the waist in the Empire style. Her gown fitted her to
perfection, he could not help but notice, and was perhaps far
more décolleté than he would have wished for, particularly
since so many of his friends had already expressed a great
deal of interest in her.

He offered his judgment with a smile. "My dear Cokie, if
I was a trifle overset this afternoon at having discovered you
were already the object of so many admirers, I suspect that by
tomorrow I shall be in a rage." He spoke nothing less than the
truth and wondered if there was any possible way he could
keep her from attending Mrs. Marston's ball in the first place.
He did not know how it was, but he could not quite warm to
the notion of seeing her sought after by so many gentlemen,
worthy or not.

"Thank you, Harley. You have relieved my mind."

At that moment, Lady Potsgrove, resplendent in a black

cap at least twice the size of her head, entered the room exclaiming, "Oh, my dear Coquette! How lovely you look! And
. . . and it is your first ball!" She then promptly burst into
tears.

"Pray, do not, Potsy!" Coquette cried. "Or I shall begin to
cry as well, and then everyone will be able to see my freckles
for the powder will have all run off!"

At that, Lady Potsgrove drew in a sharp breath and
stemmed the flood that had quickly dampened her kerchief.
"We cannot have that!" she exclaimed.

"But why are you weeping?" she asked.

"You . . . you . . . you are so beautiful and my fondest
prayer for you has actually come true; you are a lady at last,
you are in London, and in a very short while, you will be married." Once more she wept into her kerchief.

"No, no. Potsy, please, no more tears." Harley tapped her
elbow, and Coquette turned and took another glass of sherry
from him. "Here is some wine for you. See! Harley is tend-
ing to us both this evening. Is not your nephew thoughtful and
kind?"

"Thank you, Harley," Lady Potsgrove said, accepting the
sherry and letting but the smallest of sobs escape her throat,
after which she took a restorative sip. Another sniff and she
queried, "And what do you think of Coquette? Is she not
lovely?"

"Far more than I can bear with equanimity, Aunt, for I have
every fear that I shall be required to spend the evening fend-
ing off admirers at every turn."

"And so you probably shall," she agreed.

An hour later, the coach drew up before the entrance to
Mrs. Marston's town house and a footman helped first Lady
Potsgrove and then Coquette to alight. Coquette found that
she was dreadfully nervous. Her heart hammered against her
ribs and she had not felt quite so ill since the time she had
broken her arm taking a tumble from Old George several
years ago. Here she was, however, dressed to the nines, hold-

ing Harley's arm on one side, his aunt situated on his other arm, and crossing the threshold to her first London ball.

To say the event was a veritable crush was to diminish the expression completely.

"Everyone is here!" Lady Potsgrove remarked. "The entire *beau monde,* I would swear."

"So it would seem," Harley agreed.

Coquette could not speak. Her ears had grown dull with the hammering of her heart, and her eyes could not quite assimilate both the opulence of the home as well as the guests. Diamonds, rubies, and sapphires glittered upon graceful necks and wrists, even among curls. Silks adorned with gold and silver threads sparkled on elegant figures. Even a fluttering of fans revealed pearls and amethysts.

The gentlemen were arrayed in much more subdued colors, she noted, primarily a formal black as Beau Brummell wore, but interspersed with blues and burgundies, grays, and an occasional brown. *Like an opulent cottage garden,* she thought, the gentlemen forming the earth and sky, the ladies the flowers. And tonight she was a flower, just like all the other women present. The novelty of the sensation was quite overwhelming.

The thought of herself as a tulip or a geranium, so amusing in nature, brought a bubble of laughter into her throat, and much of her anxiety dissipated. Who would have thought that, a mere month past, she would be dressed, coiffed, and bejeweled as elegantly as any lady present? Not she, not by half!

As she moved through the entrance hall on Harley's arm, as she passed from chamber to chamber, she noted the lifting of quizzing glass upon quizzing glass, clearly in her direction. She knew her presence in London as an heiress had already made itself known among the *ton* by the usual method of intense, lively gabblemongering. She was therefore already known, and her fortune assessed a hundred times, before she ever crossed Mrs. Marston's portal. She smiled a little more. She felt like a horse at auction, well shod, groomed to perfection, but would she go to the highest bidder? Now there was a question, *the* question, to be answered. Was it possible that among all these gentlemen her husband awaited her? Undoubtedly.

She sighed. She wished she had been born with a different temperament, given her circumstances, something more on the order of Lady Agnes's. She had every confidence that Lady Agnes's passion to be married had been part and parcel of her desires from the time she was a little girl. How much simpler if she had felt like that.

She soon found herself before Mr. and Mrs. Marston, offering her best curtsy and complimenting her hostess on the beauty of her home. Mrs. Marston nodded, her gaze imperious and assessing. Another faint twitch of that lady's lips, and Coquette knew she would do well tonight. She was still attached to Harley's arm, as was Lady Potsgrove, and their little group continued on.

Nearby, she heard an orchestra playing a country dance and her nerves once more burned. Would she be able to perform her dances well tonight? Would she remember her steps? Would she be accounted as graceful or bumbling?

Harley leaned down to her. "Here is Templar now. Does the next dance belong to him?"

"Yes," she whispered.

She heard him laugh. "Remember, this is a ball. You are supposed to enjoy yourself."

She looked up at him and smiled suddenly. "I am grateful you reminded me, but I shan't be at ease until I go down at least one dance without tripping over my feet."

He gave her arm a squeeze. "You will dance brilliantly tonight. I am convinced of it." He then handed her to Mr. Templar.

She felt all eyes upon her as she took up her place opposite her partner. Perhaps she was the sole object of notice, or perhaps she was merely indulging in a piece of misplaced conceit. She dared not glance about, however, to see which was true. If she were to discover her fears were realized, she doubted she would be able to dance even two steps, let alone the several hundred which would comprise the country dance altogether. She therefore concentrated on Mr. Templar.

The music commenced. She moved as she was supposed to, as she had been trained to. Mr. Templar beamed when they first came together, and the next two hours became a blur of pleasure as she had never before experienced. She discovered she loved to dance—and why wouldn't she, when her favorite occupations were quite physical in nature and always had been? Dancing was merely a more orderly form of these.

Even more so did she find that she enjoyed the company of men as they sought her hand for the next and the next and the next, as they sought her attention with the telling of fine jokes and anecdotes, as they sought to engage her heart with flattery and hastily whispered poems. How strange she felt moving from one masculine arm to the next, going down a set here and there, being brought iced cups of champagne from hopeful young gentlemen, watching more youthful eyes melt with but a smile from her. She was certain had she been a more susceptible female, her head might have been quite turned by so much absurd admiration. As it was, she could not help but think how most of the gentlemen present would have been shocked to learn that but a sennight past she had been riding bareback in a silk gown.

How Harley would have laughed had he known her thoughts in this moment, as his good friend Lord Waltham gently reminded her that the next dance was his. Only she did not see him. Was he dancing? Was he enjoying himself as much as she?

She took up her place with Waltham for the quadrille and, as one who had been enjoying her London Seasons for ages, began going easily down the dance. At the same time, her gaze flitted about the ballroom. Once more, she wondered just where Harley was and whether he remembered that her waltz, which was next, was promised to him.

When the dance drew to a conclusion, Lord Waltham led her from floor. "You seemed a trifle distracted, Miss Millbrook."

She glanced up at him. "I suppose I am. Harley is promised to me for the waltz and I do not see him. Do you know where he might be?"

Lord Waltham smiled in such a knowing fashion that she was not surprised when he said, "Come. We shall hunt him down."

He led her from chamber to chamber, the town house being quite large. Even with the constant arrival and departure of guests, however, the house was still crammed with the *haut ton* and for that reason, progress was slow. Eventually, near a table laden with sliced fruits, biscuits and chocolates, she found Harley seated in a chair surrounded by several young ladies, three of whom were known to Coquette. Lady Agnes, of course, flanked his left elbow, also seated. On his right were Olivia Dazeley and Katherine Godwin. Other lesser ladies in his court were ranged behind.

"Excellent," she heard him say. "Now what of the macaroon?" He turned toward Lady Agnes and Coquette watched in some stupefaction as the young lady slipped a small piece of biscuit into his mouth. He smiled at her with just such an expression as reminded her of how a fox must feel pacing a chicken pen.

She was unable to check the words before they pounced from her lips. "What? Incapable of feeding yourself, Harley?"

He was startled by the sudden address. Seeing her, his expression darkened and she wished the words unsaid. She was quite used to speaking to him in that manner at home, particularly when he was behaving in a ridiculous fashion, as he was now, and she would never have done so in this moment except that her disgust was quite profound.

The ladies about him grew nervous and fidgety, releasing a giggle or two, but otherwise the strain in that moment was palpable for all, especially since Harley remained so very silent.

Lord Waltham's excellent manners asserted themselves. "Miss Millbrook is, I believe, pledged to you for the waltz. We came in search of you."

"Ah, yes," Harley said, his gaze fixed on Coquette with a murderous expression. He rose slowly to his feet. "You will excuse me?" he said, glancing at each of the ladies of his harem in turn.

The ladies obliged him with hints that he should return to them as soon as the waltz drew to a close. He made his bow, then took Coquette roughly from Waltham's arm.

His grip was severe upon her wrist. She glanced up at him but he was smiling and nodding to acquaintances as he guided her away from the table of sweets. If his smile seemed forced, she understood perfectly well why.

She knew she ought to apologize. She had all but made a scene, behaving as badly as ever she had at home, only this was London. "Harley," she said, "I am—"

"Hush!" he snapped beneath his breath.

She remembered the last time she had seen him this furious. Old George had thrown a shoe and she had taken out his newest hunter instead, a thoroughbred stallion. She had brought the fine horse back in a lather, and he had only barely restrained venting his fury by applying his own riding crop to her posterior. He had, however, let his displeasure be known in as profound a tirade as nothing before. She felt the same wrath spilling from him now.

She was not, and never had been, however, particularly moved by his displays of rage. Certainly he had cause, but as they made their progress in a direction that seemed quite the opposite from the ballroom, she was suddenly struck by the truth that the last thing he should be doing was permitting innocent young women, all so very hopeful, to put food in his mouth. If he meant to give her a dressing down about her conduct, then she meant to give him a little advice of her own!

After a few minutes of navigating the mansion, she suddenly found herself alone with him in a very pretty conservatory. As he closed the door and leaned heavily against it, his arms crossed over his chest, she wondered if the plants would survive what she felt certain was soon to follow.

The thought of it made her smile. This so enraged him that his cheeks darkened anew. She wondered if he was seeing her through a film of red.

"I vow, Coquette, that if you do not, in this instant, remove that grin from your face, I shan't be held accountable for what happens next."

"I am all a-tremble, m'lord," she responded facetiously. "But perhaps if I hurried from the conservatory and fetched you a biscuit, then placed it delicately upon your poor, helpless tongue, you might not feel so obviously . . . bilious."

She watched him struggle quite valiantly to compose himself, to control his temper, but he succeeded poorly. A few masterly steps and his hands were poised near her throat. "Do you know how easily I could throttle you, Miss Millbrook?"

"Oh, m'lord," she cooed in her best imitation of Lady Agnes. "Pray do not. I worship you so. You have no idea. I dream of bearing your children and being your wife and—"

A sudden smile darted through his eyes. He averted his gaze quickly, however, but not without having already betrayed himself. Finally, he asked, "Do you have any notion how utterly improper your conduct was just now? I vow the entire house heard you address me in what will certainly be passed about as a completely unladylike manner. Have you no command over yourself?"

Coquette thought the question ridiculous, nearly as much as his entirely theatrical manner of dragging her away from the ball in order to ring a peal over her head. She thought there was only one thing she could do, so she turned away from him, and gave her shoulders a slight, shuddering shake. "I have erred," she murmured, gently withdrawing from the pocket of her gown a quite useless lace kerchief. She pressed it elegantly to her mouth and gave her shoulders another sob-like ripple of affectation. She sniffed loudly.

"Cokie," she heard him say, his voice softening so suddenly that she found herself disppointed. Was he fooled so easily?

Harley resisted the sudden impulse to place his hands on her arms. He could see that she was overset, even restraining with some effort a bout of tears. He knew she had been nervous about the ball and of course she had made a dreadful mistake in making sport of him in front of so many ladies of the *ton,* but it was not as though she had committed a real crime. He began to regret his own severe reaction, especially when her shoulders shook again.

"I am so very sorry," she whispered. Another sniff.

Again, he wanted to touch her, to reassure her. He had not meant to make her cry, only to make her see that she should not have exposed herself in such a wretched manner as she just had. Her shoulders shook anew and she sniffed loudly once more.

"Cokie, please try to understand. I had only one intention in bringing you here, to give you a chance to gain command of yourself. I feared you would continue to upbraid me in what I can only say was a hoydenish, thoughtless manner." He heard a squeak of a sob escape her throat, a sound which undid him entirely. He did not restrain himself this time, but placed his hands on her arms. "Pray do not cry."

Coquette whirled around suddenly and laughed in his face. "You are nearly as hopeless as Adcock! Earlier, I batted my lashes at him as I have seen Lady Agnes do to you a hundred times, and he nearly fainted with the pleasure of it. Is your head so easily turned as well by a few feminine machinations?"

When Harley realized he had been duped, all his former rage returned to him. Coquette apparently comprehended as much and turned to slip behind a palm just as he lunged for her. In that instant, what his intention had been was something akin to a profound desire to pull her braids. Only she didn't have any braids, only a cascade of red curls separated by Grecian bands, but these were just beyond the tips of his fingers.

He reached around the palm one way, then another, but he could not grasp even a shred of her gown. She was smiling in a damnable fashion, further feeding his fury. He lunged around the palm, but she was an agile female and raced away, this time to keep him at bay with a potted lemon tree between them. What was worse, she was now giggling in a sound that reminded him of a dozen times he had chased her through the halls of Barscot. A feeling of the hunt now overtook him, something she felt as well, for he could see the glitter in her blue eyes.

She darted, he followed. She hid, he found her. She raced to one end of the conservatory, he ran after her. He caught her hair once and pulled the bands out of place. His fingers found the sleeve of her gown and he heard the seam give way in a sharp rip.

Still she laughed and glared, daring him on, provoking him, fanning his rage.

He glanced quickly about the chamber, well aware that Coquette could keep evading him merely by her agility and stamina. Finally, he saw a way that he might trap her, and so he began a slow, though exhausting, process of working her toward the only corner of the room, hidden behind an enormous palm, from which she would have no means of escape.

At last, he began positioning her into the corner. When she saw what he had done, she gave a squeal and tried one last valiant attempt to push herself by him, but he was a strong man and caught her firmly about the waist. He had half expected her to struggle, but instead, she merely smiled and said, "Oh, Harley, are we not the most ridiculous pair?"

He did not know how it was, but instead of heaping insults on her or boxing her ears, which he had done once when she was eleven after she had splattered ink purposely over his favorite buckskin breeches, he looked at her lips and cried out, "The devil take it!" and kissed her quite boldly.

Coquette had been so caught up in the familiar game of cat and mouse that she had not had sufficient time to predict the end of it. However, in more ordinary circumstances, she would have expected Harley to tie her up and leave her in one of the outbuildings, as he had done on occasion when she had been particularly naughty. She certainly would not have predicted that he would have kissed her. For that reason, perhaps, she did not struggle with him. She was far too stunned for that.

After a few seconds, though, when she might have begun pulling herself out of his rather tight embrace, she suddenly did not want to. The excitement of having found herself chased again by Harley, only this time in full ball dress, began flowing over her in a tense ripple of something that felt like desire. Her arms suddenly snaked about his neck and she held him fiercely, as though holding on to a dream she did not want to forget once she awoke. His lips were like fire against hers and his tongue, now searching in a most shocking way the recesses of her mouth, a flame that ignited her senses over and over. The longer he held her and kissed her, the more distant the conservatory seemed.

She was on her sailing vessel now and Harley was with her. The ocean breeze flowed over her in strong, vibrant waves. Harley was kissing her and she was returning his kisses with abandon. Her stomach tensed as desire built within her. There was a madness between them. Her thoughts drifted to his bed, to sharing his bed, and suddenly she could no longer feel her feet. Her knees buckled, giving way, but Harley caught her, kissing her harder still.

"Oh, Harley," she whispered against his lips.

Only then, when he heard her voice, did he draw back, his expression shocked. "Cokie, I am so sorry. I should not have done that."

She could only stare into his gray eyes, which appeared almost coal black in the dimly lit chamber. No, he should not have kissed her, but she would not have missed it for the world. She felt so dizzy, as though she had been turned in circles for several minutes. She did not know what to say to him, but as awareness dawned that her hair was in shambles, she touched a lock now hanging loose past her shoulder and said, "I believe I lost one of the bands to my hair near the large fern by the door."

He nodded almost blindly. After moving around the large trunk of the palm, he began to walk slowly in the opposite direction.

She felt her hair, her sleeve. She glanced down at her slippers and saw that they were badly soiled from having overturned a pretty fuschia and afterward treading through the soil.

Still unable to credit that Harley had just kissed her, she watched him bend down to pick up the band. Just as he was righting himself, the door opened and Lady Potsgrove appeared in the doorway. "Where is she?"

Harley gestured in her direction and she emerged from behind the massive palm. "Here, Potsy. I believe I shall need your assistance."

"What happened to you? Oh, dear, oh, dear! It hardly matters! We are in the basket, indeed! Only what is to be done?"

"Aunt, I fear it was my fault," Harley began. "I—"

"Harley, you needn't tell whiskers to protect me. Potsy, the truth is, I behaved very badly tonight. I did not like something Harley said to me, and when he tried to instruct me on proper conduct, I . . . I threw a fit. I tore my gown, broke a pot, and ruined my slippers."

"That is not entirely true," Harley interjected. "The truth is, Potsy, that—"

"Hush! The pair of you!" she cried. She drew close to Coquette and looked her up and down. "But this makes no sense," she said, adjusting her own shawl. "I was watching you earlier and you seemed to be enjoying yourself prodi-

giously and your dancing was perfection! I do not in the least
understand."

Harley gave a grunt of disgust. "Coquette only told half-
truths, Aunt. In fact, I flew into a pelter at something she said
to me and brought her here to discuss the matter with her.
However, I began provoking her, then she pretended to weep,
and I felt badly and the next moment we were . . . well, I
began chasing her about, snatching at her gown and her hair,
and here we are."

If Lady Potsgrove's eyes had grown wide at any of what he
had said to her, they were now the size of saucers. "You did
this?" she cried. "Has the whole world gone mad?" She began
to weave on her feet in an ominous fashion and after not once
announcing that she might faint, dropped into a profound
swoon.

Coquette immediately sank beside her and supported her
benefactress. "Harley, pray find Mrs. Marston and tell her we
are in need of a very discreet maid. Tell her Potsy has fainted,
that she is become ill, and then fetch both my shawl and our
coach." When he stared at her as though unseeing, she
snapped, "At once, Harley! Oh, and a vinaigrette or smelling
salts. Do not worry. All will be well."

He obeyed her and within a half hour, Coquette's hair and
torn sleeve were covered by the shawl, and she and Harley led
Lady Potsgrove from the town house as though she had been
taken dreadfully ill.

Once within the safe confines of the coach, however, Lady
Potsgrove had had enough of the ridiculous charade and
threw off their supporting hands and arms. She spoke to neither of them the entire way home, but held her smelling salts
very close.

Nine

On the following morning, as Coquette sat between Lady Potsgrove and Harley during church services, her thoughts were anywhere but on the careful sermon being delivered in a quiet monotone by the parish priest. She did not mean to be irreverent, not by half, but her mind was unfortunately still consumed by events of the night before.

Coquette knew that Lady Potsgrove was still overset by all that had had happened, most particularly that she had found her in such a ramshackle state in Mrs. Marston's conservatory, her ragged appearance the very thing Potsy had feared from the moment their small party had arrived in London. It made no difference to her that with a little playacting, they had been able to sustain a believable exit from Mrs. Marston's home and that not a breath of scandal had ensued from the incident.

She had, of course, begged for Potsy's forgiveness, as had Harley, but the long-suffering woman was only now beginning to relent toward either of them, and only because she had been greeted before the service by any number of her friends, who each inquired politely after her health. Seeing that a great scandal had not ensued from last night's debacle, Lady Potsgrove had even looked at Coquette not a minute past without actually frowning her down.

For herself, Coquette could not think of the conservatory without blushing. She still could not credit that their squabbling had turned first into a ridiculous game of cat and mouse and then ended in such an extraordinary kiss. Of course, the chasing game had resulted mostly because of habit. She could not count the number of times Harley had chased her about Barscot, particularly during the boring winter months. She smiled to herself. They had even done so once last winter when a heavy snow had stuck and there was no riding to be done, or fishing or hunting or anything.

She recalled with a start something she had quite forgot, that when he had finally caught her in one of the attic rooms, having discovered her behind an old roped mattress, he had taken to tickling her, which had set her to giggling, chortling, and squealing like a schoolgirl. And then, right in the middle of it, he had stopped and a very strange expression had overtaken his features.

Good God, she thought, *he had almost kissed me then.* And that was over a year prior.

But what did any of it mean? She placed a hand to her forehead, squeezed her eyes shut, and tried her very best to understand what was happening, but no profound insight returned to her, only the awful truth that she had enjoyed kissing Harley last night more than anything, even more than mounting a hunter and letting him have his head over miles of open turf! How was that possible?

She felt guilty suddenly as she opened her eyes and gazed up into a beautiful fan-vaulted ceiling. She should never have kissed Harley back.

Another glance toward the priest revealed that he had been looking at her for some time and nodding as though he could read her thoughts, that he believed them to be of an exalted, repentant nature, that her spirit had been engaged in silent confession. She averted her gaze quickly, afraid that he might truly read her mind, in which case the good man would be in for a shock.

As she once more reviewed the passionate kiss, a piercing question rose within her mind—was it possible she was in love with Harley? A second question followed swiftly. What had Harley thought of their shared kiss?

Harley wished Coquette would stop fidgeting beside him. The priest had stared at her more than once already and even though he seemed somehow approving of her, the last thing Harley wanted was so much attention drawn to their pew. Poor Potsy had had quite enough from the pair of them. She did not need now to think that even the heavens were taking an interest in their affairs.

If only he had not succumbed to the incredibly powerful desire he had been feeling last night to kiss the wretched girl! If only he had showed restraint—only how had it happened that he had been unable to do so? If only he had not torn her gown and destroyed her hair in their silly game, and then kissed her, the entire incident could have passed without the smallest hint of scandal. As it was, Lady Potsgrove had taken the brunt of their antics and put it about, through the help of her abigail, that she had requested to leave the ball early because of the headache and had insisted that her nephew and his ward take her home.

He still could not credit that he had behaved so abominably. Somehow, he rather thought the blame lay at Coquette's feet, for it always seemed that she provoked him into unbecoming conduct. This wouldn't fadge, however. No one had forced him to chase her about Mrs. Marston's conservatory. He had engaged in the ridiculous game himself and in truth he had loved every moment of it, especially—and here he was being brutally honest—when he had allowed himself to kiss her.

He could not help smiling, if but a little. He had expected her to struggle against him, to kick his shins, to pinch and to scratch him. Instead, she had actually thrown her arms about his neck and given kiss for kiss as though she had been doing so for years. Even this was different from the kiss at Barscot just before their departure. At that time, she had been merely receptive, wonderfully so, but had not responded nearly so ardently as last night. He found himself intrigued. Who would have thought that she would kiss with such abandon and delight? His Cokie! So unexpectedly passionate!

He glanced down at her. She was pressing her fingers to her forehead and squeezing her eyes shut, almost as though grimacing. No wonder the priest regarded her so approvingly. If ever there was penitence in a countenance, it was in Coquette's in this moment. He bit his lip to keep from laughing aloud. The last thing Coquette would ever be was penitent.

He nudged her slightly and she glanced up at him as discreetly as she could. He could see the quivering of a smile dancing upon both cheeks, saw the sudden laughter in her blue eyes. He could feel his own lips twitch. Then he looked away to keep from laughing. He felt her slip her arm about his and he squeezed her arm in understanding. All, it would seem, was forgiven and forgotten.

Coquette did not know precisely why she had taken his arm, except that when he had nudged her and looked at her, a profound affection had swelled up in her heart for him, for her dear Harley, who had always teased her to distraction. She thought she had finally come to a measure of understanding about their odd relationship, that there would always exist between them a certain bond based on both familiarity and contest that was not so much sibling in design as something akin to the best of friends. She knew herself forgiven for her antics in the conservatory and her heart felt light beyond words.

Shortly after their return to Grosvenor Square, when Lady Potsgrove had retired to her bedchamber, and just as Coquette herself was mounting the stairs, Harley bid her join him in his office. She did so at once, and saw that he was regarding her with something like wonder in his expression.

"What is it?" she asked, letting her green velvet muff dangle from her fingers.

"You are so changed," he said. "I often cannot credit that it is you I am looking at."

"Is that what you wished to tell me?"

He shook his head. "No, not precisely, but I think these thoughts very often."

She moved to the windows and dropped into a chair. "I am not changed, really, not within," she said, holding the muslin back so that she might see outside. "Which is why, I suppose, I actually encouraged you to chase me about Mrs. Marston's conservatory. Oh, dear, I can see that both Olney and Waltham are come to call. Were you expecting them?" She let the drape fall and looked back at him. He was leaning against his carved mahogany desk, his arms crossed over his chest.

He shook his head. "In previous Seasons I have enjoyed their company only at night. This call must be a compliment to you. But why are you frowning?"

"Because I suspect they both wish to wed me, or at least my fortune, and I am put in mind again of the fix I am in."

"So tell me honestly, Coquette, do you think either of them would suit?"

At that, she brightened. "Both would do famously as husbands, as well you know. They are both truly gentlemen and have a love of sports which would be pleasing to me, but what of love? Do you think I ought to consider love in choosing my husband?"

He shrugged. "I have not the faintest notion. There are but three weeks and a bit remaining in which you must choose a man and marry him. Can love develop so quickly? I do not know. How could I, when I have never been in love before?"

The door knocker sounded and Coquette rose to her feet. "Is this true?" she asked, surprised. "Not even with Lady Agnes? I thought you were rather besotted with her."

"I am. At least I thought I was." He chuckled. "You see, I am as hopeless as you. But come, let us together entertain Waltham and Olney."

"Only if we might play at billiards."

"Done."

He was about to open the door, but instead held the handle

and looked at her most sincerely. "What I wished to say to you was that I do apologize for having kissed you last night."

Coquette wished he had not said as much. She wished he was not so tall. She wished he would not be so kind to her. She drew in a crumpled breath and nodded. "I, too, wish it undone." How untrue this was, she thought. Thus far, his kiss had been the very pinnacle of her enjoyment of her first Season.

She thought he would open the door, but instead, he leaned toward her slightly, a smile on his lips. "You know, it would help a great deal if you would not look at me in that manner, as though you wanted me to kiss you again."

She laughed outright. "Oh, Harley, I do wish for it, but it is very bad of me, do you not think so, particularly since I do not love you?"

"What a baggage you are to have said as much," he complained, but by now he was laughing again.

"I suppose I just like kissing."

"Just like you enjoy being chased around a conservatory. What happened last night was your fault, you know. You always were able to provoke me into all manner of outrageous conduct."

With that, he threw wide the door which opened onto the entrance hall. Both Olney and Waltham were removing their gloves and handing them to Jenkins, who was already holding their hats.

Coquette preceded Harley, but turned back and whispered, "How very much like you to cast all the blame on me. However, no one compelled you to engage in the chase, last night or any time before. It is your soul that demands you run, not some supposedly mystical power I hold over you."

She walked briskly toward the gentlemen and queried in her strong manner, "Billiards, gentlemen?" Their response was more than enthusiastic, which led her to instruct the servant, "Cold meats, cheese, some of Cook's bread warmed and dripping with butter. Oh, and some ale."

"Very good, ma'am."

Harley watched as his friends followed after her, lambs to the slaughter. He fully expected either or both to offer for Coquette before the week was out, and why wouldn't they? What gentleman would not wish to marry a veritable goddess who would greet them on a Sunday afternoon with a promise of beef, ale, and billiards?

He joined in her wake, a familiar, powerful sensation once more gripping his chest. He resisted a profound impulse to push his friends out of the way that he might walk beside her the entire distance to the billiard room at the back of the house. Somehow the thought that she might soon be wed to either Waltham or Olney or any of his friends or acquaintance was becoming less and less appealing to him.

The remainder of Sunday was whiled away in just such a pleasant manner. After a time, Lady Potsgrove made up a fourth for whist, and as the day progressed, more of his friends and a few ladies joined in a succession of parlor games made delightful by the onset of a steady rain and fires blazing on the hearths throughout the house.

On the following day, Coquette returned from an invigorating ride through Hyde Park with her good friend Thomas Adcock. She was in a state of shock, and so it was that when Harley met her at the first floor landing, she blinked at him several times before realizing he was speaking.

"I beg your pardon?" she queried politely.

"Good God!" he cried. "Come into the drawing room and tell me what has happened? Did you take a tumble?"

"A tumble?" she asked, offended. "Harley, I have a better seat than you."

"Yes, of course," he said, smiling suddenly. "Only, I fear you were looking quite pale and I could not for the life of me comprehend why that would be." A new expression overtook his features, the smile vanishing to be replaced by a heavy frown. "Did he . . . that is, tell me at once . . . though I doubt he would . . . however, you may confide in me . . . and you may trust me to give him a hint or two."

Coquette shook her head. "A hint? What sort of hint? Of what are you speaking? You are not making the smallest bit of sense. Why are you scowling as though I have gotten into another scrape?"

"Well, have you?"

"Just what sort of scrape can one get into at Hyde Park? We had a wonderful ride, quite exhilarating and the sky was as blue as I've ever seen it, at least in London."

"Then why the devil were you looking so dumbstruck just now?"

"Oh, that," she said, as she untied the ribbons of her black riding bonnet. "He offered for me."

"Adcock?" he cried. "Of all the absurd starts."

"Yes, I know, but it was rather exciting. After all, he was the first to do so. It's just that I was so taken by surprise. He seemed nervous from the first, but I thought it was because he was astride the worst bit of blood and bone I had ever seen in my life. However, I was fair and far off the mark there." She unbuttoned her pelisse and laid it over the back of a nearby chair. "Although I have little doubt I shall expect many to follow. His mother, you see."

"Ah, yes, of course. The Matchmaking Mamas will be in full flower soon, now that you are known to be seeking a husband. So how did he make his proposals? Surely not on bended knee."

Coquette laughed and curled up in the corner of the sofa.

He shook a finger at her. "Potsy will be out of reason cross should she find you like that."

She grinned. "Only with you, Harley, would I dare. Would you pour me a sherry?"

"Of course." He turned and poured out two and after handing her the wine, he took up his place at the opposite end of the sofa. "So, tell me, did he stammer through most of it?"

Coquette took a sip of her sherry and then placed a hand

on her cheek. "It was very sweet, really, though once or twice I did have great difficulty keeping my countenance, for if you must know, he kept referring to his profound regard for me, in that way of his." She assumed a serious expression. "'Miss Millbrook—'"

"He called you 'Miss Millbrook'?" he asked, amazed. "When you have known him for ages?"

"Why, yes, of course," she responded in mock seriousness. "He was, after all, offering for me. 'Miss Millbrook, have always had a fondness, will be a good sort of husband or try to, not too demanding, et cetera.'"

"He used that particular word, *et cetera?*"

"Indeed, he did," she responded. "Could anything be of a more sublime, romantic nature?"

"I suppose not. So how did he come to the point?"

Coquette wrinkled her nose and took another sip of sherry. "Not without some difficulty. He stumbled through the rest of his speech, but it went something like, 'Mama says you are vastly improved, hopes you will not be too much trouble, my sister likes you and thinks your hair is very pretty.' He then ran a finger along the inside of his neckcloth, which subsequently bent both his shirt points in half."

"Gudgeon."

"Then he blurted out, 'Will you be my wife?'"

"Ham-handed by half."

"I fear it was."

"So am I to wish you joy?"

She shot him a severe look. "Of course not. He had no real interest in me and was only asking because he is an obedient son to a truly horrible mother, who I in turn have no interest in having as a mother-in-law."

"Were you gentle in your refusals?"

Here she laughed. "I fear I was not. I believe I said something like, 'I have never known you to be bacon-brained before, Addy. Pray accept this as my final answer.' And with that, I slapped his mount's flank with my riding crop, which set the poor gelding leaping into a gallop. Addy, though nearly losing his seat twice, held on valiantly, then escorted me home. I should perhaps mention that he begged me to say nothing of his proposal to any of our acquaintance, so I hope you know to remain silent on the subject."

"Who would I tell?"

"Precisely." She took another sip and began to smile. "I must say, it is quite satisfying to receive an offer of marriage, even if it was ridiculous."

"You are beginning to be all puffed up," he said, chuckling.

She merely laughed. "I wonder who will be next?"

"You know, you might want to curtail so much conviction, at least in polite society, that you will receive another proposal, else you will gain a reputation for conceit and arrogance."

"You sound just like Potsy. But I really only say such things to you, for I know you comprehend me perfectly and that I am not so dullwitted as to actually believe that anything but my fortune has aroused such interest in me."

Harley choked on his sherry.

"What is it?"

"Have you regarded your reflection in a looking glass of late?"

"Oh, pooh," she responded. "That is the reason a man will dance with me, but were I poor, I would not receive even one offer—unless, of course, the gentleman already had a fortune, like you, but that is quite rare, as you must know. It is no surprise to me that your home is presently being overrun by second and third sons."

Harley appeared stunned. "Are you always so pragmatic? Have I never known you in this respect?"

She offered a half smile. "It comes, I believe, from having been orphaned quite early on."

He regarded her intently. "I can imagine your sufferings only in part. I was devastated when my mother died, even though I was but a boy. You lost both your parents."

"But it is not so uncommon in this day and age, so I do not repine, if that is what you fear."

"On no account. I doubt I have ever seen you sorry for your circumstances."

She grinned. "That would have been very difficult, since not only did I have the run of Barscot but your father's affection as well."

"Still, there must have been moments."

"Of course. Early on, as such a young child, I recall going to sleep at night with terrible fears and anxieties. I did not know at the time what I was so very much afraid of, but now I believe it was being taken from Barscot and sent to an orphanage."

"There never could have been such talk in our house," he returned fervently. "Certainly it was never my father's intention."

"But you are thinking as an adult would. I was a child and thought as a child, that if my life could be so upended in one moment, why not a second time, or third, or fourth? And what child does not eventually learn about orphanages? It seemed quite rational to me that one day I might be sent to one."

He shook his head. "It seems so strange to me that only now, after we have been forced to come to London together, I am coming to know you."

"Do you realize we have not even brangled today?"

"The day is not over yet," he said, laughter in his gray eyes.

"Indeed, it is not."

"Are you in expectation of another offer of marriage today?"

She shook her head, chuckling. "No, but probably tomorrow, for Lord Henry is taking me to Astley's Amphitheater, an attempt no doubt to win my affections by denying his own. Of all your friends, he is the only one somewhat indifferent to horses."

"Horses, yes. However, he is not so indifferent to cards, which leads me to ask, do you mean to accept him should he

offer? His connections as a second son of the Marquis of Wolstonbury are even grander than my own."

She saw the concerned light in his eye and she could not
help but laugh. "The day that I accept the hand of a confirmed gamester, which I believe Binyon to be, is the day I no
longer deserve my birthright."

His smile was one of satisfaction, and he nodded his approval. "I was not certain whether you understood the depths
of his, er, *enjoyment* of every form of gaming."

"You must think me henwitted, when the first thing he ever
asked me was whether I played silver loo or not."

The trip to Astley's on the following day, however, was not
a success. Poor Lord Henry had a cold and his complexion
was rather high, indicating a fever. Before the first riders
could even break into a gallop and dazzle the audience with
every expression of supreme horsemanship, Lord Henry was
looking so poorly that Coquette rose in her seat, extended her
hand to him, and said, "Come, my lord, you need to be in your
bed with a doctor at your side."

"Nonsense," he said. But his eyes were narrowed in misery
and red from his sufferings. With a little effort, she pried him
from his gentlemanly position and drove him straight home
to his rooms in Half Moon Street, after which she saw him
settled in bed and summoned a physician. At the same time,
she sent for Harley, knowing full well that her presence in a
bachelor's abode was not at all the thing. Nor, on the other
hand, was she willing to desert her patient until she knew he
would be properly attended to.

Harley arrived within the half hour, at first appearing out
of reason cross with her for having created such a scandal,
and said as much. Coquette, however, would have none of it,
but begged him to whisper if he wished to give her a dressing
down, all the while beckoning him to Binyon's bedchamber.
He followed her, clearly prepared to ring a peal over her head,

but the moment he laid eyes on his friend, his countenance softened.

"Good God," he murmured.

"Just so."

"He is so very pale."

"He was shivering dreadfully before you arrived, but I made certain that a bed warmer was brought for his feet and another counterpane. He is better now."

Harley approached the bed. "How do you go on, Binney?"

He opened his eyes, which were still quite red-rimmed. "Oh, hallo, Tony. A trifle queer in the stirrups, but I'll be as right as rain soon enough."

"Of course you will."

"Is Miss Millbrook gone then?"

"No, she is still here. She has insisted upon remaining until your physician arrives."

"She should go. Not at all the thing to be in a man's rooms."

Harley smiled. "I have told her as much, but she refuses to leave. Says she will not desert you until she is assured of your health."

"She's a devlish fine girl, Harley."

"So she is."

Coquette felt her heart warm to Lord Henry. She did not think she had ever received so kind a compliment before. She watched Harley reach down and pat his shoulder gently.

"Rest now, Binney. I'll wait as well until the doctor arrives. We'll be in the parlor if you have need of us."

Lord Henry closed his eyes.

Harley gestured for Coquette to join him in the other room. Once there, out of earshot, he said, "I hope it is not an inflammation of the lungs."

She saw that he was worried. "We are both afraid of that, are we not?"

He nodded, but she could see that he was thinking of his

father at this moment, so she quickly changed the subject. "I hoped Potsy would have come with you."

"She had been gone for some time. Hookham's, to exchange three of her books." He then frowned at her again. "You should go, Coquette. I can manage now."

She shook her head. "Not until the doctor relieves my mind. Besides, you are here and that should be all the consequence I require to silence the gabblemongers."

"You are forgetting," he said with a wry smile. "You are now in the presence of two bachelors. To the gossips, your sin will have become even greater."

"Perhaps I am not thinking sensibly," she responded, "but I really don't give a fig for what anyone thinks of the moment. I want only to know that Lord Henry will be all right."

His man arrived bearing a basin of water. Coquette crossed the room to take it from him, then returned to the bedchamber. She sat in a chair near Lord Henry's bed, dabbed the linen in the water, and pressed it to his forehead.

"That feels wonderful," he whispered as he opened his eyes. "You are kindness itself, Miss Millbrook. I don't suppose I have the smallest chance of one day winning your hand, do I?"

"Are you actually making me an offer of marriage?" she asked, teasingly.

He sighed deeply. "Would you have me?"

She chuckled as she answered his question, "My dear Binyon, the only hand I have ever seen you truly interested in winning is one at whist, silver loo, or piquet."

He laughed, then winced. "I am so hot."

"I know. The doctor will be here very soon."

An hour later, Coquette watched the doctor emerge from Lord Henry's bedchamber, his countenance not in the least distressed. She knew the answer before ever he spoke and in turn breathed a deep sigh of relief. The fever was not of an infectious nature and should he get sufficient rest he would be recovered in a sennight or so.

On the way home, Harley glanced at Coquette. "You were always used to nurse the servants when they were ailing."

She nodded, appearing indifferent to his remark as she continued glancing out the window, watching the London scenery passing by. Harley found himself mystified. He had spoken truly on the day before when he had said that he felt as though he was just coming to know her, not less so than when he pondered not only her kindness to Binyon but also her willingness to risk social ostracism by taking him to his rooms and remaining there until she knew he would be well cared for. He wondered how many other ladies of his acquaintance would have done as much. He tried, albeit in vain, to picture Lady Agnes, Miss Dazeley, or Miss Godwin making such a sacrifice. Impossible. He knew their minds well: Their conduct was of the most sacred importance and never would they have compromised their reputations in such a fashion as Coquette had. The only question now was just how long it would take for the truth to become known generally that she had been alone with Binyon in his rooms.

"You did right today, Cokie," he said, the now familiar gripping sensation taking strong hold of his chest once more.

At that, she turned to him and smiled. "But do you think by the time the servants have gossiped sufficiently that I will still be welcome at Almack's tomorrow night?"

"Much you care," he stated, but he was smiling.

"I suppose not," she said, in some seriousness. "But Potsy will."

"Leave Potsy to me," he said.

Upon arriving at Grosvenor Square, he saw that his aunt had just returned from the circulating library, a package tucked under her arm, which she bestowed upon a waiting footman. Her carriage, a very pretty landau, drew away from the sidewalk, and his own coach followed behind to stop in front of his door.

His aunt, smiling first, then frowning, addressed Coquette.

"I thought you would still be at Astley's, my dear. And where is Lord Henry?"

"I fear my good friend," Harley said, directing the conversation away from Coquette, "was taken ill. But come inside and we will tell you everything."

"Yes, of course."

Once within the entrance hall, he drew both ladies into his office and in a straightforward manner regaled his aunt with the particulars of the afternoon. Her complexion paled more than once, and more than once she turned horrified eyes upon Coquette.

At the end of the brief history, she began to give voice to her feelings. "Coquette, how could you? When I have most especially instructed you on what is expected of young ladies during the Season! I cannot credit you could have been so thoughtless, so heedless—"

Harley meant to interrupt her, but Coquette was before him. "To do what, Potsy? To risk his health, perhaps even his life, by not seeing him properly tended to? Why, you of all women should know how indifferent, even stupid, men can be about their health. I have not been that long in Lord Henry's company without having come to understand he is not in the least attentive to the requirements of his body. To own the truth, I was thinking as much of myself as of him when I remained in his rooms and called for a physician. I could not have borne the guilt which I would most certainly have incurred had he lost his life because of even the smallest indifference on my part. No, no, you may come the crab if you like, but I stand by what I did."

"You thought he might perish?" she inquired, blinking fast several times.

"Indeed, he was painfully feverish by the time we arrived in Half Moon Street. I would no more have left him in such a state than I would have left you or Harley. Would you have wished me to?"

"Well, that is a bit of plain speaking. Only, I wonder . . .

Well, well, you did what you thought was right, and though I might have made a different decision, I think I see a way in which we might salvage the moment. Harley, I must write a missive at once! Summon a footman, will you?"

"Of course, but what do you mean to do, Aunt?" He found himself amused, for her expression had grown quite fiercely determined.

"Almeria Binyon is in town and owes me one or two favors. I shall redeem them now, see if I won't! Now, off with you both!" She took up a seat at his desk, drew forward her nephew's writing materials, then waved them away.

Harley led Coquette into the entrance hall. "My aunt has more abilities than I had ever before comprehended."

"Who is Almeria?" Coquette queried.

"Binyon's mother, the Marchioness of Wolstonbury."

Ten

On the following evening, Coquette entered the infamous Almack's Assembly Rooms and was surprised by how plain they were. With all the power attendant upon the vouchers for the assemblies, she had somehow supposed that a corresponding magnificence would follow. In this she was quite disappointed. The only elegance and display of wealth within the rooms was found upon the various persons scattered about and conversing quietly.

She was not surprised, however, that when she made her entrance on Harley's arm, the entire room fell to a hush. Ever since having assisted Lord Henry in his rooms, she had been the subject of much gossip, despite Lady Potsgrove's numerous efforts to the contrary.

To Harley, she whispered, "I vow I would be quite overset were I not so angry."

He gave her arm a squeeze as he nodded to several acquaintances. All the while, they continued moving through the gawking multitude. "All will be well. You may trust Potsy in that. Good evening, Lady Cowper."

"How do you go on, Harlington?"

"Very well, indeed. You are acquainted with Miss Millbrook."

"Of course. What a lovely gown, Miss Millbrook. That particular shade of yellow suits you to perfection."

"Thank you, m'lady," she responded, offering a curtsy. Afterward, Lady Cowper joined them as they made something of a progression about the rooms.

"You did very right, Miss Millbrook," Lady Cowper confided behind her fan. "But you must forgive those who would set propriety above so necessary a kindness as you served to Lord Henry." Setting her fan aside, she said in clear accents, "I understand Lord Henry is still quite ill. I spoke with his physician only this morning. Good Dr. Streatley expressed his gratitude at your clear thinking yesterday."

"He is an excellent man," Coquette returned. "The doctor called on Lady Potsgrove this morning as well to inform us of his progress. I was not surprised to learn Lord Binyon was still much sunk in his illness, but he will recover speedily, I am certain, for he will not like being too long absent from Mayfair's whist tables." This comment aroused a degree of laughter in those nearby who heard her say as much. She added, "Harlington sent him a basket of lemons. Cook swears by their restorative properties, especially in a cup of tea with honey."

Lady Cowper smiled then said, "Ah, here is Lady Wolstonbury."

Harley bowed and both Lady Cowper and Coquette dropped their curtsies.

"Miss Millbrook," the marchioness stated forcefully but with a warm smile. "I was hoping so very much to see you this evening, to express again my gratitude for all that you did for my son, both you and Harlington." She lifted a kerchief to her eye. "I cannot think what might have happened to him had he been left to his own devices, for if you must know, he is far too careless of his health."

Coquette could not help but smile. Her ladyship's performance was in every sense quite theatrical, but at the same time there was sincerity in her expression. "I had the very same fear myself, but he would not be gainsaid when I suggested we postpone the trip to Astley's. Once there, I could see he was growing increasingly uncomfortable. By the time

I insisted we return to Half Moon Street, he was not even capable of ordering his carriage brought round."

She shook her head, her face pinched with worry. "Then I shall only say again how deeply indebted to you I am."

"I am only grateful that I could be of service, my lady."

With that, the marchioness moved on. Coquette was not surprised when the cloud which had been above her reputation was now lifted completely. Lady Cowper alone, as one of the patronesses of Almack's, would have been sufficient to restore her position among the *beau monde,* if in time, but with Lady Wolstonbury's expressed gratitude for Coquette's care of her son, there was certainly no reason for anyone to treat her with disdain a moment longer.

For that reason, Coquette soon found herself swamped by a dozen beaus ready to take up all her dances. She acquiesced to each in turn until, too late, she realized had she not left even one dance for Harley. He merely laughed at her and moved away to take up his post amidst what she still referred to as his harem, Lady Agnes playing the lead figure and irritating Coquette to no end.

Later, after having danced a lively reel with Mr. Templar and presently partaking of a cup of lemonade and a very stale piece of cake with him, she was astonished when he suddenly blurted out, "Do make me the happiest of men and accept of my hand in marriage."

She choked on her lemonade, which caused him to beg pardon a dozen times for being such a simpleton. "I have given you a terrible shock, but, indeed, Miss Millbrook, such admiration as I feel must find expression!"

When she had finally gained her breath, she shook her head at him and laughed. "What admiration?" she asked. "All I heard you say was that you wished to be made happy."

"Eh? What's that?" he responded. "The deuce take it. I made a mull of it. But I do admire you exceedingly, and I would make an excellent husband."

"And I'm certain you shall," she responded kindly, overlaying his arm with her hand. "But I am not the wife for you. Even Harley has said as much."

His brow grew dark. "Harley set you against me, did he?"

"No, no, you are quite mistaken. Rather the opposite, I fear. He said I would make you an abominable wife, but that is not to the point. I am very flattered that you would make me such a kind, if startling, proposal, but I must agree with Harley. We would not suit, not by half."

Harley approached them both at that moment, concern writ in his eyes. "Come, Coquette, I believe the next dance is mine."

"Actually, Harley, I am promised to Lord Waltham."

"Then let us find him at once." He offered his arm and she took it. If Mr. Templar seemed a trifle downcast, she had every confidence he would recover from her refusal, particularly since she knew his heart not to be engaged.

When Coquette saw Waltham across the room, involved in what appeared to be an animated discussion with Lord Wolstonbury, she directed Harley's attention to him. Harley caught Waltham's eye and subsequently received permission to dance with Coquette when Waltham in turn smiled and nodded his acquiescence.

"Will that suffice?" Harley asked her.

"Yes, of course."

As he led her onto the floor, he whispered, "I could not help but notice that you were touching Templar in an excessively familiar manner."

Coquette frowned, not knowing precisely to what he was referring. "What do you mean?" she asked, annoyed by the tone of his voice.

"I watched you fondle his arm."

"I did no such thing," she retorted as he took her up in his arms, preparing for the waltz. The orchestra struck the first note and he swept her easily into the strong rhythm of the dance.

Once they were twirling about the room, he continued,

"You most certainly did. You choked a trifle—I suppose on the truly dreadful cake that was served this evening—Templar seemed suddenly taken aback, you laughed, and then you settled your hand in what appeared to be a quite affectionate manner on his arm."

"Oh, that," she said dismissively, but remained silent, something she knew would provoke him. She thought he was being ridiculous. Besides, she wanted to concentrate on the flow of the dance, up and back, round and round. Oh, how she enjoyed the waltz!

Harley ground his teeth. "Why will you not answer me?"

"You ought to smile, you know," she said in a low voice, "else the *beau monde* will think you are displeased with me and that, as you very well know, will never do. Potsy will fly into a pelter, and we will hear of little else all the way home tonight."

He narrowed his eyes and she felt his hand grow stiff on her back. "Not until you tell me why you touched Templar in that far too familiar fashion."

Coquette wondered if Harley knew to what extent he had just lowered his guard to her and how many different sorts of tormenting retorts sprang to her lips. So many to choose from, she thought with delight. In the end, she settled on the obvious. "As it happens, I . . . I confess I have grown quite fond of Evan, that is, Mr. Templar. I know you think him of a decidedly sensitive nature, but I could learn so much from him were I, were we, well, let us just say that modesty prevents me from saying more." She lowered her gaze as Lady Agnes always did in Harley's presence.

He did not speak for a long moment, but she knew his jaw was working strongly, since she could hear the rough grinding of his teeth. Around and around he whirled her, up and back, round and round. All the while, as she glanced at him now and then, she could see he was with some difficulty restraining his temper.

After a long moment, in which he schooled his features undoubtedly for the strict purpose of preventing the gabble-mongers from having yet one more morsel of meat on which to chew, he said, "You are the worst piece of baggage ever born."

"Come, come, is that all you will say to me? Harley, I begin to believe you are losing your touch—or have you forgotten one of the first rules of swordplay is never to lower your guard even for an instant?"

At that, he met her gaze. "You were taunting me."

"Of course."

He shook his head. "A complete novice, to be sure."

"Precisely."

"So tell me, then, of what were you and Templar speaking?"

She chuckled. For a bare moment she thought it would be amusing to say something else provoking, but in the end she decided to tell him the truth. "As it happens, he offered for me."

"What?" he cried, a bit too loudly. Several dancers nearby turned to glance in their direction. In quieter tones, he continued, "Did I hear you correctly? Templar offered for you just now, while you were eating cake?"

"Actually, I was sipping my lemonade, and nearly breathed in half the glass because of the suddenness of his declaration."

"Good God," he murmured. He fell silent for a long moment, during which Coquette allowed herself to simply enjoy the wonderful simplicity and flow of the dance. She marveled suddenly that she was actually here, dancing at the Almack's Assembly Rooms, in the arms of Harley, and speaking of a proposal of marriage she had just received. How distant her old dreams seemed suddenly of purchasing and manning a ship, then sailing away, perhaps never to return, or at least not for a long, long time.

Instead, she was dancing and speaking of offers of marriage as though she had partaken of the delights of the Season for years instead of a scant few days. How strangely life moved in all its currents. How quickly one's path could be diverted in an entirely new direction and, even more astonishing, how completely she had given herself to the pursuit of her most immediate needs.

"I hope you refused him," he said at last, looking down at her, his expression serious.

"Oh, Harley, why must you fret so? Can you not trust me but a little? Of course I refused him. How could I do otherwise with my fishwife's tongue and his gentleness of disposition? I would drive him to distraction before the cat could lick her ear."

The smile which suddenly suffused his face warmed her heart rather fiercely. She drew in a deep breath, aware that her pulse was beating nearly as quickly as the whirling steps of the dance. How strange that his smile could make her feel so exhilarated. Her thoughts traveled quite abruptly to the last kiss they had shared in Mrs. Marston's conservatory. She should not be thinking of that kiss, but then she had to admit to herself that for the past several days her thoughts had often been consumed by just how tender yet demanding his lips on hers had been. She had even had more than one rather shocking dream of a similar nature. What did it all mean, she could not help but wonder.

"What are you thinking?" he asked. Round and round, up and back.

"You do not wish to know."

"But you are quite mistaken, for I am experiencing a profound desire to comprehend just what has brought so rosy a bloom to your cheek and why your eyes are shining like diamonds."

She felt a blush begin to warm her cheeks.

"Now you are blushing. Cokie, tell me at once what you were thinking just now."

She shook her head and knew she had begun to grin. "Indeed, Harley, do not press me, else I will blush a little more and become as ridiculous as Olivia Dazeley."

The mention of one of his favorites proved to be a happy circumstance, since he lifted his chin. "Miss Dazeley is not in the least ridiculous. She is an excellent young lady of good breeding with some of the finest connections . . . in the . . . You are quite abominable, you know! Now tell me of what you were thinking."

The dance drew to a close. "I do beg your pardon, but time does not allow. Here is Sir Francis, and I am promised to him for the cotillion." With that, he was forced to relinquish her. She placed her hand on Sir Francis's arm and moved easily away with him. A glance back, however, caused her former blush to return in force, for Harley's gaze was slowly taking in her entire figure and there was such an approving, pleased expression on his face that she knew his thoughts in their entirety. The warmth on her cheeks, however, seemed to spread throughout her body. The thought that Harley clearly felt her to be attractive was quickly becoming a most heady sensation.

The next evening, Coquette walked beside Lord Waltham, her arm hooked about his, as together they traversed the numerous paths about the Vauxhall Pleasure Gardens. The narrow lanes were dimly lit and more than one amorous couple could be seen cloaked in the shadows and partaking of a scandalous kiss or two.

"How are you enjoying the Season, Miss Millbrook?" he asked.

"More than I ever expected to," she responded frankly.

He chuckled. "Harley told us you had forever resisted the notion of joining us in London, that you always felt you would be bored to tears. I am happy to hear that you are not, or do I misunderstand and was your response merely civil in nature?"

She looked up at him, thinking that of all of Harley's friends, he was her favorite. He was nearly as tall as Harley, but his hair was of a thin, blond sort and his brown eyes not nearly so interesting as Harley's. He was handsome in his way and bore himself quite regally, as was becoming of his birth. His lean figure she knew belied a great deal of strength, for he was a bruising rider, which she admired very much, and he was able on occasion to best Harley at swords. She wondered if he, too, meant to offer for her and were he to do so, what her answer would be. She realized she was actually considering such a match. Waltham was a responsible young man who would not game away her fortune, but neither, she thought, would he permit his wife to purchase a ship and sail to Brazil if she so desired. Still, should he offer, she would not be so hasty in refusing him.

She answered his question. "I was not just being civil. I have enjoyed the past sennight in London very much. Had I known so much pleasure was to be had in merely dancing and racing from soiree to ball to fete, I should have come much sooner."

"You would have been a welcome addition. I, for one, have been very grateful for your presence. Very refreshing to have a woman about who knows how to laugh and whose gaze is not always calculating and whose smiles are not in the least artificial. You possess my favorite quality, an open countenance. I believe I always know what you are thinking."

At that, she could not help but laugh. "Harley says it is one of my worst qualities, that I am not nearly discreet enough for his taste or comfort. I might have permitted his aunts to dress my hair and order a dozen far too expensive gowns that I might be properly presented to tonnish society, but they could not change my inherent nature as much as Harley might have wished them to."

He led her down a darkened path. "I would ask you something, Miss Millbrook. Is it true that you must be wed by the first of May in order to inherit?"

"Yes, it is quite true. Horridly, wretchedly true."

"I could not credit that Lord Harlington had placed such a

condition on your inheritance. I was rather appalled by it and felt he had used you quite badly, for you were exceedingly devoted to him. Indeed, no daughter could have been more so."

"That is very kindly said, my lord."

"Pray, not so formal. Call me Waltham as you did when we played at billiards on Sunday."

He smiled as he spoke, and Coquette thought it possible that he was half in love with her. She offered a smile in return. "Very well. Waltham it is."

"I realize that the conditions of Harlington's will have made your situation almost desperate, though I have little doubt you do not lack suitors, and if my friends are to be believed, you have already rejected two of them, as well as Adcock."

"This much is true, but, yes, I do carry a certain desperation about with me."

"Would you, then, consider me?" he queried softly. "Though I met you several times at Barscot, you were always too busily engaged in either riding the Chilterns or quarreling with Harley to have noticed my presence. But of all the women I have known, especially now that you are come to London and I see you against the backdrop of our fine, polished society, I find myself quite drawn to you, hopeful that you will save a dance for me or even converse with me."

"Is this a formal declaration?" she asked bluntly, since he had merely asked her to consider his suit.

"Not yet," he responded, smiling. "And it is just like you to ask for clarification. However, my pride is such that I am not willing yet to hear such a rejection as my friends seem to, but then I believe my heart to be a trifle more seriously engaged than either Templar's or Lord Henry's."

She nodded. "I will gladly consider your suit, Waltham. Of all Harley's particular friends, you are the one with whom I find I enjoy conversing the most."

"You have made me very happy in saying as much."

"I have spoken only the truth."

"There is something else I would ask you," he said, drawing her to a stop. Only then did Coquette realize they were in one of the darkest, most remote paths she had yet seen.

"And what would that be?" she queried.

"Would you allow a kiss?"

She gasped faintly, then nodded. "Yes, that is an excellent notion!"

He laughed. "Why do you say as much? Not that I am complaining, but you must admit your enthusiastic response is quite unexpected."

"Because I told Harley I meant to do some kissing while in London, and it would please me considerably to torment him with it."

He laughed more heartily still. "Then by all means, even if it is just for the purpose of provoking my good friend, I shall kiss you."

He did not hesitate, but took her chin in hand and placed a gentle, lingering kiss on her lips, which she enjoyed very much. When he drew back, she said, "I should beg for another if it was not wholly inappropriate."

His expression grew slightly intense. "And I should oblige you again, were you to say the word."

She understood then that there truly was a depth to his interest in her which she knew by instinct to protect. She merely chuckled, hooked his arm, and said, "Now, what of that waltz you have been promising me?"

In the small hours of the morning, Coquette slung her cue, struck the billiard ball of choice, and scored another two points. She was beating Harley all to flinders, but then he had had far too much brandy at White's earlier that evening to be of the smallest use to anyone.

"You owe me another ten pounds," she cried gleefully.

"The devil take it," he murmured, squinting at the green

baize. He sat on a nearby sofa. "I can see why now. The table is tipped."

"No, it is not. *You* are!" Since at that moment she rounded the table at the same time he attempted to rise from his seat, she gave him a gentle push, which caused him to flop down again, laughing.

"Then I must say you are taking shameful advantage of me!" he cried.

"Well, of course I am. It is a rare day, indeed, when you are decidedly in your cups and yet challenge me to a game of billiards anyway."

"You look very pretty in your muslin tonight, Cokie."

At that she turned to him, and lifted her brows. "Do you now mean to make pretty love to me?"

His answering smile was crooked. "Would you like me to?"

For a moment, she pondered the possibility and realized that her heart had begun to race. What would it be like were Harley to court her in earnest—to take her to Vauxhall, for instance, to kiss her in the shadowy lanes? If the last kiss they had shared were an example, she rather thought she would like nothing better than to spend an evening with him in the gardens.

She slung her cue again. After a moment, she answered his question airily. "No, thank you. Having been already kissed tonight was sufficient for me."

"What?" he thundered, staggering abruptly to his feet. Once he reached his full height, Coquette watched as all the blood drained from his face and he subsequently fainted, falling first onto the small sofa behind him, then rolling in stages to the floor.

"Harley!" she cried, tossing her cue onto the table and running to drop down beside him. "Oh, dear. You most certainly are foxed, more than I supposed."

She heard him moan and watched his eyes roll. His face

was turned into the carpet, and his right arm was stuck beneath his chest. He looked quite uncomfortable.

She took hold of his elbow and pulled his arm free. This unfortunately had a worse effect in that his face was now smashed into the carpet.

She started to laugh, for he looked ridiculous. There was only one thing to be done, however. Since she did not have sufficient strength to move him by herself, she rang the bellpull. Once Jenkins arrived, he in turn fetched two of his strongest footmen and they hefted him onto the sofa. By that time, he had come round sufficiently to protest the ministrations of his staff. He was just belligerent enough to send his servants away, but not without Coquette calling out, "Coffee, Jenkins, if you please!"

"Very good, ma'am."

She picked up her cue and began hitting the balls at random, giving Harley time to recover from his fainting spell. She had some difficulty keeping her countenance and all the while thought of a dozen things she might say to provoke him. However, he was not looking at all the thing, so she bit her lip and kept slinging her cue.

When the coffee arrived, she poured them both a cup and took up a seat adjacent to him. He was still rather pale and there was a stern look in his countenance that annoyed her. She had no doubt whatsoever as to the precise source of his severe aspect and was not surprised, after he finished one cup and had begun a second, that he turned to her and said, "What the devil were you doing kissing Waltham?" Only then did he meet her gaze.

She was astonished at what she saw. She had expected to see anger in his eyes. Instead there was so strong an expression of hurt that she was entirely taken aback. Every curt retort she had prepared died quickly on her tongue. "He is earnest in his intentions toward me, Harley. He wishes to marry me, though he did not make a formal declaration. I suppose you might say I am seriously considering his suit."

Her words appeared to have the same effect as if she had struck him with her open palm. "I see," he murmured. With that, he settled his cup on the table at his elbow, rose staggering to his feet, and bid her good night.

Coquette did not know what to think. This was not at all how she had thought her revelation would affect Harley. To some extent she was vastly disappointed since she had been looking forward to setting up his back. Never in a thousand years would she have thought anything she might say would cause him pain, but so it apparently had. Only why? Although it was possible that the circumstance of his being in his cups might have occasioned such an odd reaction. Still, as she retired to bed, she could not help but wonder what it meant, if anything.

Eleven

Harley paced the hallway near Coquette's bedchamber, having been alerted by her abigail that she would soon emerge to partake of breakfast. His head pained him severely, just as it ought given the amount of brandy he had imbibed while awaiting her return from Vauxhall the evening before.

He had rehearsed a speech of apology several times, believing that he had set a truly wretched example for her. Who was he to be criticizing her conduct when he could not even restrict himself to a proper amount of wine? He had made a fool of himself and he meant to make matters right.

The door latch clicked and a rush of air from her bedchamber swept into the hall. "Harley," she cried. "What a chance to find you here in just this moment, for I had hoped to see you this morning before you disappeared on your own round of engagements."

He was taken aback as much by her words as by the picture she made in a gown of embroidered muslin and a shawl of dark blue wool, the latter of which set off her complexion, her hair, and her blue eyes to exceeding advantage. He was caught for a brief moment, as he had been since her transformation, by how devilishly pretty she was, her beauty in this moment accentuated by the warmth of her expression as she greeted him. Beyond her, the light, airy draperies billowed in a soft April breeze.

"Your window is open," came forth as the brilliant expression of all his thoughts.

She turned back and shrugged. "I know. Isn't it a beautiful day? Not a cloud in sight and the wind smelling of heaven, for earlier it had been blowing strong and taking all the coal smoke off to the east."

"Lovely, indeed," he said, but he was looking at her. When she turned back to him, he plunged on, "I wish to apologize for my conduct last night. There can be no excuse for the depth of my inebriation. I hope you will—"

He got no further. She was grinning as she placed a gloved hand over his mouth. *"The depth of my inebriation!* Oh, Harley, if you are to become so very prosy, I will have nothing more to do with you—ever! Pray do not speak such fustian to me, especially since it ought to be clear to you I have not even had my breakfast. Besides, you cannot know what intense satisfaction I enjoyed in your sufferings of last night, particularly when you rolled off the sofa and onto the carpet. I only wish I had developed my use of the watercolors, for I should have liked nothing better than to have had the charming scene captured for eternity."

"Even paintings do not last so long," he mused, his lips twitching.

She was still smiling. "I hope you do not mean to be blue deviled over such a trifling incident—or do you suppose I have never seen you in your cups before?"

"I expect you have," he said, frowning.

"More than once," she stated firmly, nodding several times. "I remember on one particular occasion, you and your friends had been drinking heavily and I took the opportunity thereby granted me to put frogs in all your chamber pots. I have never heard so many shrieks from a set of avowed sporting men before."

He could not help but recall the moment. "I believe Templar thought he was being attacked and fired his pistol. Deuced excellent shot, for he split the pot in two."

"The frogs mercifully escaped, although your wrath found

me the next day. I believe you locked me in one of the out-buildings for the better part of the afternoon."

"Was I always so horrid?"

"In every possible way. But we have been such happy adversaries. I hope you do not mean to be all politeness now, for I vow if you do I shall never forgive you."

He felt relieved, strongly so. She had referred to the person he knew her to be, the hoydenish young woman who had behaved for most of her life like an errant schoolboy, and now he could be at ease. All the efforts of his aunts to create a lady of quality from the rough, independent creature that Coquette truly was could not keep her true self hidden always. He understood that he was quite attracted to this new form of her, which was extraordinarily beautiful, but what lay within would always, at least to a degree, be repugnant to him. Once more he felt in command of his world and offered to escort her to breakfast.

Later, however, when Sir Francis called to take her to Kensington Gardens, he found himself drawn to the windows of his office so that he might watch her depart. By pushing back the curtain just so, he was able to observe surreptitiously his good friend assisting Coquette into his new curricle. He thought with some disgust that Olney looked like a perfect coxcomb with a monstrous chrysanthemum pinned to the wide lapel of his coat. And why the deuce must he kiss her fingers before handing her up? He hoped Coquette had enough sense to refuse him should he offer for her today. Olney was a good friend, and fearless on a stretch of turf riding even the most spirited of geldings, but he was inclined to be a trifle dandified, which made him the worst possible match for Coquette's strength of manner and direct mode of speech. She should never wed a man who enjoyed bathing in rose water.

He watched Olney, who was rather heavy-handed with his

cattle, slap the reins too hard. The carriage jerked forward. Coquette, clearly up to snuff, barely moved, apparently prepared for his lack of expertise. He let the draperies fall back into place and returned to reviewing the notes his bailiff had sent by courier only that morning. How tedious such matters seemed, not just because until Coquette was married he had to review all his decisions with Mr. Jennings, but because his thoughts were more nearly consumed with the necessity of warning Coquette against wedding Olney.

He glanced at the clock, knowing full well he would see neither of them for at least three hours, then set to work.

Scarcely fifty minutes had passed, however, when he heard the steady clopping of hooves. He found himself listening intently. Olney could not have returned so soon. Besides, the clopping sound indicated but one horse, not two. A moment more, and much to his surprise he heard the front door open.

He shot from his seat and hurried to the entrance hall. There, with her bonnet a little crushed, was Coquette. "What are you doing returning so quickly, and what happened to your hat?"

She patted the green velvet confection and then laughed. "I must look a sight." Pulling off her gloves, she continued, "I fear your friend will never forgive me. Nor should he, only how was I to know Sir Francis was a mere whipster? You ought to have warned me." She settled her gloves on the table near the door, then began untying the ribbons of her bonnet.

Harley could not help but smile. He leaned against the door frame and crossed his arms over his chest. "What did you do?" he asked.

"Well, it was not entirely my fault," she responded. He could see that she was surprisingly rattled, something quite unusual for her. "But he would go on forever about his horse-flesh and the excellent points to his new curricle and though any simpleton could see the grays were short of bone, albeit well-matched in color, they were also wretchedly ill-suited in temper. I fear I behaved very badly."

"Coquette," he drawled.

"Well, he would not cease boasting about how famously he could handle the ribbons, so I suggested he hunt the squirrel."

"Where?" he cried, startled.

"Just as we arrived at Hyde Park."

"Good God," he murmured, but shortly after began to laugh. He could not help himself. He could see it all. Olney was a braggart with more bottom than sense, and in possession of heavy hands which ruined the mouths of any cattle he rode or drove. Harley had long since forbidden him the use of his horses either in London or Bedfordshire.

"Just so," she responded curtly, then rolled her eyes. "I vow he locked wheels with the first carriage whose wheels he attempted to graze—a gig, as it happens. There was a terrible splintering and the next moment we were tumbled on the pavement. The horses were terrified."

Only then did he become concerned as he realized that not only was the sleeve of her pelisse torn, but there was blood streaked down the side of her skirts as well. "You've been injured!" he exclaimed, leaving his place by the door and crossing quickly to her.

"Not so very badly. A mere scratch. Olney, I fear, was quite bruised, but I was able to take command of his team. They gentled at once, though I daresay had they not been attended to they would have very soon been beyond calming."

"I'm certain you did very right, at least by the horses." He gently pulled back the fabric and saw that she had bound her arm with a strip of muslin that was soaked through. "A mere scratch, eh?" he murmured. "Come." He took her other arm and guided her to the kitchen where Cook, who had known Coquette since a child, merely shook her head but immediately took charge of her wound.

When her arm had been properly dressed, he walked with her to the stairs. She turned to him, her eyes sparkling with amusement in that way of hers. "At least you may be easy on

one score, Harley. I daresay Sir Francis will not offer for me
now."

In this prediction, Coquette soon realized, she was greatly
mistaken. Although she viewed her conduct following the ac-
cident with complete indifference, it was soon made plain to
her that Sir Francis did not. By the following evening, while
attending Lady Sedgwick's ball, she found herself inundated
with friends and acquaintance all anxious to congratulate her
on saving not just Olney's horses' lives, but his own as well.
She thought it ridiculous in the extreme, but apparently Olney
did not, as was made quite obvious when he found her, surrounded by admirers both male and female, and made such a
fuss that she was torn between a desire to sink into the wall
or to plant Sir Francis a facer for embarrassing her so thoroughly.

Coquette tried to demur, but any such protests on her part
only seemed to make the situation worse. So it was that he
hooked her arm fiercely, carrying her from room to room,
and proclaiming her as his savior. How could she have been
surprised when, during supper, he made his intentions clear
to her. "I have never loved so completely before," he whispered ardently.

Coquette merely stared at him for a long hard moment, at
the end of which he finally had the good sense to remove the
mooncalf expression from his face and tend to his cold
chicken instead. After supper, she excused herself from his
company and would have demanded of Harley that he take
her home instantly, but he insisted upon dancing with her instead.

The diversion was sufficient to relieve her of the effects of
so much absurdity crammed into one evening. By the end of
the second set, she was in good spirits once more. Since Lord
Waltham, who was sensible as well as civil, asked her to

dance the quadrille with him, she was able to forget about Sir
Francis entirely.

Over the next several days, however, Coquette began to
feel rather pinched, as much by the ever-present Olney and
the steady Lord Waltham as by the truly wretched fact that the
first of May loomed closer and closer with each passing day.
Harley had told her that a special license required three days,
as well as an obliging bishop, to procure, so in reality she had
only until the twenty-seventh of April by which to secure a
husband.

When Olney offered for her, she refused as firmly as she
could, which sent him away appearing rather shattered. He
had somehow convinced himself not only of his profound
love for her but that she would be able to redeem all the de-
fects of his character merely by agreeing to become his wife.

In telling Harley of the circumstance, she was a little surprised to see him breathe a really large sigh of relief. "Did
you not think me worthy of him?" she asked, wondering at his
reaction.

He regarded her thoughtfully for a long moment. "I merely
thought you extraordinarily ill-suited. He delights in visits
to his tailor, while I have been assured by you a hundred times
that you had rather fall into a thistle patch than be measured
for a walking dress."

She could only laugh. "Very true. Well, I am at least glad
to hear that your answer was sensible. For a moment, I had
begun to think that the last thing you would want is to see me
married to any of your bosom bows."

Harley felt very strange suddenly as he regarded her laughing blue eyes. She had spoken the truth, more nearly than she
would perhaps ever know, but not for the reason he had once
thought.

From the moment of their arrival in London, he had hoped
she would meet someone quite unknown to him, because he
had always believed her to a large degree unfit to become any
gentleman's wife. But now, as he looked at her, he had to

admit that there was a larger reason he dreaded the thought of Coquette leg-shackled to his friends—he knew he would detest seeing her heart in any manner engaged by those closest to him. Why he felt this way, he did not in the least comprehend.

"What is it, Harley?" she asked, disturbing his reverie.

"Has Waltham offered for you formally yet?" he asked. How harsh he sounded, even to his own ears.

"No, he has not." She was frowning now and looking quite worried. "You appear to wish that he would not do so. Is this true? Would you dislike such a match so very much? Shall I cease encouraging him?"

He did not know what to say. He certainly could not tell her that the reason he wanted her to hint Waltham away was because he was entirely unable to bear the thought of knowing that his good friend would hold her in his arms and kiss her and take her to bed as his wife. No, he could not tell Coquette any such thing.

He strove to be reasonable, for Waltham would be an excellent match for her. "You must follow the dictates of your heart," he said at last.

"The dictates of my heart?" she cried. Her subsequent laugh was bitter. "The dictates of my heart involve a fine ship probably resting at anchor in either Portsmouth, Plymouth, or Bristol, maybe even one of the London docks."

"You are being absurd," he stated uneasily. He did not know what to say to her on any score.

"Perhaps I am, but unless you can give me a sensible reason why I must reject Waltham, I feel I should continue to allow him to court me, especially with the ax of time balanced upon my neck." She whirled around and flounced from the room, executing her departure with the aplomb of a lady who had been in London for years. Perhaps she was changing after all. Yet somehow the thought of Coquette becoming just like all the other ladies of his acquaintance left a sour taste in his mouth.

* * *

Over the next several days, Coquette permitted Waltham to squire her to one event after another, so much so that even she heard gossip that the Millbrook heiress had found a match at last. For herself, she was not so certain and wondered just how she was to go about discovering if she should at last give Waltham the hint he required, that his suit was indeed welcome to her.

On Thursday evening, with her arm hooked about his, Coquette walked the length of Mrs. Dalcham's property, which flanked the edge of the River Thames. The house was a fine villa and the days and nights had been so mild of late that the notion of an enchanting fete held out of doors beneath an elaborate tent had quite appealed to her. Chinese lanterns had been hung at just the right intervals to create a magical and quite romantic atmosphere.

Presently, Lord Waltham covered her hand with his own. "Are you chilled?" he inquired solicitously.

"Not in the least," she responded. She wore but a thin silk shawl of purple paisley over a satin and tulle lavender gown. Her slippers she knew to be dampened by an evening dew clinging to the grass which bordered the path, but still she was quite comfortable. "At the risk of speaking in a manner which Potsy would think was not at all appropriate for a demure lady of quality, I would remind you that I have been known to ride through the hard, frost-laden countryside in my summer riding habit."

He leaned conspiratorially close. "But one would become so heated otherwise," he suggested.

"Precisely," she responded brightly, happy to be understood so readily. She glanced up at him, at his carefully combed hair, cropped short as was the prevailing style. She realized she was quite content in his company and wondered not for the first time whether he would make her a tolerable husband.

He pointed out a star that appeared brighter than most. "I

would dub that celestial light Olney, after our friend who likes to dazzle his company with the width of his lapels." He slashed his arm across the night sky and found a row of stars. "That would be Templar, for he punctuates his speech, and the rather powerful star nearby would, of course, be Harley."

Coquette chuckled but also searched the sky until she found what she sought. "There. The two stars together. Not nearly so bright as Harley, but those I would name after you jointly. One for your steadiness of character, and the other for your great good sense."

He pressed her hand. "How kind you are, when I fear what you meant to say was that I am rather prosy and run the risk of boring you to tears."

"On the contrary," she responded quickly. "I am never bored in your company and I happen to value character and excellent good sense more than you will ever comprehend, especially since my fortune will depend on my husband possessing such qualities."

Having come to the end of the path, he paused while catching up both her hands in his. They were quite alone, and so it was no surprise to Coquette that he took the moment to press his suit. "I wish you to know that you have but to say the word, Miss Millbrook. I have come to treasure the times we are together. You are quite the most unique, artless woman I have ever known. Whatever Lady Potsgrove's opinion of your frankness and your open manner of greeting your friends, I find these qualities greatly appealing, just what I would want in the lady who would one day be mistress of my home."

Coquette could not help but be moved by the sincerity and warmth of his speech. Almost it was on the tip of her tongue to encourage him, to make him know that he was her choice, particularly since she had but a scant few days remaining in which to get a husband. Indeed, she opened her mouth and the words slid to the end of her tongue.

"Coquette!" a voice called out.

She withdrew her hands quickly from Lord Waltham's. "It

is Harley. Something must be amiss." She began walking toward him immediately, cutting across the dewy lawn and further dampening her slippers, for he was doing the same. "What is it, Harley?" she called out.

"You are promised to me for the waltz," he called back cheerfully.

Coquette glanced at Waltham and felt embarrassed. He had matched her strides and was now walking beside her. "May I take you to Hyde tomorrow?" he whispered.

"Yes, of course. I should like that."

"Harley seems most anxious for his dance."

"It is very odd, but then I did promise him the waltz."

"I believe he may be jealous."

Coquette took Harley's arm as he nodded to his friend and apologized for taking her away so abruptly. He then said to them both rather quietly, "Seames is here—in his altitudes."

"Oh, dear," Coquette murmured.

"Will you need my assistance?" Waltham asked.

"I might."

A few minutes later, Coquette watched as her cousin staggered across the dance floor, heading in her direction, and bumping into several couples. He held a glass of champagne in his hand, which sloshed unhappily onto the lady nearest him, causing her to cry out. Coquette felt her heart plummet. She had never been so humiliated in her life.

Harley, however, soon took him in hand by grabbing him beneath his arm and fairly carrying him off the dance floor.

"Hallo, Harlington!" he cried, his eyes red rimmed. "They are playing whist in the blue saloon, five tables. Care to make up a party?"

"Yes, of course, but first there is something in the garden I should like you to see."

"I do love gardens," he slurred, stumbling. Waltham caught him about the other arm and at the same moment, Coquette rescued the champagne glass from him. The gentlemen carried him quickly out of the tent, dragging him not to the house, but around the house. Coquette followed behind until she herself saw his now inert form crammed into Harley's carriage and sent away.

She remained with the gentlemen on the drive for a long moment. She did not know what to say. There was no apology grand enough to dispel the mortification she felt that her cousin would have come to Mrs. Dalcham's fete only to make such a wretched spectacle of himself.

Fortunately, both men seemed to comprehend her sentiments in that moment and escorted her in a jovial spirit back to the tent, secured her all the partners she could possibly require, and by the end of the evening her feet ached in the most satisfactory manner possible.

Later that night, after having fallen into a deep sleep, she awoke to a loud thumping noise. She sat straight up in bed, at which moment the smell of smoke struck her nostrils. She threw back her bedcovers, slipped from the bed, and ran to the door. Running footsteps in the hallway and above her bespoke the relative safety of opening the door, which she did at once.

Harley, in but his nightshirt and breeches, caught her arm. "The music room is ablaze."

"Good God! Where are Potsy and all the servants?"

"We will know soon enough."

By then, Coquette was racing down the stairs and out the front door, where she found her benefactress. As for the servants, all were accounted for, and a veritable battalion of neighboring servants and gentlemen had already begun descending on the house, forming a brigade to deliver as much water as possible to the fire.

An hour later, the flames, which had barely begun to climb the walls of the music room when the fire was discovered, had been put out.

Coquette entered the music room, her arm tight about Potsy's shoulders.

"I decorated this room," Lady Potsgrove said, her voice

quivering. "I cannot bear to look at it, and the smell is so vile."

Coquette looked up at the ceiling. The drapes had caught fire and burned upward in two quick pillars, as evidenced by the patterns of charring. "I wonder how this happened," she mused.

"A candle left burning, no doubt."

"But Jenkins is always so careful. He would not have retired without securing the house in every essential."

Lady Potsgrove also looked up at the ceiling. "Is not your room above?"

Coquette felt a chill go through her. "Indeed, it is," she said, her voice little more than a whisper. The smell was familiar now, and long-buried memories returned to her of another fire, one that had robbed her of so very much.

Harley joined them. "I do not think you should return to your bedchamber, Cokie, not tonight. I will have some of the servants sit vigil to make certain that the fire is truly extinguished and tomorrow I shall see that repairs are begun immediately." Glancing down, he laughed. "Do but look at your feet!"

Coquette looked down as well and could not keep from laughing. Lady Potsgrove had donned her slippers before descending the stairs, but Coquette had left her bedchamber barefooted. Her feet were blackened by the soot-laden, water-soaked floor. "I should have had your good sense, Potsy."

When Lady Potsgrove did not respond, Coquette glanced at her and saw that she had covered her mouth with her kerchief and that she was weeping. She immediately tended to her, hugging her warmly and turning her about in order to begin guiding her back to her bedchamber. She spoke softly to her, encouraging her to dwell on how wonderfully the entire neighborhood had worked to save their home and that indeed, only the music room had suffered.

"But look at these floors and carpets!" she wailed into her kerchief.

"Yes, I know, but they can be cleaned and repaired quite easily."

"But what of this wretched smell of smoke everywhere?"

"You know what Harley's housekeeper is like. Mrs. Lumby will not rest until all is restored to perfection, if that means scrubbing every inch of the entire dwelling. It is the host of servants at her command I am pitying in this moment, for though I do not like to mention it, Mrs. Lumby is a veritable dragon and will enjoy nothing so much as making Harley's servants slave for days at a time."

With that, Lady Potsgrove offered a squeak of a laugh as together they mounted the stairs. "You must sleep in the chamber next to mine," she said. "It is far from where the fire began and you may be at ease there."

"An excellent notion. But I shan't do anything until I see you properly settled."

"You have always been so good to me, Coquette. Like a daughter."

Coquette helped her back to bed and sat beside her for a long time, speaking softly to her and engaging her in a discussion of all the gossip she had heard at Mrs. Dalcham's fete, so that very soon she simply dropped off to sleep right in the middle of a sentence. Only then did Coquette leave her bedchamber.

The house had fallen very quiet. When she closed the door behind her as softly as she was able, she found that Harley awaited her.

"Are you all right?" he asked, holding a candlestick aloft, his expression concerned.

She held her finger to her lips and beckoned him to follow her down the hall to her room. "Your aunt has just now fallen asleep. She was greatly overset and I did not wish to awaken her just now by speaking outside her bedchamber, but, yes, I am perfectly well."

"Where do you mean to sleep?"

"Potsy said I should take the chamber next to hers, which I believe is sound."

"Yes, that will do."

She entered her room and was startled to find that the fire had charred the wall near her bed. "Harley, do but look," she cried, pointing to the dark streaks. She shuddered, suddenly aware that had the fire not been discovered as early as it had been, she and perhaps much of the staff who resided in the attic bedrooms would have perished. Only then did she begin to tremble.

"I was afraid of this," he said, settling the candlestick on the nearby chest of drawers. "I will have a servant sit here as well. Fire could still be in the walls. Cokie! You are trembling!"

"It is the stupidest thing. Until I saw these walls I was perfectly well."

He gathered her up in his arms and held her tightly. "There is nothing to fear now."

"I know. I feel utterly ridiculous."

"Nonsense. You have suffered a shock, as we all have."

She felt deeply comforted by the strength and warmth of his arms surrounding her as well as by his words. He had so easily taken charge of the situation, organizing the servants and neighbors so that in no time the fire had been mastered. Her heart seemed to swell within her as she laid her head against his shoulder. How she loved Harley. How she loved him.

The words had so easily popped into her head that she was stunned by the simplicity of their truth. She loved Harley. She understood in that moment that she always had, probably from the time she was a child and asked him to kiss her. She had never in all those years thought of him as a brother, and this was undoubtedly why—he was her dear Harley, whom she had tormented year upon year not because she disliked him, but because she loved him.

He stroked the curls which hung down her back and she

sighed with wonder. She would have wished the fire on the house all over again merely to have this moment of being held by him while at the same time having come to the powerful realization that she was in love with him. She wished he would go on holding her forever.

When she felt his fingers cease their comforting movements, she drew back and looked up at him. Some part of her knew of the extreme impropriety of this embrace, particularly since she wore but her nightgown and he was in only his nightshirt and breeches. "Oh, Harley," was all she could think to say as she met his gaze.

What he might have been thinking in that moment, she could not possibly know, except that he had grown very quiet, but his expression was rather intense. Impulsively, she threw her arms about his neck and kissed him. Once more he took her in his embrace, this time crushing her against him and returning her kiss as though he feared she would fly away did he not hold her so tightly. Coquette quickly became lost in the feel of his lips on hers. A third kiss. This was a third kiss, but so different even from the first two. Different perhaps because she had finally admitted the truth of her heart and she wanted him to feel how much she loved him and always would. He was her dear Harley.

"Coquette, my darling," he murmured against her lips, only to kiss her more forcefully still. Her lips parted and his tongue dipped within, first a tender assault and then a powerful thrusting as though he was taking possession of her once and for all. How she loved this kiss, which spoke of the future and all possible happiness.

Harley could not believe the passion exploding between them. He had never kissed a woman in this fashion before, as though his entire happiness depended upon it. Somehow the very thought that had the fire not been caught so early it might have resulted in her death heightened his present feelings. What would it be like to lose Coquette, he wondered.

His heart ached at the thought of it. But why? When had she become so precious to him?

He drew back for a brief moment and looked into her eyes, mere shadows in the dim candlelight, her expression wondrous and tender. Was this Coquette, truly? The hoydenish young woman who had plagued him most of his life? Was she changed enough to rule over Barscot as she would be expected to, with grace and dignity?

He felt her withdraw slightly and he let her go. He saw something pass through her eyes, a powerful emotion he could not at present comprehend, of fear perhaps.

"You would not want me always at Barscot," she said, her eyes wide. Had she read his mind?

He shook his head slowly, the small movement crushing her, evident in the manner in which she turned away from him and sank down onto her bed. She sat staring at the floor. "Barscot was never my home," she murmured.

"Of course it was. It still is. It always will be."

She looked up at him and laughed, too brightly perhaps. "I never believed it, or did you not know as much?"

He wanted to leave her room. He felt angry and overset, but why he did not know. "You are being absurd."

"Just as you were in permitting me to kiss you. Why did you?" Her question was all belligerence.

"No man would ever reject a woman clad in only her nightgown."

A bright spot of color appeared on each cheek. "I daresay Waltham would have taken more pleasure in it than you."

No man could have enjoyed kissing her more than he had, but for some reason she was as she had always been, stubborn and challenging. "You will never change," he shot at her, then quit the room before she had a chance to respond in kind.

He marched down the hall to his rooms, entered, and with the greatest of efforts kept from slamming the door behind him. What had just happened, he wondered. How could he have been kissing her so passionately one moment then brangling with her the next, except that he finally understood something about her—he believed, more deeply than he had previously thought, that she was wholly unworthy of his mother's post.

With that, all the fight left him and this time, he sank down on his bed. Good God, was that the truth of it then? Coquette was unworthy of being mistress of Barscot and for that reason he kept at bay all the powerful feelings he clearly had for her?

Of course. She was everything a lady was not. She rode bareback with her skirts hiked up so far that even the stableboy saw the full length of each leg. She spoke stable slang whenever it pleased her. She rode for hours on end, ignoring all her social duties. She did not give a fig what anyone thought of her. She was hoydenish, coarse and in every sense a disaster.

Except that she had changed.

Only, had she?

Twelve

"Will you marry me?" How easily the words spilled from her lips.

"My dear Miss Millbrook, have you gone mad?"

"I assure you, M. Dubois, I have not. For the first time since the will was read to me, I am thinking clearly." She then outlined what the terms of their marriage would be, that it would last three months and would be followed by a very quiet divorce, at which time he would receive thirty thousand pounds, a sum which would make him completely independent. She smiled. "You would never have to teach another lesson in deportment or dance again."

She could see that he was tempted, sorely, but that at the same time his conscience smote him. "What sort of man would I be to take such dreadful advantage of a lady?"

"The kindest and most deserving, which you certainly are. Please try to understand my predicament. If I do not wed, I lose my fortune. If I wed a man with the intention of truly being his wife, I will lose my fortune. I believe you are a man of honor, and as such I would trust you to hold to our agreement even though by right, once we were wed, you would have legal command of my fortune. Am I correct in believing that I could trust you?"

He stared at her in disbelief. *"Mais oui, bien sur.* But I cannot. You must see that I cannot marry you."

She felt weary suddenly and looked away from him. She rose from her seat and moved to the windows. He lived in rooms on a very busy street and had a view of hundreds of smoking chimneys. She could well imagine the torment of her request and was convinced more than ever that she had made the right decision in placing her proposal before him.

After Harley had left her in the small hours of the morning, she had remained sitting on her bed, long past the moment the candle guttered in its socket, and had not risen from her seat until well past dawn. She had been devastated by his frankness, and something more. A great hole had been exposed within her heart in that moment, of loneliness and abandonment. Of course she was unworthy of him, of Barscot Hall. She was an orphan.

She turned suddenly to M. Dubois and unburdened herself to him, of how desperate she felt, of what it was like to be alone in the world and how her fortune and what it could purchase for her had come to mean everything to her. She knew he would understand, for he had been orphaned as well. The revolution in France had done as much to him.

At the same time, she did not speak of her love for Harley. How could she do so, when so much pain flooded her the moment even the smallest thought of him crept into her mind? Instead, she dwelt long upon her desire to travel the world, to create a life that would belong just to her, that could never be taken from her.

M. Dubois smiled. "Except by a hurricane or typhoon."

She smiled in return. "And I could not think of a better end were I to lose my ship and my life in such a fashion."

He shook his head anew. "You are an oddity, Miss Millbrook, but I tell you now I will accept of your offer, but not for thirty thousand pounds."

"Do you wish for more? I am amazingly wealthy."

He shook his head. "No, I shall be content with five thousand, but I insist that you have a solicitor prepare all the proper papers in advance. In that way, your fortune would be secured to you."

"I had not thought of doing so, but it is an excellent notion.

Very well," she said, stretching out her hand to him, "it is agreed. A marriage for five thousand pounds to last three months and to end in divorce."

He took her hand, holding it between both of his. "Even five thousand will purchase my freedom, you must know that."

With that, she began to grin. "This must be the first moment in which I have had any contentment in the nature of these conditions to my fortune. That it has become a blessing to you has thus far been my only recompense."

With that, she left M. Dubois and called in Upper Brook Street, startling Lord Waltham's butler. Fortunately, Waltham was at home and received her warmly in his morning room. "To what do I owe the honor of this visit?" he inquired in his gentle manner. "Though I must confess you give me hope." He searched her face, then added, "Or perhaps not."

She took up a seat adjacent to his and once he was seated, she said, "I have debated my situation time and again and I have decided to choose another man to wed, but not because he was in any manner superior to you. Indeed, Waltham, I was very much tempted to encourage your suit, for I knew you would make an admirable husband. However, I did not feel such a marriage would be at all fair to you since—" She could not finish her thought.

"Since you do not love me?" he inquired.

She nodded.

"Is it Harley?"

She was astonished that he would have guessed the truth. "Why do you say as much?"

He shrugged. "There were times when I watched you with him that I thought not only that you were very much in love but that he was as well. Even last night at Mrs. Dalcham's, though he had reason to interrupt us, I felt he had done so because he could not bear to see us together, not simply because your cousin was foxed."

She looked away from him, her heart sinking lower and

lower. "Harley did not offer for me, if that is what you are thinking. He wouldn't, you know. He does not believe I would fill the post as mistress of Barscot with even the smallest degree of distinction."

"Then he is a fool."

At that, she looked at him again and saw that he was most sincere. "You were always so very kind to me. I shall be forever grateful for your support during these trying weeks." She rose to her feet and offered her hand to him. He took it and, in his sophisticated manner, placed a soft kiss on her fingers.

"May I ask," he queried, frowning slightly, "whom you are to marry if not Harley?"

She shook her head. "It does not matter, for the ceremony will be very private, but I will tell you this much—I have made arrangements with this gentleman to be divorced within three months."

"Good God," he said, his frown deepening. "You are not serious?"

"I never wanted a husband," she said.

"Just your ship?" he inquired, smiling a little sadly.

"Precisely. But I have told you these things in the strictest confidence because I know that I can trust you. I beg you will say nothing of this matter to anyone."

"You may trust me, indeed."

With that, Coquette felt all the fatigue of a sleepless night settle upon her, and she returned to Grosvenor Square proclaiming the headache. She informed Lady Potsgrove that she would be unable to partake of the evening's festivities, to which declaration Potsy took not the smallest exception, and retired to her bedchamber.

That night, Harley sat in Lady Portslade's drawing room. The town house was decidedly overcrowded and stifling. Lady Agnes was situated on his left, her leg touching his rather scandalously, and Olivia Dazeley was on his right. For the past fifteen minutes, each had been teasing him about his need to have his hair trimmed and both were using the opportunity to entwine their fingers in his locks. There was much laughter, and he had to admit that for the first few minutes he had felt happy, relieved, and grateful to be surrounded by young ladies he knew would not once cross the bounds of propriety.

However, at a certain point, perhaps when Lady Agnes let the tip of her slipper slide down his ankle, he began to be less content. She had been the primary object of his attention for an entire twelvemonth, and once or twice he had almost hinted of his desire that she become the next Countess of Harlington. He turned to look at her now. Her lashes flirted with him, her bow lips smiled enchantingly, revealing even white teeth, her hair was coiffed to perfection, and jewels which belonged to her well-connected family had been draped over her with the skill of an East End hawker. He should have been gratified, since Lady Agnes was an excellent match for him. She was the daughter of an earl herself and would know quite well how to take up the reins of Barscot.

He met her gaze fully. Her eyes were a very light shade of blue, but where was the laughter, the amusement, the delight?

He turned to Olivia, who had just pinched his neck. He smiled at her and met her gaze. Her eyes were a delicate green-gold, but were nearly as icy as Lady Agnes's. Katherine Godwin approached him in that moment and immediately took up a seat at his knee on a footstool. His harem was now complete. That was what Coquette had called the ladies who fairly prostrated themselves before him. He could almost laugh at the thought of it, for each of them would have been mortified had they known they were being referred to in such a manner.

Katherine smiled brightly at him, her face turned toward him in an adoring manner. "How do you go on, Lord Harlington? Is this not a lively soiree? Although I must say I should not have placed the ferns so near the fire. They will be wilted before midnight with so much heat. Do you not agree?"

Olivia pinched him again, and he turned to her. "Harley, do

you mean to dance with me at Mrs. Chelwood's ball this week?"

At nearly the same moment, Lady Agnes inched closer to him, if that was even possible. "Harley, you have not told me if you like my hair done in this particular manner."

Suddenly, he was on his feet before he even knew what he was doing and nearly toppled Miss Godwin over, so hasty were his movements. He was awkward in his apologies but he had just recalled an extremely pressing engagement.

With that, he quit the premises and instead of climbing aboard his coach, told his man to return to the mews, that he would have no further need of him the rest of the night, and began walking in the direction of St. James Street and his club.

The entire distance he kept shaking his head, unable to comprehend what had prompted him to make such an erratic, thoughtless departure . . . except that he found himself bored beyond belief. What did he care for the way a lady styled her hair or whether or not Lady Portslade's ferns were too close to the fire or why he must promise to dance with this lady or that for a ball that would not take place for another sennight? He wished suddenly that he was anywhere but in London, for on the one hand he was beset by ladies pursuing his title, fortune, and connections and on the other, he was being tormented by a hoydenish creature who felt like heaven in his arms!

He longed to be at Barscot, riding hard across the turf, giving his best hunter his head, and letting the exertions of such a gallop ease the tension from every muscle. Coquette at the very least would have appreciated his desire to do so, only, of the moment, she seemed to be the cause of his greatest disquiet.

Four days later, Harley sat in his office staring at his bailiff's letter, yet not seeing a single word. He had seen very little of Coquette recently and had begun to wonder if something more than his own criticism of her was troubling her. She had refused to accompany Potsy on the usual round of social events, even going so far as to send a note to his aunt during breakfast stating that she would not be attending the masquerade that night. Harley knew that Coquette had been looking forward very much to her first masquerade, so it was with some sense of alarm that he learned she was absenting herself.

A soft scratching on the door interrupted his thoughts. "Come," he returned forcefully.

When his aunt peeked her head in, he sat back in his chair. "Oh, it is you," he murmured.

"Were you expecting Coquette?" she inquired, slipping into the room as though involved in a scheme of some treachery.

He could only smile. "No," he responded, shaking his head. "But why are you skulking?"

"Am I?" she asked. "I had not meant to. It is merely that the workmen have arrived and I heard Coquette just now order them from her bedchamber. There is much work to be done within, Harley, as well you know. I am wondering if you ought to speak with her."

He frowned slightly and searched his aunt's face. Her expression was sufficiently disingenuous to set him on his guard. "She must have some reason for wishing them elsewhere."

Lady Potsgrove advanced into the chamber. "Very well. I see I cannot be subtle with you."

"No, you should not, as you very well know."

"Yes, of course you are right. You are very much in the mold of my brother, and he had to be hit with a brick before he could see what was just beneath his nose."

"And what is just beneath my nose that I am not seeing?"

"Only that Coquette has chosen a husband and will be leaving us soon."

These words, he confessed, had precisely the effect of a brick striking him right upside the head. He blinked several times. "You are mistaken," he said at last.

"How else then do you explain her conduct?"

"You mean her refusal to attend the scheduled events?"

"More than that. She has left the house early each day and returned late with dozens of packages."

"Most London ladies of *ton* do so," he countered, but he had begun to feel uneasy.

"Not Coquette. I have had to beg her to accompany me to Bond Street to purchase much needed gloves, let alone anything of a frivolous nature like a new cap or bonnet. No, something is amiss. Mark my words, Harley."

"Why do you not ask her yourself, then, if you are distressed?"

"I did. She began to weep, gave me a kiss on the cheek, told me not to bother my head over her difficulties, then dismissed me. She would have none of my questions or comfort or even a pat on the shoulder. When I attempted to do so, she turned me about by the shoulders and asked me very gently to close the door behind me when I left."

"Good God."

"Just so."

He was on his feet before he knew he had made a decision to even take his aunt's advice. After a few bounds up the stairs and a hurried march to her door, he knocked briskly. "Coquette? 'Tis Harley. Will you speak with me a moment?"

"Yes, of course. Do come in. There is something I must needs ask you, as it happens."

He opened the door and at once regretted having succumbed to his aunt's persuasions. He had not realized until this moment just how much he had been avoiding her and how relieved he had been that she had been keeping to her rooms. Now, however, he could not escape her, since he had begged admittance and was presently standing not ten feet from her.

She was by the window, dressed in a rather summery frock of flowered calico in shades of green and peach, her hands clasped before her. Her curly hair hung in a red mass about her shoulders, though she had tucked, albeit in a rather absent manner, a white rose behind her left ear. She was an absolute portrait of beauty even if she had left off her powder and rouge and her lashes were not darkened in the least.

"Are you scandalized by my appearance because my hair is not dressed properly?" she queried. There was a smile on her lips, but her tone was rather caustic. "Is that why you stand there gawking at me like a country gapeseed?"

Was he doing as much, he wondered. Perhaps he was. He should not have come here. Coquette could manage her own troubles, which he knew involved her desperation to be married by the first of May.

"Of course not," he retorted, disliking the tone in her voice. He wondered why the deuce she was overset. "You look very pretty."

"Indeed?" she queried. "Do you truly think so?"

He frowned. "Why the devil are you on your high ropes?" he asked.

"Am I?" she returned, shrugging.

"Of course you are. Your nose is higher than your forehead at the moment."

She sighed and turned away from the window. When she moved to her bed and rolled a pair of silk stockings, only then did he realize that a portmanteau lay open on her bed half-filled and two trunks rested on the floor, awaiting her pleasure.

"What the deuce is this? Are you going somewhere?"

"Yes, to France in approximately a fortnight."

He scowled at her. "You are making no sense. Why the devil would you go there, particularly when you are supposed to be married by then?"

"Even if I am married, why would I not be able to go to France—or do you suppose my husband will not desire to go?"

"You do not even have a husband yet," he snapped.

"That much is true," she said, matching a silk glove to its mate and smoothing them together.

"I have never seen you so sadly in the mopes before, save perhaps when you first learned of my father's conditions to your inheritance. What is going forward? I still cannot credit that you have declined attending the masquerade this evening. I thought you were very desirous of going, or have you suddenly lost all interest?"

"I suppose I have," she responded, with another shrug.

He lost his temper, took a long step forward, and with a brisk movement closed the portmanteau with a snap. "Now, my dear girl, tell me what the devil is the matter with you."

"Nothing," she responded, taking a step backward, her eyes wide. "But for some reason your overbearing and quite beastly conduct puts me in mind of what it was I wished to ask you."

"Yes?" He could not imagine what she would say next.

"I need you to procure a special license for me. I intend to be married on Saturday."

"What?" he thundered.

Only then did she smile, clearly taking pleasure that she had succeeded in shocking him. "Did you think I would be unable to get a husband?"

"Of course not. You rejected a dozen suitors as it was. But who did you finally succeed in bringing up to scratch? Good God, not Waltham?" He felt ill suddenly, panic seizing his heart.

"No," she said.

The relief he felt was so profound that he sank onto the bed. "Who, then?"

"You will not like it, Harley, not one bit. So you should prepare yourself and not go off on a fit of apoplexy when you hear my choice of husband."

He sought about in his mind for the man to whom she might be referring, but he could not picture anyone of late whom she had been encouraging, except Waltham. "Very well, who?"

"M. Dubois."

He could not have heard correctly. "The Frenchman? Your dancing instructor?"

She nodded.

"Of all the absurd starts! Why in heaven's name did you choose him, particularly when you had your pick of the *beau monde*'s very best? Well, I tell you now, I shan't countenance such a match, not by half, so you may forget wedding him. I know my duties as your guardian. I absolutely forbid you to marry Dubois."

She crossed her arms over her chest. "Why? What difference does it make to you whom I wed?"

"What difference? What about consequence and connections? He is a parasite on our society, an exile without friends or family, without a single advantageous attribute to bring to you except his knowledge of all the ballroom dances!"

She tilted her head. "Is that how you have seen me all these years, like a parasite?"

"I was not referring to you in the least. I was speaking of M. Dubois!"

"But I have no connections, no family except my horrible cousin. Did you resent my presence at Barscot and in your home all these years?"

"Of course not. You are twisting everything around."

"Am I? You seem to forget that except for my fortune, I am an orphan. I have no connections, no home, nothing. The same may be asked of me in this marriage I propose. What do I bring to M. Dubois? As for M. Dubois, he is a gentleman, and was once an heir to an excellent property near Paris. His family, several sisters and a brother, his parents, all died at the guillotine. Because of ill fortune and nothing he did, he lost everything. Does that make him unworthy of me? "

He stared at her for a long, long time. He felt uneasy, as though he was being shown a part of himself that he did not like. "I am very sorry for his misfortunes, but I shan't permit you to scandalize my family, my aunt, by wedding a mere dancing teacher. I forbid it."

She shook her head. "It is as though I have never known you before. You are not sorry for his misfortunes in the least. Your sole concern is how my marriage will affect your consequence. Really, I am quite glad you came to discuss the matter with me, for I promise you I am not nearly so blue deviled as I was before."

"Say what you will, I shan't allow the marriage."

She returned to the bed and once more opened the portmanteau. "In this I believe you to be mistaken, Harley. I have seen my solicitor—your solicitor—and he assures me you have no such power in this case. I do not need your approval to marry anyone. The choice was mine to make. That much at least your father made clear in his will. All I need for the present is a special license, and if you cannot provide one, I have every intention of leaving immediately for Scotland, which I daresay you would dislike even more than the actual marriage. How would that appear to your friends and acquaintance—your ward married *over the anvil?*"

Harley was too angry to continue the discussion, particularly when she was being so obstinate. "We shall see," he stated harshly, rising from the bed. He headed for the door.

"If you mean to speak with your solicitor," she called after him, "he will tell you what I have already said."

He refused to answer her and walked briskly down the hall. As soon as he reached the landing he began shouting orders. Lady Potsgrove emerged from his office, having waited to see how his conversation with Coquette went.

"Harley, what is the matter?" she asked when he reached the bottom step.

He ground his teeth. "She means to marry Dubois!"

"What? The dancing instructor? Oh, my head feels so faint."

"Not now, Aunt! For I mean to see my solicitor at once and put an end to this absurdity!"

* * *

Coquette had not continued packing once Harley left her bedchamber. Her heart had grown so heavy in her chest that she could not have lifted even her pair of gloves, so sad was she. Instead, she moved to the window and watched as Harley paced up and down the street waiting for his coach to be brought round from the mews. How she loved him—so hopelessly, so completely, and without the smallest chance of fulfillment. She was only now beginning to understand the prejudices with which he viewed her, this most recent conversation sinking her spirits further.

Only when he had driven away did she return to her bed, and then not to continue packing but to stretch out facedown on the counterpane and subsequently shed so many tears that her only wonder was that she had not soaked the entire coverlet.

Harley returned three hours later deeply sobered by what Mr. Jennings had told him. If he had thought her marriage to Dubois was bad, the knowledge of all the stipulations and supporting documents to her actual arrangement with the man was a hundred times worse. He could not credit that she could be so indifferent to propriety as to have actually planned a marriage in which she would very soon after seek a divorce.

However, the documents had been signed by both of them, and only a special license was needed to see the deed done. He first considered refusing to oblige her in this, but he felt it would be infinitely worse were she to scramble to Scotland instead.

In truth, he was sickened by her decision and more so by the arrangements she had made with Dubois. What sort of man was he, anyway, to have agreed to such a thing? Hardly a gentleman.

Suddenly he knew what he might do to put an end to this charade and a strange calm settled over him. So when he next met Coquette as she was arriving in the drawing room that evening before dinner, her hair still hanging free about her shoulders, he addressed her. "I have been to my solicitor and it is as you have said. I beg your pardon for any unkindness I might have spoken to you this morning, but the suddenness and strangeness of your decision proved a considerable shock. I wish to atone, however, and hope that you will extend an invitation to M. Dubois for dinner tomorrow evening."

Coquette in turn stared at Harley as though he had just grown horns. For her part, she did not trust the nature of the proffered olive branch and wondered just what he meant to do next. Still, she did not hesitate. "How very kind of you, Harley. I think it an excellent notion. He was very shy of the idea but now, with your blessing, he will be more at ease."

She did not mistake the martial light which subsequently entered his eye or with what ill pleasure he let his gaze drift over her coiffure. When Lady Potsgrove entered the chamber at that moment, she immediately murmured, "Oh, dear. Have the pair of you begun brangling again? And you had been doing so well of late. Oh, dear. Oh, dear." She pulled at her cap, covered in white dove feathers, which sent several flying in all directions.

On the following evening, Coquette debated for nearly half an hour whether to permit her abigail to dress her hair properly. She was so out of patience with Harley that she wished to torment him, if but a little, and could easily have done so by not wearing her hair in the traditional knot or cascade of curls. As it was, she felt obligated to M. Dubois to set aside her desire to engage in her usual warfare with Harley in order to set her betrothed at ease. She knew his sensibilities well enough to comprehend that he was not especially looking forward to dinner this evening.

So an elegant cascade of curls it was, punctuated by Greek

bands. She wore a gown of simple white cambric with a three-quarter overdress of dark green patterned silk edged with a narrow gold braid. Draped over her elbows was a fine shawl of Merino wool in a shade of deep violet which she wore low to the back, as was the fashion. When she caught sight of her reflection just before she quit her chamber, she was struck again by how greatly she had been transformed in the past several weeks. For the barest moment she wondered if she truly wanted to purchase her sailing ship after all.

This, of course, was the most ridiculous thought ever and she quickly cast it aside. The hour had come, however, to face Harley again, for she had little doubt he did not intend to be entirely pleasant this evening. She therefore lifted her chin, lifted a brow, and prepared to do battle with her nemesis.

She happened to arrive at the entrance to the drawing room just as Harley snapped a book shut he had ostensibly been reading. She stopped on the threshold and met his gaze squarely. Lady Potsgrove had not yet arrived, nor had M. Dubois. She lifted her chin anew but said nothing.

He rose to his feet as was polite. "I see you have dressed your hair."

"I did not want to," she returned coldly. "I did so only for M. Dubois's sake. Were it not for his feelings, I should have delighted in nothing more than wearing my hair all a-tumble."

He narrowed his eyes, but merely nodded his understanding. "Sherry?"

"If you please," she responded coolly, moving slowly across the chamber and taking up a seat near the fireplace.

He brought her the glass of fortified wine, which she took, thanking him politely, but in a quick afterthought spilled a couple of drops on his leather shoes. "Oh, dear," she gushed. "Look what I have done? I do beg your pardon!"

He glanced down and saw the beaded droplets, which he leaned down and wiped away with his kerchief. He pocketed the kerchief and moved to the fireplace, where he planted a shoe on the hearth and glared at her. She sipped her sherry, feigning innocence.

The room grew so quiet that only the ticking of the clock on the mantel could be heard. Harley picked up a blackened poker and began pushing at a layer of black powdery coals, burned the night before. He then twirled the poker and moved leisurely toward her. All the while, the poker remained in motion. "I hope you are well." The poker dropped in a long swing toward the carpet and just happened to brush against the white cambric of her skirts. "Oh, dear, I am sorry! I have left a black streak on your lovely white gown. Do forgive me." He removed his kerchief and swiped at the streak which of course spread the black soot into an even wider pattern.

"Do stop!" she cried, pushing at his hand.

He backed away and returned the poker to the nearby stand. She let false tears well up into her eyes, and rose from her seat. She dabbed at her cheeks which were indeed damp, and moved toward him. "Harley, pray do not be angry with me. Please try to understand, I beg of you."

She moved closer still, then pretended to stumble, fell into him, and wiped her rouged cheeks across his neatly tied neckcloth. When he set her to rights, she held her kerchief to her cheek once more, this time in make-believe astonishment. "Look what a dreadful thing I have done!" she cried. "Rouge on your neckcloth!"

"The devil!" he cried. There was a small mirror over the table nearest the fireplace to which he moved. Once seeing what she had done, he turned on her in a flash. She gave a squeal and ran from him so that for the next few seconds he was chasing her madly about the room, as he had done so many times before at Barscot.

She raced from the chamber, crossed the entrance hall and tore down the hallway. He was close on her heels, and once she felt his fingers brush her hair. He had done that so many times, catching her by her hair, which hurt dreadfully. Such memories made her move more quickly still until she had passed from the house into the small garden beyond. The night was dark and the air damp, but there was nowhere to go except behind a plum tree.

"Harley, no!" she whispered. "Enough! I am sorry. Indeed, I am."

"I am not finished with you yet," he cried, also on a whisper. He lunged to the left, quickly to the right and caught her about the waist. He tore the overdress from its buttons and pulled the bands from her hair but she could not help herself and began to giggle, then laugh, until she was squealing with the delight of their silly game.

"You should be in tears!" he exclaimed hotly, giving her shoulders a shake.

But she laughed once more, so hard that tears began to course down her cheeks. "I love you so," she said, quite without thinking.

He released the hard grip on her shoulders. "What did you say?"

She stopped giggling. "I do not know. Nothing of consequence, I daresay." She could not have spoken her heart aloud, could she? No, that was impossible.

"I believe you said you loved me."

She shook her head. "I would never have said anything so ridiculous."

She recognized a familiar, even roguish light which entered his eye, and was not surprised when, in the next moment, she was engulfed in his arms and he was kissing her forcefully.

How much she longed to give herself to what had proven to be the absolute wonder of kissing Harley. For a brief moment, she did just that, sinking against him and feeling the strength of his arms all about her. She could have remained with him forever, beneath the plum tree, quivering from head to foot, as he kissed her over and over.

Common sense, however, asserted itself quickly and she pushed away from him. "No, Harley! You are not to be kissing me again, for I cannot bear it. My heart aches for days afterward, and if you remember, I am to be wed in but three. I will have a husband."

"But you will divorce in another three months," he retorted bitterly.

"What difference were I to be married for three months, three years, or a lifetime? I will tell you, none at all! Either way, I am leaving England before the summer is out, and I doubt I shall ever return."

He appeared shocked, and she took the opportunity to examine the damage he had inflicted on her. Glancing down at her beautiful overdress, she said, "You have quite torn all the buttonholes. What a beast you are, but then you always were. Do you know, I wonder that you disapprove of me so very much when, with the smallest provocation, you forget you are a gentlemen and engage in the most childish of games with me!"

With that, she moved back toward the house and once inside, climbed the servants' stairs and returned to her bedchamber. She looked a sight, but her eyes were shining and her complexion had taken on a wonderful glow. She ought to have been very sad because of what had just happened, yet somehow, having spoken the truth of her heart made her heart lighter than it had been in days.

Thirteen

Harley remained near the plum tree for a very long time, repeating over and over in his head precisely what she had said about kissing him. *My heart aches for days.*

And she had said she loved him. Good God! Coquette was in love with him. How strangely this truth acted upon his heart and mind. Under such circumstances, he would have expected to feel a mild disgust, for he did not esteem her as he did the majority of the ladies he knew. Instead of disgust, however, there was such a warmth coursing through his veins that he felt as though he had touched a life spring of sorts that had now flooded him with a deep peace and contentment he had never before known.

Coquette loved him. Beautiful, wild Coquette. Darling Coquette.

But this was madness to be thinking that he either liked or approved of her affection for him. She would always be the hoydenish vixen who had plagued him at Barscot ever since he could remember.

Yet not always. There had been an equal number of joyous times with her, either riding through the Chilterns, or board games at Michaelmas when the snows were deep in their favorite gorges, or music whenever his father requested she play. She had been a presence in his house who had resided near the nursery all her life and descended to join his family for every occasion, much to the consternation of his proprietous aunts but to the delight of his father, his uncles, and occasionally himself. Life had never been dull when Coquette was around.

Eventually, he began a slow progress back to his bedchamber to change his neckcloth. Whatever he might have thought of M. Dubois, he had no intention of greeting Coquette's future husband with rouge smeared over his neckcloth.

Later, Coquette greeted M. Dubois politely and received in return a warm, grateful smile. She realized at that moment, as he bowed to Lady Potsgrove and Harley, that he was, indeed, very much the gentleman. He was much older than she, of course, as well as Harley, so that even Potsy was a trifle in awe of him. Now that he had been invited as a guest into the home of one of his former employers, he lost all obsequiousness and conversed with each of them as an equal.

Coquette had been nervous from the beginning, knowing that Harley's dislike of her present scheme would not prevent him from making his displeasure known at some point in the evening. By the time she was sipping her turtle soup, however, she had begun to relax, for Harley seemed to be on his best behavior.

She had just lifted her spoon to her lips and sipped the savory soup, when Harley blurted out, "So, M. Dubois, you will be a free man in but a handful of days."

"Harley!" his aunt cried.

Coquette would have remonstrated as well, but she was too busy choking on her soup. She coughed a dozen times, sipped her wine, and sputtered a little more. Through watery eyes, she turned to her nemesis. "How could you be so coarse?"

"You would speak of coarseness, Cokie, when your sole intention is to cause my family an enormous scandal by divorcing M. Dubois as soon as you are able?"

She sat back in her seat and glared at him.

"Harley," his aunt called to him. "You've said quite

enough. The matter is settled. I do not know why you must kick up a dust now."

"Because," he said, narrowing his eyes at M. Dubois and settling his linen on the table, "I wish to know how he can live with himself for having agreed to appropriate part of a lady's fortune merely to secure his own."

Coquette rose to her feet and slapped her linen on the table as well. "If that is not the outside of enough, I do not know what is! Just how many young ladies of fortune marry gentlemen who promise to insure the protection of that fortune, then whistle it away at White's or Boodles or one of the East End hells? A score, I am certain."

"That is very true," Lady Potsgrove said, joining in the fracas without the smallest regard for the manner in which Harley scowled at her. "I knew a Miss White who entered into what was supposed to be an excellent match with the Viscount of Heathfield and within the year he had lost her fortune of some eighty thousand pounds. Coquette is very right, Harley. Marriage does not in any manner protect either a lady or her fortune."

"Quite so," Coquette added, once more taking up her seat. "But M. Dubois has requested a mere five thousand pounds, which you very well know I can afford and rejected the thirty I originally offered him."

"Thirty pounds?" Lady Potsgrove inquired. "Only thirty? Oh, then it is too bad of you, M. Dubois, to have afterward demanded five thousand."

"No, no, Potsy! You have greatly mistaken the matter. I offered M. Dubois thirty thousand pounds to marry and divorce me, not thirty!"

"Good heavens!" she cried, glancing from M. Dubois to Coquette and back again at least a dozen times.

"Just so," Coquette said, offering a warm smile to her future husband.

"Indeed?" Harley queried, now frowning mildly as he surveyed M. Dubois.

M. Dubois, however, felt obliged to speak, which she wished he had not. "I comprehend your concerns perfectly," he said, with but a whisper of an accent. "Indeed, until Miss Millbrook pressed me, I was not inclined to accept of her offer. I did so after a frank discussion of her past at Barscot Hall, her disinclination to marry where she did not love nor was not loved, and her desire to purchase a sailing vessel by which, if I have understood her, she means to travel the seas quite extensively."

"What do you mean, her past at Barscot?" Harley asked defensively.

M. Dubois shrugged. "Only that having been orphaned, as I was, Barscot never felt like her home. But then, I believe it would be quite difficult for you or anyone who has not lost both parents at a young or relatively young age to comprehend these feelings. Only when I saw her general despair did I feel compelled to accept of her offer."

"Despair, Cokie?" Harley asked.

Coquette felt exceedingly uncomfortable. "I suppose I would not have referred to my sentiments in such a manner, but yes, there is an attendant despair when one is alone in the world, a sense, perhaps, that one will never truly have a place to call one's own."

Lady Potsgrove interjected, "Is that why you were always so wild?"

Coquette shook her head. "I was always so wild because it pleased me. I do not think there is a connection, but I suppose there might be."

After that, everyone fell silent. How odd, Coquette thought, as she glanced from one to the other, that in their silence as each mulled over the situation, there could be a sense of great chatterings in the air, as though each thought was spoken aloud. She returned to her soup, which was now rather cold, but in the absence of anything else to do, she dipped her spoon until the bowl was empty. At least Harley no longer seemed prone to argue the value of her proposed wedding scheme. He, too, she noticed, seemed consumed with eating his soup.

Friday night, quite late, Harley sat around a table with his dearest friends at his club and thought that with one or two more glasses of port he would be completely foxed. He glanced about. Given the various slouching postures of his friends, he realized they were foxed as well.

"Coquette," he slurred, "is to be married tomorrow. I wish you all to attend."

A general sighing of disappointment went round the table. "I should have liked to have married her m'self," Olney said, turning his emerald ring as he leaned his chin heavily on his fist. "I loved her. I think I always did, even if she did look like a witch half the time at Barscot."

Harley started to laugh. "She did look like a witch. A few centuries past, with all that violent hair of hers, she would have been weighted down with stones and tossed in a pond to see if she floated."

Lord Henry, quite recovered from his illness, blinked several times. "I loved her too. I don't think she believed me, though. Prettiest legs. Did you ever see her ride bareback?"

A different sort of sighing went up about the table this time. Harley smiled sloppily, remembering the last time she had ridden bareback. "She did not want to come to London," he said, measuring each word. "I think she wanted to stay in Bedfordshire always."

"She loved the hills about your house," Waltham said. "I don't think she would have cared for Kent nearly as much. The land is very flat where my house is, not nearly so pretty as your . . . "—he hiccuped—"Chilterns."

"Parts of Kent are not in the least flat," Templar said.

"No," Waltham mused. "There are as many curves to the land in the northern parts as there are to Coquette. God, what a figure."

Harley nodded, then drew himself up sharply. "Do not speak about Coquette in that vile manner."

"Oh, beg pardon. Forgot you were in love with her. Now, why is it you are not marrying her?"

"Yes, why?" Lord Henry inquired, squinting at Harley.

Harley puffed air through his cheeks in a disparaging manner. "Did not say I was in love with her," he began. This protestation, however, was greeted with a general round of guffaws. He realized even in his stupor that all his friends believed he was very much in love with her. "Whatever you think, she is not worthy to be mistress of Barscot."

His friends began protesting quite hotly at this declaration, even throwing things at him. Olney's snuffbox hit him in the chest. "What did I say?" he asked dumbly.

"You should be ashamed. Coquette is a goddess," Lord Henry slurred. "She would be worthy to be mistress of Zeus's palace on Olympus. So why not your paltry mansion in Bedfordshire?"

"Well done," Olney cried, his head slipping from his hand and hitting the table with a loud thump. "Ow."

"Just so!" Waltham intoned. "Coquette would be brilliant as mistress of Barscot!"

"Do you all think so?" Harley asked.

"Indeed," Templar and Lord Henry cried in unison.

"Well!" he responded. "But I had always thought I should have had Lady Agnes rule at Barscot."

"No, don't do that!" Olney stated, squinting at him.

"Why? She is quite as elegant as my mother ever was and Barscot should have elegance and grace. I have always thought as much."

Waltham queried, "Why would you want that for Barscot when you could have wildness and beauty? Coquette is like Windermere or Grasmere. She has majesty. Lady Agnes, good God, she is like a piece of stone. A statue, really."

"Quite cold, your mother," Olney interjected. "She once

sent me from Barscot because she said she did not like her
son having such friends as me."

"She did not," Harley said. "Oh, wait a minute. She did, did
she not? I remember now. She was very intent on only boys
of rank playing at Barscot."

"Then she died," Waltham explained helpfully.

"So she did." Harley pushed his glass of port away. He
knew that something momentous was happening in how he
viewed his world, but still his mind was foggy. He rose un-
steadily to his feet. "Must go home now. Good night."

Apparently, he did not get far. When he awoke with sunlight streaming on his face through a truly reprehensible
crack in the draperies, he discovered he was still wearing
evening dress and was propped in a painfully awkward position on a short sofa in Olney's rooms. A glance about the
chamber found a clock which reported the news that it was
ten o'clock in the morning. He tried to sit up but his neck was
stiff and he flopped backward instead, only to hit his head on
the rather hard, albeit padded arm of the sofa.

He groaned and rolled himself off the torturous couch and
finally found his feet. Olney could be heard snoring loudly
from his bedchamber.

Ten o'clock on Saturday. What would he do today, he wondered. Waltham had mentioned a couple of days ago that he
was interested in selling his very fine black gelding. He might
have a look . . . at . . . good God! Coquette was to be married
in an hour in his drawing room!

However ill he felt, however stiff his entire body, his athletic limbs responded well and before the cat could lick her
ear, he was standing on the sidewalk hailing a hackney. Fifteen minutes later, he walked through the front doors of his
home and without saying a word to the small party assembled
and ready in the drawing room, he raced upstairs where his
valet, whose knowledge of his master was significant,
awaited him with hot towel and razor.

Twenty minutes later, which left his neckcloth tied rather

shabbily, he walked down the stairs and into the drawing room. He swallowed hard as he took in the countenances of his aunt, Waltham, Lord Henry, Templar, Mr. Jennings his solicitor, a parish priest, and a quite somber Coquette. He noted that Olney was not present, undoubtedly still snoring happily.

"Good morning," he called out, ignoring Potsy's severe, disapproving shake of her head. "Ah, I see we want five until eleven, time to spare." He glanced at Coquette again, but she would not meet his gaze.

Coquette for her part could not look at him not because she was disappointed that he had arrived in such a haphazard, tardy manner, but because he had arrived at all. She had awakened with a terrible weight on her chest, aware that from this moment on, this hour, her life would be changed forever. From first leaving her bed, a panic had seized her, and though she had tried to encourage her spirits with thoughts of the vessel she would be purchasing within the next sennight, still her pulse would race and her throat had grown unbearably dry. She wondered if she would even be able to make the proper responses during the ceremony.

She had scarcely spoken to Harley in the intervening days since their dinner together with M. Dubois. She had scarcely spoken to him because she had hardly seen him. She had ceased attending social events, and he apparently wished to be anywhere but in Grosvenor Square. She was grateful for that, until this moment. Now she had to face the unfaceable, that she would be leaving England soon, forever perhaps. She would therefore probably never see Harley again and simply did not know how she would bear that.

She finally glanced at him and saw that he was looking at her with a deeply troubled expression. Almost there was fear in his eyes. She blinked and wanted to look away but she could not. *Harley, why could you not love me,* her heart asked.

He took a step toward her and she took one toward him. Over and over, she asked the question silently. *Why could you not love me, why, why?*

He took another step in her direction. She followed suit. There was but five feet between them now. "Is this truly what you want?" he asked.

She nodded, but it was a lie. What she wanted was so impossible that she could not even frame the thought in her head. Snippets came to her of a possible future, of sitting beside Harley on a cold winter evening and playing at backgammon between kisses and brandy, of riding hard through the Chilterns with Harley close behind, of letting him chase her in the orangery until she was out of breath from laughing.

"Cokie?" he whispered, drawing very near her.

"Harley, you beast," she responded.

"I am in love with you, my darling."

"Oh, Harley!" She was in his arms and somewhere in the great distance she could hear the good vicar protesting. But she did not care because Harley was kissing her wildly and she clung to him with all her might, until the next moment she was falling and he was falling, and she was sprawled in a completely unladylike fashion on him, laughing so hard that she thought her corset would burst.

Then she was on the floor with him, sitting up, and he embraced her. "I have been such a fool," he said. "Waltham told me as much, but I didn't believe him until just now when I truly understood—Coquette, you are the only woman for me, the only lady who could ever make me happy, and if you wish never to wear your hair in gold bands, or put rouge on your cheeks, or use a lady's saddle, I will not complain, not once! I love you. I love you. The way I have always known you, like Windermere."

"Like what?"

"Wild, untamed beauty, my love. Only tell me you love me, now."

"I already did, remember? By the plum tree."

"Then I was not mistaken?"

"No."

"I say!" the vicar cried out. "What is going on here? I have never seen such a careless abandon of propriety."

Lady Potsgrove, who had tears in her eyes, placed a gentle hand on his arm. "All will be well. You'll see."

Harley rose to his feet and assisted Coquette in gaining hers. He immediately turned to M. Dubois. "A thousand pardons. But you shall still receive what Coquette agreed to, never fear." When M. Dubois opened his mouth to protest, Harley added, "I would not have it otherwise, my friend."

"I shall accept your generosity," he said. "Though I believe this is the best and happiest ending possible."

Coquette then gasped. "Oh, but it is not! Harley, we do not have a license and I strongly suspect that the bishop will not wish to grant another to the same young lady in so short a span of time."

"No, indeed!" he responded, laughing. "Well, I can see there is only one thing to be done. Gretna it must be."

Fourteen

Coquette had never known that such happiness was possible. She sat beside Harley in his traveling coach, one trunk and a portmanteau strapped to the back. Every time she pondered the marvelous circumstance that she was eloping to Gretna Green with the man she loved, a delicious shiver passed through her. She was having an adventure, and one more potent than any her imagination had ever conjured. She had never, in all her four and twenty years, considered the possibility that love would one day find her. She had been long since resolved to a destiny of solitary exploration, one in which she knew she would have found a measure of contentment but surely nothing as she was experiencing in this moment.

As she glanced up at Harley, who met her gaze, smiled, and squeezed for perhaps the hundredth time the hand he held in a tight grip, she wondered at all that had happened to have brought her to this place. And it had begun with his father's will.

She began to see the absolute wisdom in Lord Harlington's interference in her life. Harley never would have looked twice at her as she was, her long red curls rarely combed thoroughly and never dressed properly, her manners a disgrace, and her stubbornness wholly unchecked. At the same time, she never would have pondered the possibility that all this time she had been quite desperately in love with him.

She leaned her head against his shoulder and her throat

grew painfully constricted. She felt as though she had come home after an absence of years.

Home. Something about that word disturbed her, but she could not explain it. She would now live at Barscot the remainder of her life, the place she had called home from the time she was four years old. Only it had never truly felt like home. Again, her heart seemed to skip a desperate beat. She glanced up at Harley's face, barely seeing more than his shirt-point from her awkward position, squished into his arm as she was. Did Harley truly want her there? Part of her knew he did, but there was another part that was not so well convinced. After all, he had thought so meanly of her for so long. How could he change so quickly?

She closed her eyes and forced herself not to dwell on her worries overly much. After all, he had publicly proclaimed his love for her to a greatly startled priest of the church, to a weeping Potsy, and even a grinning Lord Waltham. He could hardly retract his professions now that they had been witnessed so thoroughly.

She drew in a deep breath and released a great, if quite silent sigh. Of course she was being ridiculous. Of course.

The coach stopped, but not for long, at Alconbury Hill, where Coquette took only a cup of tea. She was not in the least hungry and said so. The coach labored north toward Scotland. Her worries were soon displaced with the exigencies of travel, of being alternately charmed by some part of the passing landscape, then bored with the sheer drudgery of getting from one place to the next.

When night fell, even the advantage of the scenery was lost and she felt as though she had become a mere series of regular jostles against Harley's arm. His coach was well sprung, but the ruts in the road were frequent and deep.

Once at the Bell in Stilton, she fell gratefully into bed. Sleep conquered her quickly, and before she knew what was happening a serving maid was rousing her gently, a cup of hot

tea in hand and a message that Lord Harlington wished to
leave within the next half hour if it pleased Lady Harlington.

"I beg your pardon?" she asked, looking up at the maid.
"Oh, but I'm not . . . that is . . . " She blushed hotly, thanked
the maid, took her cup of tea and bid her return in ten minutes
to help her dress.

She hoped she would not be so silly as to make that mistake again and only wondered what the maid thought of her.
Not that it mattered, of course. She would probably never see
either the Bell or the serving maid again so long as she lived.

Once in the coach, she told Harley of her slip, but he did
not seem in the least concerned. "They are used, no doubt,
to seeing all manner of elopements on this road."

"Yes, but it was very lowering to be so missish and
thoughtless when I quite pride myself on the contrary."

With that, however, he kissed her, a gesture which had
the wonderful effect of soothing away her feelings of fool-
ishness.

The journey progressed without incident, another day
and night spent in exhausted slumber, on sheets Lady Potsgrove had insisted they carry with them. For that, Coquette
found herself deeply appreciative. Whatever care the housekeeper and servings maids showed at Barscot, not even a
tithe of such fastidiousness had yet appeared in any of the
inns along the Great North Road. Still, she was not in the
least dismayed, merely grateful that she had been prepared.
After all, a journey around the world as she had planned
would surely see worse habits of cleanliness than poorly
aired sheets.

She had been buttoning her nightdress at an inn in York
when this last thought struck her. Her trip round the world.
All that was gone now. She would soon be Harley's wife and
all her adventurous plans cast aside. A familiar ache, almost
a loneliness, seized her chest. From the moment Harley had
confessed his love for her she had been so taken with feelings
of adoration and joy that she had not thought what an actual

marriage to Harley would mean for her daily activities. There was Barscot now to think of, and children to be birthed, her new duties.

The ache in her chest turned to panic as she began to realize just what she had done in agreeing to his madcap scheme to forsake M. Dubois and race to the border of Scotland. She would be his wife, mistress of Barscot Hall, a countess!

She slept fitfully, nightmares teasing her through the early hours of the morning, of being cast over the side of a sailing ship, of falling hard from a horse who galloped across an uneven field, of having climbed a cliff only to fall backward into nothing.

She awoke at dawn, her nightclothes damp with perspiration. She did not know what her frightening dreams had meant, but she did know that today she must begin conforming herself to what would be her new role and position in society.

An hour later, Coquette sat rather stiffly beside Harley as his coach rolled from York. Scotland now seemed but a breath away, every mile pressing her toward a future she had never desired nor sought. She found it difficult to think of things to say to Harley and wondered if he had yet noticed how quiet she was.

"What is amiss, Cokie? I have not seen you so sullen since you first learned of my father's will."

She sighed heavily.

He nudged her gently. "That does not bode well. What thoughts are rattling through your head and clearly cutting up your peace?"

"You will be angry," she stated.

He chuckled, a sound which gave her some relief. "I do not doubt it. I only wonder that we have been so tolerant of each other these scores of miles past. Tell me, my dear, in what manner have I offended you?"

"Oh, but you have not," she said, turning toward him. She

watched him catch his breath as he looked down at her. "What is it? Do I have coal dust on my face?"

"Not by half. You are so beautiful, and sometimes I cannot believe how much I love you."

She felt incomprehensible tears flood her eyes. "You make everything wretched by saying as much," she complained.

He barked a disbelieving laugh. "I had always thought ladies wished to hear professions of love. Am I that mistaken, or do you, in particular, dislike the sound of my voice?"

She shook her head and covered her face with her gloved hands. "Harley, you do not understand. I know I shall disappoint you."

"What do you mean?"

She let her hands drop to her lap and again looked into his face. She thought for a very long moment, then said, "I know how to navigate by the stars."

He frowned slightly and shook his head, but he did not speak. Instead, he appeared to be pondering her words. "I see," was all he said.

There. Even in saying as much, she had brought a troubled look to his face. She could guess at his thoughts, that she was an oddity and could never truly be mistress of his home in any graceful, appropriate sense.

Harley stared out the window of the coach, watching the rather desolate moorland pass by. Occasionally the sound of a bleating sheep would strike his ears, but otherwise he was quite fully engaged in interpreting what Coquette had meant by her cryptic words. He knew she had learned to navigate by the stars. She had told him as much six years past, the same year she had refused a come-out ball. He had thought her ridiculous at the time and had told her as much. Was that why she had made reference to her knowledge of navigation? Because he had ridiculed her?

He could not be certain, but he felt the weight of her words fully. She was not one to be blue deviled very often, but the moment he had seen her crestfallen face this morning, he had known something was distressing her. Was she then expressing her wish to be sailing, or the circumstance that much of her knowledge was unrelated to domestic matters? He could not be certain. On the other hand, he knew her well enough not to dismiss her present unhappiness. Indeed, he intuited that something darker lay beneath her words. He wondered if he should offer to take her on an extended honeymoon to the Mediterranean, but he sensed that wouldn't fadge. No, something more potent than merely her desire to have adventures lay beneath her words.

For the moment, therefore, he merely wrapped her arm tightly about his and held her close.

Coquette wished Harley was not being so kind to her in this moment, for he could not imagine her thoughts. Indeed, the rapid succession of images which kept passing through her mind had more to do with running away from him than anything else. She was beginning to understand that she could not bear the thought of being married to him or any man and to therefore be bound to her husband's home and notions of what she should do each day, how she should live, what her activities should be. She had studied how to navigate by the position of the stars and she had so long pictured herself on the ocean that she realized now she would do anything to get her ship.

But how? If she did not marry Harley, she would lose her fortune and therefore any possibility of owning a sailing craft of any sort. Yet if she married him she would be bound to Barscot. Oh, what a dreadful mistake she had made in accepting his hand in marriage! How much better to have wed and divorced M. Dubois! How foolish she had behaved and now, unless some other scheme occurred to her, she would be bound forever to Harley.

A brilliant thought flooded her mind. Once she arrived at Gretna Green, she could find a man to wed her in name only, for a fee, just as she had concocted the earlier notion of marrying M. Dubois. Yes, that would do. Only, how was she now to be rid of Harley?

That was a much more difficult matter. Although she could begin the process even now by setting up his back, a skill at which she was certainly expert.

She drew her arm out of his strong clasp and untied her bonnet. As quickly, she pulled her hair from the coiled braids which had kept her thick curls in check. She then rose, turned, and sat herself opposite him. She crossed her arms over her chest. "I just think you ought to know, Harley, that I have no intention of spending most of my days at Barscot." She lifted a challenging brow.

He did not seem much moved by this comment. "I do not blame you in the least," he responded reasonably. "A young lady who has imagined herself walking the streets of Rome, Lisbon, even Calcutta, can hardly be expected to be content forever in my home."

She narrowed her eyes at him. "Then you will let me have my ship?"

He shrugged. "I did not say that, precisely. As it happens, I have great plans for your fortune. There is a tidy property in Sussex I have been hoping to purchase and now, with your vast wealth, I mean to do so. Do you not think that an excellent plan?" Before she had even opened her mouth to protest, he added, "Of course, once we are wed, I will not need to ask permission to spend your funds. Ah, Cokie, life does not bring much greater joys than this, would you not agree?"

She felt the heat in her face and could only imagine how red it was from the sudden rage she was experiencing. "If you think for one moment I will simply let you do whatever you wish with my—oh, Harley, you beast! You were teasing me."

"How readily you rise to the fly, dearest. I hope you continue doing so, for it is one of my favorite pastimes."

"You always could put me in high dudgeon. Only answer truthfully, what do you think of my purchasing a ship once we are wed? Though I suppose I would have to return occasionally to visit Barscot."

"What of me?" he inquired. "Do you mean to be a real wife to me, or will I need to find consolation elsewhere?"

She might have been a maiden, but she was neither naive nor ill-informed on the habits of men. "I suppose you must find a bird of paradise, as men are wont to do."

"Will you help me choose one?" he asked, his expression all innocence.

She gasped and was about to read him the riot act, when she saw the devilish light in his eye. She clamped her lips tightly together, but this did not in the least stop him from laughing very hard at her expense. She crossed her leg over her knee and let it bounce several times, causing the sharp toe of her half boot to strike his leg repeatedly.

When it hit him a fifth time, he leaned forward suddenly and grabbed her ankle. His smile was wholly wicked. "I do not know what bee has got into your bonnet, Cokie, but if you kick me again, you shall answer for it!" He then released her leg.

She could not resist. All the old, former patterns returned and she kicked quite hard.

He leaped upon her and began tickling her so roughly that within a few seconds she was squealing, laughing, and begging him to stop, which he did, at least the tickling, but he did not release her. Instead, he began kissing her neck. A minute passed and then two, perhaps three. Her mind soon became quite liquid and she could no longer remember why she had moved to the opposite side of the coach in the first place. He moved from her neck to her ear to her cheek, and then his lips were on hers. She was squished against the seat, but did not care. His mouth was like heaven, the sweetest of reveries she could have ever imagined.

Somehow her arms found themselves wrapped about his neck and then he was holding her close and exploring her mouth so deeply that she thought she might perish then and there from the sheer pleasure of it. His kisses continued for a very long time and only ceased when the coach hit a particularly deep rut and he was jostled away from her.

He returned to his original seat but pulled her to sit next to him. He then spent the next hour or so continuing to help her forget just why she had wanted to overset him in the first place.

Thus the day was whiled away, so pleasantly that Coquette continued to relegate to the back of her mind her decision to find a different husband once she had arrived in Gretna Green.

Darkness fell. "How long now?" she inquired, glancing about, but there was not even a moon to show a local landmark by which she could determine their proximity to the Scottish border town.

"I would imagine we are very near now." His arm was about her shoulders and he was squinting into the dark. "At the last inn, the hostler said it was but a few miles more to Gretna. We must have traveled six as it is."

Coquette felt her heart begin to hammer against her ribs. She wondered just how she was to tell Harley that she had changed her mind, that she could not marry him after all, that even though she loved him she felt certain she could never be content enslaved to the duties of his life. She also wondered if he would be willing to help her select a husband from among the inmates of Gretna in order to fulfill the conditions to her inheritance while at the same time not in any manner jeopardizing her fortune. She shuddered faintly. She did not think Harley would like either notion very much at all.

Another mile passed. Gretna grew closer still. She felt obligated to at least give him a hint of the changes she wanted to make, but just as she opened her mouth to speak, a light blazed suddenly to the right and the next moment three hooded horsemen rode onto the highway, forcing the coachman to draw the conveyance to an abrupt halt.

"Harley, what is it?" she cried. "Thieves? Oh, but this is too wonderful! An adventure before we have even reached Scotland!"

"Can you see by the lamplight on your side just how many there are?"

"Only three. The shadows are fairly well lit and the land open enough. Oh, I see the light is a flambeaux which must have just been lit. How brightly it shines."

"I see two pistols. The third man approaching us appears only to have a sack. So we are to be robbed, eh?" He reached under his seat and from a hidden compartment withdrew a pair of pistols.

"How famous!" she whispered. "Do give one to me, Harley. You know I am a crack shot."

"I do, indeed." He turned, smiling at her faintly. "Are you not in the least unnerved?" He handed her the gun, shot and powder and she immediately primed her weapon.

"What? By this? Good God, no. I am more overset by the thought of marriage than by being robbed."

She heard him choke on his laughter, but he bid her keep her weapon low and hidden.

She nudged him. "Do you wish me to prepare your pistol?"

"No, I think not." He then secured it into the waistband of his breeches. "I have another notion entirely as to how this encounter might proceed."

The man with the sack approached. "Yer jewels, me lord, or the lady dies!"

"We have no jewels," he retorted sharply.

"No jewels," the man cast over his shoulder.

"Then ask fer wat money he carries." There was a slight brogue to the second man's speech.

"Money, me lord, and be quick about it."

"It is in the trunk, strapped to the back. I shall have to retrieve it for you."

The robber seemed uncertain but backed away, holding his pistol level, and finally gesturing for Harley to descend from the coach. To Coquette, Harley whispered, "When I am fully behind the coach, set up a caterwaul."

"As you wish," she murmured.

He quickly left the coach, and she watched him walk slowly to the back. Once he was there, she began to scream, bloodcurdling sounds which she had learned to do as a child when she most particularly wished to torture Harley. She felt the coach rock suddenly and then she fell silent, feeling certain he had accomplished his task.

"What gives?" the second bandit called out, urging his horse forward. "Billy? 'Ave you the blunt?"

But his compatriot was silent.

Coquette waited, her body tense. She raised her pistol slightly. The horseman was not approaching by way of the door but on the opposite side, so she knew she was not in danger from him. On the other hand, the third man, his pistol raised, gave his horse a kick and headed straight in her direction.

She understood at once what his intentions were. If Harley had succeeded in disabling the first man, and the second man succumbed to a similar fate, then she could serve as a hostage. She felt a strong sense of determination flood her such as she had never known. She would neither become a hostage, nor would she be injured in any manner. She had but to keep her head and all would be well.

The hooded man dismounted and shouted to the coachman to keep his seat or he would soon feel the sting of a pistolball. His voice was hoarse and deep, but these were but a shallow disguise. Coquette felt the blood drain from her face. She realized she knew the masked man and a sickness of understanding and real fear flowed over her, for the man now near the door had only one true intent this night.

As soon, therefore, as he cracked the door, she took aim, and fired at the arm holding the pistol. Her aim was true. He spun around and fell face first in the road.

Chaos erupted. Another shot, which must have been the

robber's. A horse's hooves. She quickly primed her pistol and by the time she was ready to fire again, Harley was before her, the first bandit held in his tight grasp. The second bandit had ridden away. The man weaved on his feet and his eyes rolled. "You must let him go," she said.

The man looked at her and blinked, trying to focus. "Please, mum. I beg ye."

"We will not let either of these culprits go and did I know the moors even a trifle, I should mount this fellow's horse and pursue his bosom bow."

Coquette merely shook her head. "You must let him go, now."

Harley frowned at her, but after a long moment, queried. "Are you certain?"

"Very much so. The identity of that man"—here she pointed to the ground—"will explain everything. But I have little doubt that another coach or traveler will be along shortly, so I beg of you to release your man now, then draw the injured one into our coach that I might tend to him. Tie his horse to the back and let us be on our way."

He stared at her very hard for a long moment, then nodded. "As you wish."

The bandit was gone in seconds, though Harley had appropriated his pistol in case he had thoughts about returning for another go. He then went to the prostrate but groaning form of the man still lying on the road and carefully removed his hood. "Good God!" he cried. Glancing back at Coquette, he added, "You knew, then?"

"Yes. Is he incapacitated? I wish to know if I might disarm now."

"He will hurt neither of us." Harley then found the man's pistol and spoke to his coachman. Coquette could hear his words clearly. "You will have to pretend, I fear, that none of this happened. Do you understand me?"

"Of course, m'lord."

Only then did Harley pick Rupert Seames up from the road and toss him none too gently into the coach.

"You are killing me," he complained.

"Nonsense. Your wound is but a scratch! Although if I did not have my soon-to-be wife to consider, I would turn you over to the magistrate in Gretna or, better yet, leave you to the wolves."

Rupert glared at him.

"You meant to kill me," Coquette stated, eyeing him angrily.

"Of course. I failed the first time when I stole into the music room and set both pairs of draperies on fire. And I might have succeeded tonight if that nodcock had not been tricked by your squealing, throwing his attention away from Harlington."

Coquette frowned slightly. "Then your drunkenness at Mrs. Dalcham's fete was merely a ruse."

"Precisely."

"You are something of a simpleton," Harley offered, smiling. "Eh, Seames? But all's well that end's well."

"What do you mean to do with me?"

"I should like to cut you to pieces," Coquette said.

Rupert merely laughed. "You always were more of a man than a woman."

Harley threw out his left arm to keep Coquette from launching herself on her horrid cousin, then threw out his right and planted Rupert such a perfect facer that he slumped down onto his seat unconscious, in which state he remained until the coach rolled into Gretna.

By then Coquette had worked out a plan with Harley.

Once Rupert awoke, Harley explained to him that as soon as could be managed, he would find himself on a ship to New South Wales, where he would be required to remain forever. If Rupert chose to return to England, Harley made it perfectly clear that he would be prosecuted for attempted murder, by fire—at his own admission—a few nights past and most recently by the attack on Harley's coach.

Coquette added, "I will give you a purse of five hundred pounds by which you might become properly settled in your new country. It should serve you well if you can train yourself to even a mite of self-control."

"Five hundred pounds," he spit bitterly. "A paltry sum when you have a thousand times that amount."

"And had you been worthy of it, I should have given you more. But, Rupert, you are the most worthless, feckless creature on God's earth. I warn you to be silent, however, even though I can see you wish to give me a dressing down for all my supposed abuses to you. If you choose to speak, you will forfeit even the five hundred I intend to give you. Do we understand one another?"

He merely stared at her, his eyes hard and resentful, but he did not again open his mouth.

Once at Gretna Hall, where Harley secured rooms for all three of them, Coquette found herself suddenly fatigued. She had meant to discuss her new scheme with Harley, but she was much too tired and bid him good night. As she fell asleep, she reviewed with some pleasure the nature of the entire attack and how well she and Harley had performed as a team. He had proved, as she had always known he would, to be a man she could rely on with swords, pistols, or fisticuffs. As she drifted into her slumbers, she smiled again at the thought that she ought at least ask him if he wished to accompany her on her adventures after all.

The morning broke overcast but not too damp in the Scottish border town. Coquette was nervous, however, knowing that she must finally lay her decision before Harley and help him come to a quick acquiescence so that their subsequent search for an acceptable husband could commence as soon as possible.

While sitting across from him, she tried to summon her courage to address the subject, but she could not. Instead, she asked, "How fares my *beloved* cousin?"

Harley shrugged. "The physician arrived last night and actually removed the pistol ball. It appears you inflicted a trifle more damage than we both suspected. Seames lies feverish, but well enough. He appears to be enjoying the use of as much laudanum as he desires, so his spirits, though not entirely present, are not in bad form."

She smiled in return. "He will do well in New South Wales. I am convinced of it."

She was a little startled when Harley suddenly possessed himself of her hands. They were partaking of their breakfast in a private parlor, so he was perfectly free to do so without offending anyone. However, she realized the time had indeed come, so she gently withdrew her hands, though she could not meet his gaze.

"I knew something was amiss. I have known it since yesterday. Only, please speak your mind to me, Coquette. If you do not, how else will I know how to answer you?"

She could hardly breathe as she stared back at him. "I am so very sorry, Harley, but I cannot wed you after all."

He blinked and seemed a little startled but then his lips twitched.

"Now, you must take my words seriously. I am not joking."

He strove to compose himself. "Very well. Do you mean to tell me why I am no longer worthy of your hand?"

"No longer worthy?" she cried. "No, no, it is nothing like that, I assure you. You are very worthy, more than I deserve, no doubt. But I just cannot be mistress at Barscot. I wish to travel the world."

"You mean you wish to hide from Barscot."

She frowned and shook her head. "No, not in the least, but what a very odd thing to say."

"Well, then let me ask you something. Are you able to converse with Mrs. Heyshott?"

"Of course." Mrs. Heyshott was the housekeeper at Barscot whom Coquette had known all her life

"And my butler?"

"Well, yes, I have known them both for ages."

He lowered his voice conspiratorially. "Then, in truth, you would be able to be mistress of my home, since all that is really required of you is to let each of them know your pleasure, and your pleasure shall be done."

She really detested Harley the most when he was being reasonable, for somehow he always seemed to miss the point. "It is not so simple," she returned.

"Oh, but it is."

"No."

"Yes."

"You are being stubborn again," she accused him.

He crossed his arms over his chest. "I mean to be very stubborn if it means that I shall be deprived of your company across my breakfast table every morning for the next thirty or forty or perhaps even fifty years, so you ought to be prepared for a real fight this time, Cokie."

She felt her will assert itself, as it always did when Harley came the crab. She crossed her arms as well. "As it happens, Barscot is only part of the difficulty. The other is that I mean to have full use of my fortune. I mean to purchase a sailing ship and I intend to see every port of call ever created on the face of the earth before I die."

His lips twitched anew, and she was further incensed as much by his refusal to take their conversation seriously as by his attempts at high-handedness.

"Very well. Agreed. You may have your fortune and your ship, but I will accompany you on your travels. There is still much piracy about, and you will need a hand on your ship capable of using swords or pistols to advantage."

She stared at him. She knew he could not possibly be serious. Besides, she meant to travel alone, not with a husband.

"I wish to go alone."

He shook his head. "I fear I cannot allow it."

"You are not in a position, my lord, to allow or to not allow anything!" she responded hotly. "I will not marry you, and all I need now is for you to assist me in finding a man similar in temperament and honor to M. Dubois."

"I will not leave you, Cokie."

He was being absurd. "Yes, you will."

"No, my darling. Never."

"I will most certainly, then, be leaving you."

He considered this. "No. You will try, but I will find you. Again, I say, I will never leave you. Never."

She did not quite understand him, but suddenly she was disturbed and a faint lump had formed in her throat. "I do not know why you are being so obtuse, but I am going on a ship and you are not."

"Then I will purchase my own ship and follow you about for decades, if necessary, until you come to your senses. You cannot possibly escape me on every continent." He was now smiling, and that so warmly that the lump in her throat grew even more painful.

"Harley, I wish you would not be so absurd when I am try-ing tell you in the plainest manner possible that we can never be married. I do not wish it. I wish for only my fortune, my ship, and my loneliness . . . I mean my solitude."

At that, he rose from his seat and rounded the table to her. He took her hands and lifted her to her feet. "You spoke truly the first time. Your loneliness. That is what you have been try-ing to tell me."

"No, I have not," she whispered, tears now starting to her eyes. "I meant my solitude. That is how I have always pic-tured my future."

"I say again, Coquette, I will never leave you. I mean to hold you close always, to keep you in my bed, to keep you by my side, to ride my horse next to yours, to surround you with children that will belong to you and me alone. There is only one circumstance over which I have no control, and that would be the same circumstance that brought you to dream your lonely dreams . . . and that would be death. Beyond that, again, I promise with all my heart I will never leave you."

She gasped, for now she understood what he had been trying to say all along. He drew her into his arms and held her so tightly she could hardly breathe.

"I will not leave you, my darling Coquette, my dearest love. I wish that I had known all these years how you suffered even at Barscot."

A small sob escaped her throat. "I was not unhappy. Your father was very dear to me."

"But you were alone. I see that now. I see that even all my aunts and uncles, cousins and friends could not replace a true family. But I will be your family now and we will make, God grant us, a family of our own. I know as well what it is to be lonely. I had no brothers and sisters, only this little termagant who ran the halls of my house and with whom I was at war for at least two decades."

"Longer, surely."

"Yes, from the first, but only because one day I was to discover in her the very wife I needed."

She drew back that she might look into his eyes. "Truly, Harley? Is that how you truly feel?"

"Yes, my darling. Only tell me I may accompany you on your voyages. You will break my heart otherwise."

Coquette looked into his gray eyes and a sudden memory returned to her, of being on her father's knee. He was bouncing her, and she was laughing. In his eyes was an expression of constancy, one that she now saw in Harley's eyes as well, the same expression she had always seen in his father. The past met the future at this moment in her life. She felt as though even in death, her father had made bridges for her in the shape of first Lord Harlington and now his son, all of which had given a beautiful and surprising continuity to her life. She understood, as Harley had already come to understand—the dreams of her beloved ship had been her protection, a refuge she no longer needed.

She smiled, though her eyes were misted with tears. "I will never leave you, either. I promise. I did not know, I did not understand myself, but I do now. But when did you discover the truth?"

He stroked her hair and touched her cheek with the back of his fingers. "I am not certain. Somewhere between comprehending your obvious enjoyment of society during the London Season, and a growing awareness that when you felt threatened you always spoke of your ship."

"I'm frightened," she confessed. "I feel as though I am stepping off a very high cliff into nothing but air."

"Your cliff, I daresay, will probably prove no higher than your bed, off of which I know you to have jumped a thousand times in your youth. In which case, jump now, and I will catch you."

"Oh, Harley!" With that, she kissed him and had all the pleasure and delight of feeling his passionate response. He nearly broke every rib hugging her as he did and as for her tender mouth, which had abused him so sorely over the years, well, it would be wonderfully bruised for a very long time indeed. She was sure of it.

Coquette enjoyed very much being married over the anvil that day. With her fortune now made secure, and her life made complete in her marriage to Harley, she returned with him to London, where their nuptials were celebrated by family and friends. A long honeymoon ensued, which lasted several years. Harley encouraged her to fulfill her dreams, to purchase a ship, to hire a crew, and together they sailed the oceans, at least for a time, at least until they brought home two babes and a third growing within and decided it was time at last to tend to Barscot. Besides, it was much easier raising the little ones on the backs of horses than fretting that a sudden wave would rise up and sweep one or the other away. Better to fall off a horse than a ship.

Thus the years appointed to her were whittled away in the enjoyment of her numerous children and beneath the approving, satisfied gaze of her husband. If occasionally the halls rang with not the squeals of her children, but her own as Harley chased her from room to room and occasionally up into the attics, who was present to disapprove anyway?

More Regency Romance
From Zebra